The Candidate

He gaped at the tattered photograph that had just been slipped into his hand. His heart raced, and Senator Matt Steele, Democratic candidate for president, halted so abruptly his Secret Service agent bumped into him.

"Keep moving, sir," Joe Venuto urged. "Stand still and you invite trouble."

Matt barely heard the warning.

"Senator Steele!" A lilting, accented voice shouted above the noise of the crowd. "I must speak with you."

Matt curled his fingers around the photograph as if to protect it. He raised his gaze to search for the voice.

A man's face with high Asian cheekbones and uncharacteristically blue eyes appeared over Joe's shoulder. The man fought the jostling crowds to stay close to the rope that separated Matt and his entourage from the press of people who had come to the rally. "Please, sir! I have to see you."

Matt took another look at the dog-eared snapshot, then turned to Joe. "Bring him to the bus."

"Sir, that's not a good idea. We don't even know who he is."

"Pat him down. Run a check on him with that phone of yours, or whatever you want, but I need to see him. In my bus. Now." Matt turned and strode toward the campaign bus, heedless of the crowd still hoping for its brief moment of his time. Joe hustled to keep up. Matt heard him speak to another man in the detail. He tuned Joe out. Tuned out his chief of staff and his press secretary who were probably confused by Matt's sudden departure from the planned handshaking opportunity. He tuned out everything, except the photograph in his hand.

What They Are Saying About

The Candidate

"A timely, edge-of-your-seat account of how secrets come to light and affect the outcome of a National Presidential election. Skye Taylor is a new and talented author to watch closely."

Elizabeth Sinclair,
Best-selling, award winning author
of the Hawks Mountain Series

The Candidate

by

Skye Taylor

A Wings ePress, Inc.

Mainstream Novel

Wings ePress, Inc.

Edited by: Jeanne Smith
Copy Edited by: Joan C. Powell
Senior Editor: Jeanne R. Smith
Executive Editor: Marilyn Kapp
Cover Artist: BJ Jaynes

Wings ePress Books
http://www.wings-press.com

Copyright © 2012 by Anita Skye Taylor
ISBN 978-1-61309-744-1

Previously published: ISBN: 978-1-61309-927-8

Published In the United States Of America

Wings ePress Inc.
3000 N. Rock Road
Newton, KS 67114

Dedication

To all the people who encouraged me to follow my dream and believe in myself, especially my Mom and Dad, my children, and my critique partners: Elizabeth Sinclair, Nancy Quatrano, and Kat McMahon

One

He gaped at the tattered photograph that had just been slipped into his hand. His heart raced, and Senator Matt Steele, Democratic candidate for president, halted so abruptly his Secret Service agent bumped into him.

"Keep moving, sir," Joe Venuto urged. "Stand still and you invite trouble."

Matt barely heard the warning.

"Senator Steele!" A lilting, accented voice shouted above the noise of the crowd. "I must speak with you."

Matt curled his fingers around the photograph as if to protect it. He raised his gaze to search for the voice.

A man's face with high Asian cheekbones and uncharacteristically blue eyes appeared over Joe's shoulder. The man fought the jostling crowds to stay close to the rope that separated Matt and his entourage from the press of people who had come to the rally. "Please, sir! I have to see you."

Matt took another look at the dog-eared snapshot, then turned to Joe. "Bring him to the bus."

"Sir, that's not a good idea. We don't even know who he is."

"Pat him down. Run a check on him with that phone of yours, or whatever you want, but I need to see him. In my bus. Now." Matt turned and strode toward the campaign bus, heedless of the crowd still hoping for its brief moment of his time. Joe hustled to keep up. Matt heard him speak to another man in the detail. He tuned Joe out. Tuned out his chief of staff and his press secretary who were probably confused by Matt's sudden departure from the planned handshaking opportunity. He tuned out everything, except the photograph in his hand.

As Matt approached, the driver of his campaign bus opened the door, and Matt took all three steps in one leap. "Wait outside, please."

The driver looked at him in surprise, but then rose and climbed down out of the bus.

Matt sank onto the soft faux-leather recliner of his mobile headquarters and opened his hand. The photograph remained curled so he set it on the coffee table and pressed it flat.

A group of laughing, smartly dressed Marines stared up at him, his much younger self among them. Matt raked his fingers through his carefully groomed hair, dislodging the difficult lock of bangs that immediately fell onto his brow. He pushed them aside and studied the photo.

His cousin Sam Davis stood in the center of the group, grinning broadly. He had one arm draped across Matt's shoulders, and the other around a slender young Vietnamese woman. Sam had been his best friend and the closest thing he'd ever had to a brother. Matt remembered the day the photograph was taken. More than thirty years ago. A week before Sam had been killed.

The door swished open, and Joe stepped up into the stairwell. "Sir, this man is not a voter. He's not even an..."

"Let him in."

The Secret Service agent frowned but stepped aside to let the visitor pass by him in the narrow stairway.

"You can leave, Joe."

"But, sir!"

"Out. Please."

Joe's expression said he wasn't happy about any of it, but with a brief salute, he turned and left. When Joe was gone, Matt invited his guest to come up the stairs and join him.

"I will only take a moment of your time, sir."

The stranger stopped on the other side of the coffee table, and Matt found himself looking up into an eerily familiar pair of sky-blue eyes. He felt as if he'd met the man before, but he couldn't think where or when. An emotion he couldn't identify squeezed into his chest. He rose slowly, fought to ignore the intense feeling of disorienting familiarity, and extended his hand.

"How may I help you?"

His guest smiled and accepted Matt's hand. "It is good of you to see me, sir." His precise English held a trace of the singsong accent of Southeast Asia. He was several inches shorter than Matt's six feet four inches, had straight black hair, and those blue eyes that were so unexpected in an Asian face.

Matt gestured for the man to sit and resumed his own seat.

"I am Thanh Davis."

The surname added to Matt's confusion and jangled emotions. "Davis?"

"Yes, but please, you may call me Thanh." He perched gingerly on the edge of the couch that matched Matt's chair. "We met. Sort of…" Thanh continued.

I have met this guy. No wonder he seems familiar. Matt pointed to the photograph laying, still slightly curled at the edges, on the table between them. "W-Where," Matt cleared his throat, "did you get this?"

"*Bà ngoai*, my grandmother, gave it to me. I am sorry. I have distressed you. I did not think, after all these years..." Thanh's face creased with concern.

Matt shook his head, still trying to make sense of the photo and this unknown man's connection to it. "It's just the shock of seeing it out of the blue like that. I don't understand...."

Thanh leaned across the space that separated them to point to the young woman in the photo. "This is Mai Ly. My mother. And this man was my father." His slender finger tapped Sam's chest.

"That can't be," Matt protested in disbelief. "Surely Sam would have told me if..." Matt trailed off, shaking his head in denial.

"Perhaps he did not know. *Bà ngoai* told me they were hoping to marry, but before they could get his commanding officer's permission, my father was killed." Thanh's expression clouded. "Then Saigon was overrun, and all the Americans left in a hurry. My mother was taken to a re-education camp where I was born."

Another wave of disorienting memory flooded over Matt, this time piercing him with an overwhelming sense of guilt.

"S-she never came," Matt whispered through the anguish crowding into his throat. "I got her name on the list, but she never came."

"The list?" Thanh, asked, clearly baffled.

"Your mother came to me just before the evacuation of Saigon. She thought she was coming to meet Sam, but..." Matt broke off, swallowed the painful lump lodged in his throat and started again. "I had to tell her what had happened to Sam. She was distressed. Both about Sam and about what would happen to her when the Americans left."

Matt closed his eyes while the scene from so many years ago played out in his mind as if they'd happened just last week. Emotions unbelievably raw and fresh washed over him.

4

~ * ~

"We can marry? Yes?" Mai Ly's gaze scanned the room beyond Matt, looking for Sam. Finding it empty, she looked back at Matt with a question in her eyes.

She looked so delicate, but beneath the beautiful, fragile exterior was a tough, determined survivor. Sam's fiancée had lived through more of hell than anyone Matt had ever known, yet she remained confident, sunny and resilient. It was one of the things that made her so attractive to men, especially to Sam. And to Matt himself, if he was honest about it. He prayed she would be strong enough to bear the latest blow life had delivered.

Sam was dead. He shouldn't have been in harm's way at all. He'd only been sent to guard the perimeter at the DAO headquarters from unruly mobs, not from enemy shells. And Matt had to tell Mai Ly that Sam wasn't coming back.

Mai Ly reached for the paper in Matt's hand. The precious bit of paper she and Sam had been waiting for authorizing their marriage.

"He's gone, Mai Ly."

Mai Ly scanned the page, and then looked at Matt in confusion. "Gone home? To the USA? Without me?"

"He was killed."

Mai Ly's eyes widened. "No! Sam is at the embassy. Nothing bad can happen there." Her gaze searched the room again with desperate disbelief.

Matt watched the hope in her eyes give way to agonized despair. "Sam was guarding the airfield. He was in the wrong place at the wrong time."

Matt wanted to smash his fist through the paper-thin walls of the apartment he and Sam had shared. Walls that had sheltered the growing love affair between his friend and Mai Ly. He was furious

with the ambassador and all the foot dragging that had cost Sam
his life. Furious that any of them were in Vietnam at all.

~ * ~

"Wrong place," Matt muttered aloud. Then his voice faded to a broken whisper. "Wrong time."

Thanh leaned closer. "Excuse me?"

Brought abruptly back to the present, Matt gazed at the young man leaning toward him, his brow furrowed, the tilted blue eyes questioning.

They were Sam's eyes. That's why they looked so familiar. Matt tried to remember the exact shade of Sam's eyes. Eyes that had twinkled in devilry, softened in concern, grown hard at injustice. Eyes Matt had known as well as he'd known his own. He tried to bring a mental picture of Sam into focus, but it had been too many years. He focused instead on Thanh Davis. The son Sam had never known.

"I'm sorry. I was just remembering. It's been a long time." Matt shook his head to clear the cobwebs. "You said we've met, but I must apologize. I don't recall where."

"At the Vietnam Memorial Wall. A week ago?" Thanh prompted. "We bumped into each other."

Memory and understanding sluiced over Matt. "I was late for a meeting. You must have been searching for your father's name, and I almost ran you down. I should have stopped. I should have apologized."

Thanh shook his head. "No need. It was my fault. I saw you tracing his name with your finger, and I was curious. Your man started to shoo me away, but then you turned so quickly. That is when I realized who you were. You are all over the television because of the campaign. But seeing you right in front of me gave me a strange feeling as if I knew you personally. Then you hurried away without speaking, and I could not think why I felt this, this strange connection.

"The next day, it came to me. I took out my photograph and studied it closely. That is when I am sure the man my father embraces in the picture is you. You have not changed, not very much." Thanh finally stopped speaking and waited for Matt to respond.

Matt gazed out the window at the broad shoulders of Joe Venuto who stood guard by the bus door. The sound of Sam's joking voice came back to him.

"Say cheese, everyone. You never know who'll be looking at this one day, maybe years from now. Can't have 'em thinking we were unhappy about being here, can we?" Sam laughed and repeated a vulgar little ditty that set them all to sniggering, and the camera snapped.

Reluctantly, Matt returned his gaze to the worn old photo. Young people who appeared carefree and happy. Two of them were in love. And all the time the enemy edged ever closer, gaining control of village after village. Determined to take possession of Saigon by the end of April.

"Sam Davis was my cousin. He was also my best friend," Matt said at last. "We grew up together."

"It hurts you to speak of him, even after all these years?" Thanh's inflection made it a question.

Matt didn't try to deny what his observant visitor had already sensed. "His death was so senseless, but no more so than what happened to you and your mother. I promised her I would get her name on the evacuation list. I gave her my radio so she could listen for the coded warning to come to the embassy when it was time. But she never came. I thought maybe she changed her mind about wanting to leave. I should have gone to look for her, but everything was so..."

"You must not blame yourself," Thanh assured Matt hastily. "Many people were responsible for what happened in the end, but not, I think, the soldiers. I have studied the history of those years. Especially since I have come to this country where I am able to read less biased accounts."

"But, your mother," Matt protested, "I should have gone after her."

"You had a job to do. You had orders to follow. If my mother chose not to come to you when you had promised to help her, perhaps it was because she felt loyalty to her own mother. *Bà ngoai* never said anything of this list you speak about. I think she did not know of it." Thanh reached for the photo and tucked it back into his breast pocket. "But, I did not come here to distress you, sir. I just want to learn about my father. I want to find his family, and I hoped that you would be able to help me."

Matt shoved his hair off his brow again as he studied Thanh Davis's face. *His eyes are so incredibly blue. I don't remember Sam's eyes being quite that bright. There must have been a blue-eyed Frenchman somewhere on Mai Ly's family tree.*

"Your father was a good man, Thanh," Matt began, not sure where to start.

"Was he smart? Was he a good student? And a brave soldier?" The questions began to pour out of the son Sam had never known as if a dam had burst. "Am I like him at all?"

"You resemble him, a little. You have his eyes, and his height for sure. Sam Davis was a brave man and an outstanding soldier. Perhaps just an average student, but he had a devilish sense of humor. In fact," Matt pointed toward Thanh's pocket, "he was trying to be sarcastically funny when that picture was taken."

"But my mother did not think it was funny?"

"She didn't understand English very well."

"What was my father like before he became a soldier? When he was a boy?" Thanh moved even closer to the edge of the couch, clearly eager for anything Matt could tell him about his father.

Matt didn't have to wonder what it was like to feel as though a piece of who you were would always be missing. He, too, had been born in the midst of a war that had taken his father's life before Matt's birth. *But I was luckier than Thanh. I never knew my birth father, but Mom married a man who loved me and reared me as his own.*

"How long have you been in the United States? Have you come to Washington just recently?" Matt asked, with apparent irrelevance as another thought came to him.

Thanh's eyebrows lifted. He was clearly puzzled by Matt's abrupt question. He opened his mouth to answer, but Matt lifted a finger to forestall him.

"Hold that thought..." Matt reached for his cell phone tucked into a holster on his belt. He tapped the *on* button, then told the phone to call Eve at home and waited. A smile tugged at his lips for the first time since the photograph had been pressed into his hand. When his wife answered, Matt winked at Thanh.

"It's much too complicated to explain on the phone, love, but I promise to sort it all out for you when I get home. I just wanted to warn you that I'm bringing someone with me for dinner."

~ * ~

Eve climbed into bed and settled into the crook of Matt's arm. "After all these years together, I'd have thought nothing you did would surprise me, but I have to admit, I never could have guessed who you were bringing home for dinner."

"You can't be nearly as surprised as I was when Thanh shoved that snapshot into my hand as I was leaving the rally this afternoon," Matt replied as he arranged the sheet around his wife's shoulders. "I thought I was going to faint for a minute when I saw that picture." He held his hands up in front of their faces, palms open as if he were reading the lines crossing them. "My hands were like ice. It was weird."

"Weird how?" Eve tipped her head back to look up at him.

"Well, I haven't really thought about Sam in--in ages I guess. But last week, I got a letter from a chaplain in San Diego. From the veterans' home where Bill Nickerson was being cared for once his cancer got out of hand. The chaplain knew Bill and I had stayed in touch, and since Bill didn't have any family, he took it on himself to tell me Bill had died."

Eve lurched up onto one elbow. "Bill died? And you didn't tell me? What about the funeral?"

"There wasn't a funeral. Bill left his body to science. Besides, you were out of town when the letter came, and by the time you got home, I forgot about it."

"What a shame. I really liked that old coot." Eve sank back against Matt's side. "But it was inevitable, I guess. And probably a relief to him."

"The chaplain said Bill told him his only regret was that he wouldn't live long enough to vote for me."

"I'm sorry. I know he meant a lot to you." Eve traced the line of Matt's jaw with one finger. "But how does Bill's passing have anything to do with Thanh? Or Sam, for that matter?"

"Nothing really. Except that after I read the chaplain's letter, I got this crazy impulse to visit the Wall. My Secret Service guys weren't happy about the unplanned visit and neither was Rick. I was due at GWU in half an hour, and we'd already had a busy day, but I just felt like I had to stop there on the way." Matt shrugged and rolled toward her.

"You ever get a feeling like that? Like you don't know why, but there's just this thing you have to do?"

"Yeah, all the time," muttered Eve. "Like sleep. God knows why I should need to sleep, but I just get the feeling—ouch! What's that for?"

"I'm serious here. I'm trying to tell you how I met Thanh. I think it was meant for me to go there."

"Meant how?" Eve stopped rubbing the place Matt had pinched and draped an arm across his hips.

"I've been all over the news. On TV and in ads. And Thanh had seen my picture dozens of times, except he never put two and two together and realized I was the man in his picture until he ran into me at the Wall. Actually, I ran into him."

"I'm surprised Joe let a total stranger get that close. How did you just happen to run into him anyway?"

"Joe wasn't on duty that day, and I don't know what was up with his sub. I was too busy tracing Sam's name with my finger and thinking how symbolic it was that the reflection of the letters etched into the stone was written right across my heart. Like he's still a part of me, and he always will be. And then I was remembering the last time I saw him and..." *Sam had been strapping on his gear, getting ready to head out to Tan Son Nhut Airport, saying he was going to go play soldier again even if it was just guarding the Defense Attaché Office compound. He'd been laughing when he'd said it. Then he'd hoisted his duffle onto his shoulder and disappeared out the door. Forever.*

Matt's chest tightened again. The way it had that day at the Wall. As it had when he'd looked down at the photograph that afternoon. Thirty years should have been long enough to take that sense of guilt and pain away.

"It got to me. Suddenly, I just needed to be gone from there. The long and short of it is that I bolted, and I nearly ran into this guy who'd been trying to see around me. I didn't really look at him. I was in a rush.

"Turns out, it was Thanh. And he apparently got a better look at me than I did at him because it stuck in his mind. And when he had a chance to think about it, he realized I was the man standing next to his father in this old photo he had tucked away."

"Explains why it took him all this time to track you down." Eve turned her face into the crook of Matt's neck and snuggled closer. "Thanh showed me the photo. I forgot how handsome you looked in a uniform."

Matt harrumphed. "You just think all men look handsome in uniforms."

"Maybe," Eve agreed in a sleepy voice.

Neither of them said anything for several minutes, and Matt thought his wife had fallen asleep when she added, "I just hope Thanh showing up like this won't stir up all those nightmares you used to have."

"Why should it?" Matt asked, blithely ignoring his irrational reaction to the photo earlier that afternoon. "This kid never knew his dad, and it's like I get to do this one last thing for Sam. I should've gotten Thanh's mother out and I didn't. I let Sam down."

"You did what you could, but it was a treacherous time, and bad things happened. Things you didn't have any control over. So stop blaming yourself."

"But I could have gotten Mai Ly out." *I could have done a lot of things differently. I could have...*

Eve hugged him tighter for a moment, and then relaxed again. She mumbled something Matt couldn't make out, her voice trailing off as sleep overtook her. But for Matt, the comfortable drowsiness of approaching oblivion edged farther out of reach as a fresh wave of guilt crept into his heart.

"I'm sorry," he whispered into the still darkness.

Two

Roland Miller stood in his DC hotel room window gazing down at a garden where a fountain merrily sprayed water into the decorative little basin surrounding it, wishing he were somewhere else. He wanted Ash. He wanted Ash with a hunger that made everything in him ache. But the gossip would be shattering and giving in to his hunger could destroy his campaign.

At times, he wished the Republican Party hadn't picked him as their golden-haired boy. Or that the image he presented didn't fit so neatly into what they thought the voting populace wanted in its next president. He represented everything the current incumbent didn't. Old family. Old money. Fiscally and socially conservative and a hawk.

His team had managed to enact unprecedented entitlement overhauls at the state level. Now they wanted him to do the same with the underfunded federal programs. He had championed Bush's campaign to topple Hussein and bring the enlightenment of democracy to the Middle East. In spite of continued calls for some kind of exit strategy, he strongly admonished that announcing troop withdrawal dates would just give the fanatics a light at the end of their tunnel and a reason to hang on until the Americans left. He also felt the US needed to strengthen its position militarily, both in the minds of the insurgents and those of America's allies. Bases already occupied by US troops anywhere in the world should not be abandoned, and it was foolish to suggest otherwise.

But personally, he felt he was a long way from the ideal candidate. He'd married Jean Anne to avoid the draft all those years ago, and a deep and abiding friendship had grown between them. A friendship more like that of siblings than spouses. They'd managed to bring two sons into the world before he could no longer bring himself to sleep with her, and her early demise due to breast cancer had brought more relief than grief. But the world didn't see it that way. And he'd let them. If anything, he'd gone out of his way to foster the image of the grieving widower. It made life easier.

Louis Castillo, his campaign manager, came through the door from the main room in the suite, a bundle of irrepressible energy. "The car's waiting for you."

Louis shifted his weight from foot to foot, rubbing hands together in his impatience. Rolly shut his eyes and pushed the longing for Ash down somewhere deep inside of himself where even he wouldn't notice it. Then, smoothing his features, he turned around.

"You okay, Rolly?" Louis peered at him with uncharacteristic perspicacity. "You missing Jean Anne? She was always there for you, and this has got to be hard."

"Jean Anne's been gone for over a year. I've adjusted." Rolly felt uncomfortable with his manager's sympathy.

Louis grinned. "Then maybe all you need is to get laid."

"I don't need to get laid," Rolly replied with dismissive finality. He grabbed his jacket off the back of the chair and shoved his arms into it. "And take that smirk off your face."

"Your wish is my command." Louis bowed low and doffed an imaginary hat.

"I get no respect around here," Rolly threw Louis a playful frown and chuckled, his mood lightening. "We better get moving. You can brief me in the car."

~ * ~

Blair Cabot held himself with an arrogant tautness to his shoulders, drawing himself up to the full extent of his five feet eleven inches. He'd long ago stopped wishing he were taller and settled into exploiting the assets he did have. He had his crew cut hair trimmed every other week, and he worked out faithfully to keep his body just as ruthlessly controlled as his hair. He knew his broad shoulders and barrel chest tended to intimidate, and he liked it that way.

He watched Roland Miller make his usual elegant entrance without a hint of jealousy. Miller was nothing more than a well-heeled, well-educated, effeminate fop. In Blair's opinion, neither the life he'd lived, nor the politics he subscribed to, added one wit to his consequence. He might be ahead in the polls right now, but that was about to change. Both Blair and Matt Steele had been steadily gaining on him. And Blair was gaining more rapidly with the backing of a huge, dissatisfied middle-of-the-road populace who felt ignored by their parties' extremes.

The American people had finally realized there was viability in a third party candidate. They were so fed up with the same-old-same-old they were willing to take a chance on something completely different. All Blair had to do to win tonight's debate was point out the failure of either of his opponents' parties to accept accountability for the fiscal train wreck they'd both helped put in motion, then hammer home the reminder that neither appeared willing to make the compromises required to stop it. Blair's successes in the business world spoke for themselves. He knew how to clear out deadwood and make things profitable. And there was plenty of dead wood in D.C. to be cleared out.

Blair's confidence came from the knowledge that he was good at what he did. He wasn't afraid of hard work. He was single-minded and disciplined. He could see the larger picture when others couldn't and be ruthless in making things happen. He was more than capable of achieving the goals he set for himself. With the sole exception of earning his father's esteem.

He loved and admired his father more than any other person he'd ever known, and all his life, he'd desperately wanted to prove he was just as good as the old man. But no matter how well Blair had done, it had never seemed enough to gain the praise he felt he deserved. He'd been captain of the football team in high school and graduated *summa cum laude* from Dartmouth College.

Rachel Marie Westmoreland had been sought after by dozens of men, but she'd married Blair Cabot. Blair had taken over the family business when his father wanted to retire and then turned it into the biggest foundry in his state, casting everything from church bells to cannon barrels, before going global and acquiring roots in more than a dozen additional enterprises. Then he'd married all four of his daughters off to highly successful men and seen to it they would lack for nothing. There was only one thing left on his agenda.

Beg, bribe or blackmail, one way or another, the US Postal Service would be delivering Blair Cabot's mail to 1600 Pennsylvania Avenue in four months time, and Howland Cabot III would finally have to admit his son had amounted to something after all.

When Miller nodded in his direction, Blair dipped his head in recognition, and then turned his attention back to the discussion about Matt Steele.

"Steele's begun to buck his own party." TJ Smith, Blair's campaign manager, leaned in close to offer a warning. "Be sure to steer clear of the issues he's already started compromising on. And don't give him a starting block to launch any new ideas from, either."

"I know. Stick to his record and attack the party line," Blair agreed. "Where is he anyway?"

TJ shrugged. "Not like him to be late."

"Or unprepared."

"Remember that." TJ shoved a small stack of index cards into Blair's hand. "Talking points."

"There he is now. Who's that guy talking to Steele's daughter?"

TJ jerked his attention toward the lobby entrance.

Matt Steele and his family made their way through the busy foyer surrounded by staff and trailed by reporters hoping for a quotable comment. Blair squinted slightly, trying to bring the faces into focus. He refused to concede to wearing glasses, or to admitting he needed them. In college, he'd been on the rifle team and never lost a single long-range competition. He didn't like to accept that age might be eroding any of his youthful competence.

They moved closer, and Blair got a better look. He didn't think he'd ever seen the uncharacteristically tall Asian man strolling casually across the polished tile floor with Megan Steele's hand tucked into his elbow. Perhaps he was a new boyfriend, but it did seem odd that he'd have been included in the family group tonight.

"Find out who he is," Blair commanded, tersely.

"Right, boss." TJ moved off quickly, his cell phone already at his ear.

Blair studied the newcomer for a few moments longer, checked his watch, and then began reading the cards TJ had given him.

~ * ~

After the family had gone to their seats, Matt Steele looked out over the heads of his chattering staffers and studied his opponents.

Roland Miller certainly looked the part. Slender and distinguished, with steel gray eyes and hair to match, Miller carried himself like a winner. He never simply arrived—he made an entrance. He was gracious in a way most men seeking the highest office in the country had not been for generations. Matt didn't think he'd ever heard Roland Miller say anything personally disparaging about another politician. Perhaps he left that to people on his staff, but somewhere beneath that air of old world courtesy and southern charm, must lay a calculating, determined core of steel, because Roland Miller generally got things done. Often, the seemingly impossible.

Lately, with polite respect for the current president's preferred role of peacemaker, Miller had been coming out forcefully on matters of foreign policy. On the campaign trail, he'd effectively made references to Matt's record of involvement in predominantly domestic affairs and Blair Cabot's complete lack of political experience on any level.

Matt's stock rebuttal was that brandishing a big stick abroad only worked if America was strong enough internally to back it up with action. Then, stifling his personal animosity toward Miller's draft-dodging past, he generally changed the subject to Miller's failure to outline a coherent plan to reduce the soaring deficit. A deficit made that much larger by the repeated deployments of the military to every corner of the world and a failure to rein in the defense budget.

Blair Cabot was a very different adversary. Anyone in his presence felt the power of his personality. Another man who got things done. His sturdy, shorter-than-average stature didn't command the instant impression of competence Roland Miller did. But Cabot was far more ruthless. He'd come from a family with a long history of success in business and had exceeded even his father's achievements. Matt could only guess at how many men Cabot had crushed getting to where he was today. He didn't have a career full of voting history for Matt to pick apart. For the most part, they agreed on the need to close their bases in Europe and let the Europeans start defending their own socialist societies. Societies that had gotten to where they were because America paid their defense bills. Matt wasn't so confident about the Middle East. Or Korea and the rest of Southeast Asia. Their biggest points of contention were in healthcare, education and immigration.

Cabot was the first independent with a real chance at winning the election. He was drawing the support of moderate Democrats who were willing to at least consider reining in runaway entitlements and less than hawkish Republicans sick of being the world's police force and ready to bring their boys home. At the moment, Roland Miller was ahead in the polls. Matt's campaign had been gaining steadily in the last few weeks, but so had Blair Cabot's.

Tonight's debate was anyone's to win.

Three

"So, what out-of-the box idea are you planning to introduce today?" Matt's running mate leaned in to ask.

"Do you have to stand so damned close? You make me feel like I'm shrinking." At six foot two, Matt didn't often have to look up at other men, but Hal Weymouth, a former UNC point guard, towered over him.

Hal grinned, his good-natured charm as unconscious as it was infectious. "You'll get used to me. You're going to have four, maybe eight years, if you change your mind about seeking just one term." Hal jerked his head toward the seething crowd. "I think Jack's trying to catch your eye."

Matt followed Hal's gaze. A slight, vigorous, black man wove agilely through the crowded room. Whenever he had a clear line of vision, he directed his dark eyes at Matt.

Jack Holland had been Matt's press secretary ever since he'd been elected to the Senate and had become an indispensable asset to his campaign. Jack's instincts when dealing with the press, were flawless. Matt couldn't have asked for a more dedicated or tireless colleague.

"God, it's a circus out there," Jack complained when he got close enough.

"Politics *is* a circus." Hal chuckled.

"Hey, Hal," Jack grimaced as he cocked his head back to acknowledge Hal's wry comment. Then he turned back to Matt. "Did you get to review the stuff I sent over?"

"Yeah." Matt grabbed Jack's elbow and steered him toward a small, unoccupied anteroom. "Mind running interference for a bit? I need a few minutes to collect my thoughts."

"How come Winfield isn't here throwing last minute instructions at you?"

"Couldn't stand still long enough, I suppose," Matt said, excusing his campaign manager's absence.

Jack shoved hot-off-the-press newsprint into Matt's hands and pointed to a front-page column. "Well, you might spend a few minutes reading this and be prepared to answer some probing questions on the education bill your committee just pushed through the Senate. Wagner brought up a couple of angles that are sure to raise more than a few hackles."

"I'm sure he did!" Matt subsided into a comfortable armchair and spread the paper across his lap. "Oh, Jack?"

Jack had already disappeared, leaving Matt alone except for Joe Venuto standing guard by the door.

Matt read quickly down the page. The article continued on page eighteen. He rearranged the paper, finished reading the article, then let his gaze travel to the opposite page headed *Letters to the Editor.* He started to refold the paper, then stopped, one particular letter catching his attention.

Your recent editorial, 'The Greatest Democracy and The Twenty-first Century,' is indicative of what is wrong with our government.

Matt scanned quickly down the column, saw his own name and went back to read the letter again. He stared at the name appended to the letter and wondered about Edna Jordan from Illinois. In spite of her obvious naïveté, he understood her frustration and couldn't suppress the unexpected urge to agree without reservation. Once upon a time, he might have written just such a letter. Instead, he'd gotten involved and discovered things were not so easily undone as he'd once thought. The wheels of government ground relentlessly forward, thwarting would-be reformers by its sheer enormity.

Mrs. Jordan's sweeping summation, characterizing America as a country of indolent, self-centered people recklessly condemning future generations to an escalating and crushing debt, Matt could forgive. Her opinion that politicians weren't to be trusted was shared by many. That she tarred him with the same brush, he found disquieting. That was the very thing he'd been trying to change during the course of this campaign.

He'd given his word he'd be a one-term president and spend all four years of his time in office making decisions based on what was best for the country, not what would guarantee his re-election. What further reassurance, what other promises had he not made that he, perhaps, should have made? How many others felt as Mrs. Jordan did?

His mind still on the letter, he flipped back to the front page and glanced through the usual collection of disheartening news, then folded the paper and set it aside. He closed his eyes for a moment and rested his head against the chair. The steady hum of voices filtered in from the room beyond, but he managed to block it out.

He pictured Eve making her way to her seat directly in front of the podium where he would stand. His daughter, Megan, would be there, too. And Thanh. Matt smiled. His personal cheering squad.

"Senator?" Jack hovered at his elbow.

Matt stood quickly. "Time?"

"Rick's here. He said to tell you to stay on target and not get started on one of your rants. And stay away from entitlements." Jack wagged his eyebrows, and then hurried away.

Matt started to follow, then turned back. Without stopping to wonder why he did so, he dug through his pocket for his penknife. He thumbed through the paper to page nineteen, and cut out the letter, folded it into a small square and tucked it into his wallet.

~ * ~

Ten minutes later, the moderator brought his gavel down on the central podium to quiet the audience.

"Ladies and gentlemen, I have the honor of welcoming you to the second in our series of presidential debates between Governor Roland Wallace Miller, of the Republican party, Senator Matthew Graham Steele, Democrat and Mr. Blair Howland Cabot, representing the Coalition of Independents."

Enthusiastic applause interrupted the introductions several times before the three men shook hands and stepped up to their respective podiums. With another rap of his gavel, the moderator quieted the audience before introducing the members of the press who would be presenting the questions. Then he repeated the ground rules, which didn't preclude impromptu rebuttals even if they interrupted another man's response.

With half an ear paying attention to the moderator, Matt found Eve where he had known she would be and returned her steady gaze, finding strength, as always, in her presence. She made the quick, familiar, gesture with her hand that was her unique way of saying *I love you.* Matt copied her, touching his thumb to his chest before wagging it in her direction. Eve smiled, and Matt winked back. Then he turned his attention to the moderator.

The first question was directed to Roland Miller and might have been written by Matt's own staff, considering the way it laid out the debate on defense. Miller stuck to the party line, repeating his hawkish stance on beefing up the military, then launched into the need for additional infusions of cash to fund the ongoing and a long-contested development of the F-35 alternative engine.

"That jet is a black hole even without a new engine!" Blair Cabot interjected with a scornful sneer. "It's time to face the facts. Our air superiority is already uncontested. Why do we need to sink billions into new research at a time when our country is mired in debt of unprecedented proportions?"

Miller pursed his lips until Cabot shut up and the supportive applause died down. "Maintaining that superiority is key to preserving our leadership in the world. If we did not…"

"What kind of leadership are you pushing?" Cabot spat contemptuously. "Acting as the world's self-elected policeman? Protecting Europe while they fund their outsized welfare systems with the cash they don't have to spend on defense? Or perhaps you think imposing democracy on countries that have no appreciation for it is more essential than shoring up our own economy?"

"Are you suggesting we take a back seat and let Russia reclaim what they consider their rightful ascendancy?" Miller asked with gentlemanly poise.

"Russia is as dead as conventional warfare. It's a new world out there, and it's time you woke up and took notice."

"What about China?" Miller finally had an edge to his tone.

"China just wants to be a trading partner. They have no plans to take over militarily."

"Your grasp of international politics appears to be seriously lacking," Miller retorted, finally riled enough to take a personal jab at his opponent.

"And your grasp of economics is more than seriously lacking," Cabot shot back.

The moderator cracked his gavel down. "Senator Steele, do you care to comment on the defense budget in general, or the fighter jet procurement in specific?"

"I agree with Mr. Cabot," Matt began. "That we shoulder far too great a share of the defense of Europe, and about our need to be everywhere in the world. But I agree with Governor Miller on the issue of China. The most recent report to congress suggests that China's military buildup could become a destabilizing issue throughout Southeast Asia, and that they have as many as twelve hundred short-range missiles aimed at Taiwan, which we have promised to defend in the face of an attack. Added to which, China is developing anti-ship ballistic missiles with the potential capability of attacking American aircraft carriers. This should be a primary concern in our defense planning along with continued training and arming of covert operators to combat pockets of terrorism wherever it threatens peaceful civilizations and American interests."

"Which leads us right back to being the world's police force," Cabot turned on Matt with the same aggressive disdain he'd shown Miller.

"We cannot revert to the isolationist stand we took before World War I," Matt asserted calmly. "There are too many out-of-control governments and rogue terrorist organizations, and like it or not, we are currently the only country with enough clout to take the lead in protecting ourselves and the rest of the world from them. The United Nations can vote for sanctions and approve troops to be sent into troubled spots, but that still requires the might of the United States. Our economy is inextricably woven into that of the rest of the world, and we cannot allow anarchy to take over or we'll all be back to the dark ages."

Cabot snorted and opened his mouth to lob another volley, but the moderator shut him down a second time, and then turned the mike over to the journalist from Chicago.

They sparred less heatedly over the education bill just passed in the Senate and soon to be on its way to the House. Cabot wanted to privatize the entire public school system, and he made a great case for it. Miller was Little Johnny One Note on the subject of vouchers. Neither addressed the poor and falling ranking of American students measured against other developed countries, and Matt felt he might have gained points both for himself and his bill.

"Senator Steele. In his recent book, *Fiscally Sound*, Ron Hamilton points out that the only effective plan to pay down our country's enormous deficit will require sacrifices by all of the so-called middle class as well as the very well off. Can you explain to those young Americans just entering the work force how you plan to work toward ensuring their own financial future, as well as that of their children?"

It was the opening Matt had been hoping for.

"*Fiscally Sound* is probably the best thought-out treatise on what needs to be done to put our country back on sound economical footing," he began. "And I agree with Mr. Hamilton. The only way to restore the American Dream is to recall what that dream *is* and what it is *not*.

"Every year, the number of people requesting permission to immigrate to the United States increases. And thousands of others come without permission." A ripple of disapproval followed and Matt paused a moment before asking, "Why do so many want so desperately to come to America?"

Matt's campaign manager frowned. Immigration was an issue Rick wanted Matt to avoid as much as possible. Matt ignored him.

"It's the cradle of economic opportunity," Blair Cabot interjected. "We live in a global economy and everyone wants the best shot at making it to the top."

"What about people who have no chance at ever becoming rich? Why do they come, legally or illegally?" Miller's challenge was directed at Cabot, but his cultured, equitable tone had reappeared.

"For the freebies," Cabot snarled. "Because the bleeding liberals give them free medical care, free education, free food stamps. You name it. And it's there for the taking for anyone with guts to find a way across the border without getting caught."

"Mr. Cabot makes a valid point," Matt cut in. "But he's forgetting all those who leave behind family, homes, heritage, social standing and careers to be here. Why do so many give up so much to come to a country where they will have to start all over again? Because…" Matt kept his pause brief lest Cabot interrupt again, "they seek opportunity and freedom. Because they seek the American Dream."

Cabot made a scoffing noise, but before he could voice an opinion, a reporter in the front row shot to her feet.

"Senator Steele," the reporter called out, and Matt turned toward her. She was sleek and poised. Sleek like a shark, and not one of the regular entourage of reporters. Matt wondered where she'd come from. "Is there any truth to the story that an illegal immigrant has been seen regularly in your company recently?"

It took Matt a full minute to realize the shark was referring to Thanh Davis. A pregnant pause, that went on much too long, followed as gasps of salacious interest rippled through the crowd.

"And that you pulled strings to get him a green card?" The shark grinned in triumph and sat down.

Four

Matt had realized his moment of confusion had created the impression there might be some truth to the reporter's suggestion, and he'd forced himself not to scramble for a denial that would only lend more credence to the allegation. As he rode home, he reflected on the answer he had given and knew that in spite of his best effort, there would be people digging for dirt in the days to come.

Illegal immigration was another hot button issue and any discussion of amnesty drew forth heated, emotional arguments from both extremes. Matt had been trying to stick to an equitable middle of the road for years, but Congress had done nothing and states had begun to take matters into their own hands. Which in turn, dragged the courts in to decide what was constitutional and what wasn't. And all the while, millions more poured in, some of them bringing the worst elements of the societies they'd left behind.

The initial antipathy toward Vietnamese immigrants, who'd been classified as refugees, had faded and their cultural priorities toward education and family had made them good citizens and welcome neighbors. But that wouldn't stop detractors from trying to paint Thanh's status in a darker light, or questioning Matt's connection to him. He could only hope it would be quickly eclipsed by some other tidbit sensationalized by a rabid media hungry for scandal.

~ * ~

Joe Venuto pulled the car into the Steeles' driveway and came to a stop. Megan didn't wait for the door to be opened for her, but bolted from her seat with an excess of energy, flew up the stairs and began fumbling with her key. Eve followed more slowly, while Matt stopped for a few words with Joe before ascending the steps to his front door.

"You did good tonight, Daddy." Megan shoved the door wide and stepped back to admit him.

"Did well," Eve, forever a schoolteacher, corrected absently, as Matt bid Joe good night and then closed the door to help her off with her coat.

"Did well," Megan repeated obediently. "The bit about remembering that America is the land of opportunity and not just about getting something for nothing was cool. Mr. Winfield looked like he was going to have a hissy fit."

He probably had, Matt thought. Rick Winfield and Matt were on a collision course, and Matt wondered how much longer it would be before they collided with a deafening crash. Winfield had managed every campaign Matt had run, but he was as entrenched in the entitlement and special interest rut as any man Matt knew. Matt's hints that he'd had an epiphany and intended to share it with the voters before the election had Winfield in a twist. Winfield didn't like to lose, and he wasn't about to let Matt throw the election away on a quixotic quest, however well intentioned.

"We were talking about JFK in my poly-sci class the other day and…" Megan broke off at the sound of the phone ringing and loped off down the hall.

Eve started up the stairs, exhaustion in every line of her still-slender body. "That phone better not be for me. I'm desperate for a hot bath."

"Need help?" Matt leered suggestively.

Eve lowered her voice to a dulcet whisper. "If you don't take too long."

Matt watched her until her legs disappeared around the curve of the staircase.

"Daddy!" Megan's voice preceded her down the hall. "It's Ben. He wants Mom. He probably needs money."

"I'll talk to him." Matt took the portable handset from her. "I suppose you're headed to bed? Don't you have an early class tomorrow?"

"Way too early." Megan covered a huge yawn. "Remember when we used to sit in the kitchen and drink hot chocolate after everyone else was in bed? We always solved all the world's problems, just the two of us."

"I remember," Matt murmured as he gave his daughter a quick hug and kissed the top of her head.

Megan returned the hug and bounded up the stairs, blowing a kiss in his direction as she went.

"Ben?" Matt wandered into the front room and sank into his favorite chair. "How's grad school going?"

"Okay, Dad. Pretty normal, I guess. I watched the debate. Mostly the same old crap. But I've got to admit you surprised me tonight. Interesting call to arms."

"Is that what you called to say?" Matt tried to decide if he was being set up for an ambush. The past few years had often felt like all-out war between him and his son. They rarely agreed on anything, and the disagreements always felt like personal attacks. It hurt that the son he loved so intensely seemed to enjoy baiting him and sometimes chose an opposing point of view just to be contrary.

"Actually, I asked to speak to Mom."

"She's gone up to soak in the tub. Is there a message I can give her?"

"Just tell her I said hi. Why I really called was..." Ben cleared his throat. "I'm kinda in a bind, and I need some cash."

"But you've only been back at school three weeks."

"I know, Dad, but the apartment rent had to be paid, and the security deposit. And you wouldn't believe the stack of books I had to get this term."

"I thought you had a part-time job lined up?" Matt wondered when Ben was going to get serious about taking on responsibility.

"It fell through. Anyway, I found another one, but I don't start 'til next week."

"How much?" Matt got up and moved toward the library while he talked.

"Five hundred anyway. A thousand would definitely get me through to my first paycheck." Sounding relieved, Ben pushed his luck. "I still don't see why I have to work my way through school. It's not like we're poor."

"I did. Your mother did, too, and it didn't hurt either of us." Matt sat down at his desk and pulled out the checkbook.

"Spare me the lecture. I've heard it before."

"Then don't ask," Matt snapped, stung into letting his exhaustion show.

"Sorry, Dad. Look, I know you only want what's best for me." Ben's voice lost the bitter edge it so often held.

Matt tried to recall the last time he'd hugged his son or told him he loved him. "Ben, I've made out the check for fifteen hundred. I'll put it in the mail tomorrow. Try to make it last. Okay?"

"Thanks, Dad. That's really generous. Tell Mom I love her, and I promise I'll call again soon. And not for money."

"She'll look forward to it."

"Well, I've got to get back to my homework." Ben's voice trailed off.

Matt swallowed. "Ben?"

"Yeah, Dad?"

"Take care of yourself."

"Right. G'night."

Matt turned the handset off and sat with it cradled in his palm, staring at it without seeing it.

His family meant everything to him. Why couldn't he just tell Ben that? He'd give Ben just about anything if he really needed it. Why couldn't he just say the words like he had when Ben was small? Why did everything have to be a struggle between them?

For a man who was good with words, it seemed ridiculous. Clever and persuasive with everyone else, when it came to Ben, the words just crowded around inside him and he couldn't summon them forth.

With the women in his life, it was a little easier. He hugged them often and told them he loved them. But far too often the things he felt in the depths of his being didn't get said even to them. Megan was his princess. He even used to call her that, but she'd asked him not to when she started dating and thought it too childish. So he'd stopped calling her princess and had never found another way to tell her the things a father would always feel for his little girl.

And Eve, whose name had been a song in his heart for as long as he'd known her. A song grown more poignant with every year, but he'd never found the words to tell her that. Was there some flaw in his personality?

He thought about Eve, stepping from the tub, slick and smelling like roses. His body responded to the thought with sweet desire.

Matt grabbed an envelope from the drawer and addressed it to Ben. He hunted for and found a pad of sticky notes. Peeling one off, he stuck it to the front of the check. With his pen poised, he hesitated. The momentary vision of a small, tow-headed boy, arms clutched trustingly about his father's neck, flashed into Matt's head. Then, quickly, before he could change his mind, he wrote, "*I love you - spend it any way you like. I'll always be here for you. Dad.*"

He sealed the envelope and carried it out to the kitchen. He took his keys from his pocket and placed them with the envelope on the counter so he wouldn't forget to post the check in the morning.

Then he went upstairs to keep a promise.

Five

"You do not look as though you are enjoying yourself very much."

Annie Santos jerked her head up toward the voice that had interrupted her self-imposed isolation. "Not much," she conceded cautiously. The man was younger than most of the men in the room. About her age, she guessed. And obviously of Vietnamese descent. It was the only reason he could've had for attending this affair. She'd been coming to these meetings to keep her mother company for years, but she couldn't recall seeing him before. "You're new?"

"I am," he agreed with an engaging grin. Now she was certain she'd never seen him before. She'd have remembered that smile even if the blue eyes hadn't been remarkable enough. "I saw the poster on the church bulletin board. May I join you?" He put his hand on the back of the chair opposite her and waited for her permission to sit. She nodded.

"I hope you weren't too disappointed. It's mostly just a bunch of old fogies who come to chatter about their kids and their kids' kids and remember the good old days that actually weren't all that great."

"I can see how that would leave you out." He lowered himself into the rickety folding chair and glanced about before returning his gaze to an appreciative assessment of her.

Annie felt a flush of pleasure at the implied compliment, not in his words so much, but definitely in his eyes. If she weren't careful, she could get carried away by those eyes. "I come when my mother hasn't got any other ride. It's the height of her week."

"I am sorry. I should have introduced myself. I am Thanh Davis. And you?" His brows lifted in invitation.

"Annie Santos." She reached across the table.

"It is a delight to meet you, Annie Santos." The hand enveloping hers sent a frisson of excitement rushing through her. She jerked her hand back at the unexpected and not entirely welcome zip of electric current. She didn't want to get involved with anyone. Not for a while, anyway. Not until the humiliation of having given her heart to Alejandro Garcia was forgotten.

If Thanh was fazed by her reaction, he didn't show it. "I think you have been living in the area for a while, if your mother comes here regularly."

"I grew up here. Since I was about eight, anyway. How about you? You don't sound as if you grew up anywhere in the States."

"I did not. I emigrated two years ago. I stayed in San Diego for a few months, then followed a friend to Virginia. He helped me to find a job and a place to live. And then he fell in love with a lady from Philadelphia and moved north. So here I am, making new beginnings again."

"He was your only friend?"

"Well, no. But I have been busy with my job and...other things. It is why I came tonight. I thought perhaps to meet people I have something in common with."

"I take it your father was an American?" Annie figured that had to be true. It was the only thing that could have made him think this meeting might fill some hole in his life.

"Yes," Thanh answered simply.

"Does he live around here?"

"Unfortunately, not." A shadow passed over Thanh's handsome features. "He died before I was born. I came to the US to find his family. That was my hope, anyway."

"Was?"

"Apparently, he was an only child and his parents are deceased."

"Is that what kept you so busy? Finding out your search was in vain?"

"Yes and no. It did keep me busy running into so many dead ends. I knew very little beyond his surname, which my mother bestowed on me in an effort to give me respectability. But I did meet his cousin. So it was not entirely in vain. And your father? Have you found him?"

Annie smiled conspiratorially and leaned toward Thanh. "Promise not to tell my mother?"

"How could I tell your mother? I do not even know her."

"True." Annie felt drawn to this man who seemed so easy to talk to, and she so rarely got to talk about her father. "My mother found him for me, although sometimes I think she wishes she hadn't. But I'm glad she did.

"He's a nice guy, for the most part. Although he didn't always play by the rules, or I wouldn't be here. My parents had an affair. How sordid, huh? He was a civilian pilot and they met in a bar in Saigon. He always came to her for a day or two whenever his schedule brought him to Vietnam, which was pretty much every week. It lasted for over two years. Mother thought they would marry, especially after I was born, but then one day he just stopped coming."

"And she came to the United States to find him?"

"I was just a baby at the time, but Mother managed to get us on a plane out of Vietnam before the fall of Saigon, and she tracked him down. But it turned out he was already married and had a family in California. I have two half brothers, even. But Dad did the best he could. He swore to his paternity, secured my citizenship for me and sent my mother checks every month to support us. What he did to her and to his wife wasn't right, but he's always been good to me."

"So you see him often. How fortunate you are."

"Not as much as I'd like. He's divorced and retired now, but he still likes to fly, and he owns a little airplane. Sometimes he flies out to visit me. Sometimes, I go to visit him, but my mother doesn't know. She thinks I am visiting a college friend. She was very angry and hurt when she found out he had a wife already. I guess she had a right to be."

"Perhaps she would not be so angry now. It has been a long time. Feelings heal eventually."

"Maybe. But she likes to keep up the pretense of hating him, so I don't argue with her. She gave up a lot for me. I owe her that much, at least."

"That and coming to these meetings?"

"Yeah." Annie grinned, then her sobered again. "Here she comes now. Remember, nothing about my dad, okay?"

Thanh pressed his lips together and winked, then stood as Annie's mother approached. All of a sudden, he looked stricken and bent to whisper. "How should I address your mother?"

Annie scrambled to her feet, reaching a hand toward her mother. "Mom. This is...my friend, Thanh Davis. Thanh, my mom, Mrs. Luong."

Her mother pursed her lips as she scrutinized the tall stranger, then she smiled her approval at what she saw. "It is my pleasure to meet you, Mr. Davis."

"And mine as well." Thanh took both of Annie's mother's hands in his. "But please call me Thanh."

"Blue, like the sky." Mrs. Luong murmured with a fleeting frown.

"What are you talking about, Mom?"

"His eyes are blue like the sky, daughter. That is what Thanh means." Mrs. Luong turned her gaze back to Thanh. "We will see you again, I hope?"

"I hope so, too." Thanh freed her mother's hands and reached for one of Annie's. "Meeting you has been the height of my evening. Of my whole week, as it turns out." He placed special emphasis on the word height and winked again as he said it.

Annie felt a blush rushing up into her face and prayed she had enough of a tan to hide the incriminating color. "I aim to please," she muttered in confusion, then took her mother's arm and turned toward the door.

"Until next week?" Thanh's voice lifted above the scraping of chairs as others gathered up their things and prepared to step out into the night.

Annie turned back to find Thanh's gaze fixed on her with the hint of a smile still tilting the corners of his mouth. 'Maybe,' she mouthed silently. Then she turned away and hurried her mother toward the door. She wasn't sure how she felt about furthering this friendship.

She couldn't recall ever feeling so comfortable with a man. Certainly she'd told him things she'd never told anyone else. Things about her parents. About how she felt toward her father. But Alejandro had hurt and humiliated her. Letting a man get too close wasn't something she was prepared to let happen again.

Alejandro had been her whole world for those crazy lust-filled months. He'd made her blood hot, and left her pining for their next moments together. She had believed, as her mother once had, that the passion would last forever. And Alejandro had been just as faithless as her father. Maybe all men were like that.

But had Alejandro ever felt like a friend? It was hard to remember anything beyond the infatuation, and the ultimate betrayal, now. Perhaps it would be as well to keep Thanh at arm's length. To keep whatever there was to be between them just a friendship. It would be safer that way.

"I like your young man," Mrs. Luong said as Annie settled her mother into the passenger seat of her beat up little Corolla.

"He's not my young man, mother. I just met him, for Pete's sake!"

"Nothing like Alejandro," Mrs. Luong persisted, ignoring Annie's protest.

"Why? Because Alejandro wouldn't be caught dead at a meeting like this?"

"Because he is polite. He knows how to behave toward his elders," Mrs. Luong said dismissively.

That Annie couldn't deny. Alejandro had been flippant rather than civil to her mother on the few times they'd been together. But that had been Alejandro. He'd treated his own mother the same way. At the time, Annie had seen it as confidence in himself. He'd been smart, hardworking and eager to make his way in the world. Not willing to let old world expectations slow him down.

In retrospect, it was easy to see Alejandro had been self-centered and rude. She doubted he'd ever really cared for her beyond the fact that she was pretty, happy to be charming to his clients and willing to let him into her bed. Even there, it had been more about what he wanted than what might please her. It had been more than a year since Alejandro had walked down the aisle with a plain, bossy little woman with a huge fortune and all the right connections. Almost a year since Alejandro had shown up on her doorstep one night, confident she'd still let him into her bed in spite of his marriage.

What did Annie know about Thanh anyway? He could be just an Asian version of Alejandro Garcia, looking for company because he was lonely. Maybe even seeking a sexual relationship, but having no intention of anything permanent. He had admitted coming to the meeting for the sole reason that his friend had moved away and he'd been looking for a new diversion.

"Did Mr. Davis say if he would be returning next week?" Annie's mother asked, intruding on Annie's cynical assessment of Thanh's motives.

"No. He didn't mention it," Annie answered as she slid into the driver's seat and shut her door.

"Oh. That's too bad. I liked him," Mrs. Luong repeated wistfully.

"You barely met him. How can you know if you liked him or not?"

"You would have much in common," Annie's mother persisted.

"Why do you think so?"

"He is Vietnamese, and I am guessing he has an American father, just as you do."

"That's where anything we have in common begins and ends. Except his father died before he was born and his mother shortly after. He grew up with a grandmother in Ho Chi Minh City where he would have been considered less than acceptable among his own people. And you know that better than most. I've had advantages Thanh never dreamed of. When you came to America, my father did what he could for both of us and he supports you still."

"Tony Santos treated me like a whore." Mrs. Luong flared angrily.

"He was a lonely young man whose job took him a long way from his home and family much too often. Perhaps it wasn't fair not to tell you he had a wife, but you were a willing partner in that affair," Annie shot back.

"Do not speak to me so, daughter. You know nothing about it."

Annie started to reply, but bit back the retort. Who was she to find fault with her mother, after all. Annie knew what it was to think yourself in love. Blinded by the heady passions of the body and deliberately ignoring questions that should have been asked.

"I'm sorry, Mother. But I don't think Thanh and I have that much in common, even if he does have nice manners." Which was all too true. Thanh and she could hardly have had more radically different upbringings. She was surprised he'd even gotten a college education, considering the plight of children growing up in Vietnam with no fathers to give them status. And that was just the cultural difficulties his grandmother would have faced. Persevering in the face of the Communist takeover must have made his childhood even more different.

"He seemed very taken with you." Her mother refused to be deterred, her voice soft and lilting again. "Perhaps if you will let yourself see it, you will find you are more alike than you think—I like his smile," she added after a pause.

A smile, Annie had to admit, that had caused her heart to feel like it had lurched to an unexpected stop for a moment. Just the memory of Thanh's smile that her mother's observation conjured up caused this odd sensation. Annie pressed her fingertips against her heart to suppress the sudden flare of excitement.

Six

Darkness was already closing in as Matt Steele and Thanh Davis stepped out onto the porch of the McLean, Virginia house Matt's family lived in when he had to be in DC. It was a sure sign fall was on the way in spite of the fecund scent of damp earth and green growing things. The haunting perfume of Eve's favorite moonflowers that grew up the latticework and twined around the porch railing pervaded the warm night air as Matt and Thanh settled themselves into a pair of Kennedy rockers with steaming mugs of hot coffee. Eve and Megan were in the kitchen cleaning up after supper and would join them in a bit.

For a while, neither man said anything, then Thanh set his mug on the table beside his chair and turned toward Matt. "You can not know how happy this past month has been for me. Finding you and getting to know your family and your kindness...especially when it is such a busy time. I..." Thanh broke off and tapped his fingers anxiously against the arm of the chair.

"It has been a pleasure for us, too," Matt started to assure Thanh before the younger man took a deep breath and went on.

"When the woman I once hoped to make my wife chose another man, and soon after that my grandmother died, I had no one left to care about. I felt very alone, and life seemed very unfair. Then it became my greatest desire to find my father's family. I had no idea if they would even be happy to meet me, but that dream kept me hopeful as I worked through the bureaucracy to get a visa and then a green card. I persevered even when my search took me to the home of the wrong Samuel Davis, which was rather embarrassing. Then you told me my grandparents were gone and there were no aunts or uncles, and it felt like a door slamming in my face again. I truly had nothing left.

"But, in the span of just a few weeks, you have made me feel as if I have always been part of *your* family. You welcome me even though you have no reason to do so. You make me feel…" Thanh broke off again, his voice wavering.

Matt cleared a sudden knot in his own throat. Thanh had just put words to a feeling that had been nagging Matt since they'd first met. The inexplicable sense that Thanh belonged in Matt's life and had always belonged there. The only thing Matt regretted about the last few weeks was that the campaign had left so little free time. No time to take Thanh to the small town Matt and Sam Davis had grown up in. No time to show Thanh all the places Sam and Matt had known as boys, to recount the adventures they'd had, or even to take Thanh to the graveyard where his father had been buried. All that would have to wait. But in the meantime, Matt prayed Thanh was in the country to stay. He thanked God for the chance that brought them together that fateful day at the Wall.

"I'm the one who is blessed. Sam was my best friend, and it's hard to accept that you have been out there all these years, and I had no idea."

"I wish I could have known my father." Thanh's soft-spoken words held a world of longing.

Matt felt the depth of sorrow in the younger man's voice and understood the yearning. Neither man spoke for a while. Matt took a swallow of his now-cold coffee and glanced over at Thanh. The chirping of crickets under the porch and the creak of Matt's rocker were the only sounds to break the quiet communion. Thanh picked up his mug, but didn't drink from it. Matt watched him rubbing his finger over the painted surface, feeling, but probably not seeing, the emblem of the United States Senate.

"Did he love my mother very much?" Thanh asked suddenly.

The statement-question caught Matt off guard, and he brought his rocker to a sudden halt. He'd been thinking about the day Thanh had come to his office. And wondering, what if a woman, stripped of her home, her family scattered and her daughter shamefully pregnant, had not saved one insignificant snapshot? What if he and Thanh had never met? Matt dragged his thoughts back to the moment.

"He wanted to marry her," Thanh prompted.

"Loving your mother convinced Sam that everything he'd lived through in Vietnam had been worthwhile. He was a good soldier, but we had fought an unwinnable war. By the time he met your mother, our own president had declared a truce with honor that didn't feel very honorable to the men who'd sacrificed so much. Especially your father. " Matt returned Thanh's probing gaze.

"I used to wonder." Thanh's voice sounded strangely hushed and far away. "Growing up, I heard a great deal of propaganda about the American aggressors."

"Unfortunately, much of it probably more true than false." Matt's mind skittered away from the arrogance he knew to be fact, and he looked back into the blackness of the yard, unwilling to see the reproach he might find in Thanh's eyes. He concentrated on Sam and the honorable things about that long ago war. "Sam loved Vietnam and its people. He thought them beautiful and deplored the violation of so much that was good."

44

"When I was a little boy," Thanh began with a wistful note to his words, "I used to pretend my father did not really die, and someday he would come and find me. I knew he could not be as perfect as I liked to imagine. But just to know him and for him to know me..."

"That, I understand." *How well I know that desire.*

This time Thanh set the mug down hard enough to slosh coffee onto the table. "You cannot know..." His voice had an unaccustomed edge to it.

"But I do," Matt interrupted. He turned in his chair to look at Thanh in the dim light spilling out of the kitchen door. It outlined Thanh's profile, accentuating the high cheekbones and smooth skin. "I do know," Matt repeated. "My father died in a war, just as yours did." He waited for Thanh to return his gaze, but the younger man stared resolutely ahead. Matt drummed his fingers on the arm of his rocker, debating how much to tell of a story that really belonged to his mother.

"My real father's name was Harry Stuart," Matt said after a long pause. "He was a pilot in Korea. He came home one summer to say goodbye to his family and friends before being shipped out. Harry had grown up next door to my mother, and even though she was promised to marry another man, they spent most of his last few days on furlough together.

"When his leave ended, he blew her a kiss and climbed aboard a train, and she never saw him again. In September, two officers showed up on Mrs. Stuart's porch with the news that Harry had been killed. I was born seven months later."

"Please forgive, I did not know," Thanh apologized in a horrified voice, his gaze meeting Matt's at last.

"I was four when my stepfather finished his hitch in the army and married my mother in spite of what she and Harry had done. I was old enough to have fantasies like yours, and I insisted they'd made a mistake. I told them my real father was a prisoner and someday he'd get free and come home again. My mother finally took me to the cemetery. She stood me in front of his marker and told me in cold, hard detail about his funeral. I think I cried enough for ten little boys that day."

Matt wanted to reach out and touch Thanh. He wanted to make a physical connection as real as the one that seemed to twine them together emotionally. But perhaps it wouldn't be welcomed. He thought about how different they were, yet how alike. Worlds apart, they'd grown up wanting the same thing, struggled against the same unanswerable longing and arrived at adulthood, scarred by the same loss. Things that were an indelible part of the men they had become.

Then Thanh leaned across the gap between their chairs, and his fingers brushed hesitantly over the back of Matt's hand. Before Matt could react, the back door burst open and Megan stepped out, coffee pot in hand.

"Anyone need a refill?"

~ * ~

At first, the dream was just tangled wisps of images: a handsome young flier from a bygone era grinning with insouciance as he climbed aboard his fighter plane, a small boy, shoulders heaving, in a pathetic heap before a polished granite stone. And another little boy with almond eyes and bare feet staring into the distance, watching for a father who would never come.

Then, just before dawn, Matt dreamed of his childhood.

Matt and Sam rode a cake of ice down a swiftly moving river. They screamed, half with excitement, half in fear, as icy water lapped over the edge of their bobbing vessel and soaked the hems of their corduroys. They clutched each other for support as the slab of ice surged under the bridge into a dark tunnel of rushing water and jostling ice chunks, the sounds echoing in the confined space.

As they shot out the other side into blinding sunlight, realization dawned on them that they had not thought how they would get off their icy raft before it reached the sea and plunged into the turbulence of the incoming tide.

"We gotta jump," Matt yelled, his heart pounding with sudden panic. He pointed to the narrowing gap between their raft and the trunk of a long dead tree that stuck out into the river. It was their last chance to reach safety.

"Jump, now!" Sam bellowed above the rush of water, then took the leap, not checking to see if Matt followed.

Matt hesitated. Finally he made a desperate leap, his foot connecting with a protruding log, then slipping. He felt himself falling. Then Sam reached back and grabbed the collar of Matt's jacket. Sam tugged, gasping for breath, as Matt finally managed to get a toehold. Together they made it to shore. They scrambled up the steep banking through snow-covered brambles. Their hands ached and bled as they dragged themselves to the top and stood panting with relief to have made it off the river.

"That was kinda dumb," Sam gasped as he surveyed their current predicament.

"I know," Matt agreed, still shaking with the sure knowledge that without Sam, he'd have fallen back into the river and probably drowned. "You saved my life."

"That's what friends are for." Sam shrugged off the thanks.
"No, I meant jumping off on this side of the river." Sam waved his arm toward the chain link fence that now barred their route to home.

"Not that we had a choice." Matt checked to the left and then the right. The fence went as far as he could see in either direction. "Now what?"

"Climb over it," Sam answered, grabbing the fence with both hands.

Matt hesitated as Sam hauled himself up and tried to find purchase with his rubber-toed boots in the two-inch squares. Matt tugged at his mittens and reached for the fence.

"I don't think I'm going to make it." Sam's oddly adult voice came from somewhere above Matt's head. Heat had begun to replace the cold and Matt, was perspiring. He tried to pull himself up, but people were jostling all around him. Voices everywhere, speaking a language that sounded familiar, but he didn't understand a word. Couldn't figure out where all the people had come from.

"Sam!" Matt called for his buddy, but couldn't find him in the milling crush of bodies. Women holding babies up to the soldiers barricading the fence. Men shoving everyone in their way. Kids whimpering, eyes big with fright. What in hell was going on? "Sam!"

Sweat dripped into Matt's eyes, stinging and blinding. His heart pounded loudly. Almost as loud as the whop-whop of helicopter blades overhead. He should have been on the other side of this fence. What the hell was he doing out here? Matt glanced over his shoulder, then remembered why he'd come outside the embassy grounds. He'd promised Mai Ly he'd get her out. When she hadn't come, he'd gone looking for her. Now it was too late. It might even be too late for him.

"Let me in. I'm a Marine!" Matt shouted, elbowing his way to the gate. A hand reached out, grabbed the front of his sweat-soaked uniform. "Let me in!" Matt shouted again, his voice hoarse with the effort to be heard.

"You're in already," a soft voice told him as the hand clutching his pajamas let go. Matt glanced down at wrinkled folds of his sweaty pajamas, then up to the owner of the voice.

"You going to be okay?" Eve asked as she kneaded his shoulders.

"Yeah, I think so." Shaken and sheepish, he sat up and swung his legs over the side of the bed. His brain felt foggy, his eyes heavy with lack of sleep.

"That must have been a doozie of a nightmare," Eve commented as she continued to rub his shoulders and back. "Where were you, anyway?"

"Outside the embassy."

"Saigon, I have to presume." Eve stopped massaging his shoulders and moved to sit beside him. "It's been awhile since you had any of those nightmares. You sure you're okay?"

Matt felt disoriented. "I was dreaming about Sam. About a crazy adventure we had as kids. At least, that's how the dream started out. But the ending didn't make any sense."

Eve slid off the bed, then bent to brush her lips over his. "Nightmares don't have to make sense." She grabbed his hands and pulled him to his feet. "Take a shower. Maybe that'll help shake it off." She kissed him again. A long, lingering, soul-healing kiss.

"Or we could go back to bed and fool around," she suggested, circling his waist with her arms and pulling him close.

"We could, but you've got a breakfast meeting to get to, and I've got a campaign to win."

Seven

Nightmares don't have to make sense, Matt reminded himself as he rode toward Union Hall on his way to a VFW-sponsored event. He stared blindly out the window at the early morning traffic. Eve's cheerful efforts to distract him had not banished the lingering effects of his nightmare. Neither had the shower rinsed away the nagging guilt the nightmare had rekindled.

The nightmare hadn't made sense because he never *had* gone looking for Mai Ly. He had not been outside the fence that awful day. Perhaps he should have gone earlier, but he'd been confident she would come to the embassy. He'd given her the radio and told her what to listen for. She should have come.

By the time he'd realized she wasn't coming, it was too late. The radio might have gotten stolen, or maybe she'd forgotten the code. He should have gone to find out. But maybe she'd changed her mind about wanting to leave. At least that's what he'd told himself. Whatever her reason for not showing up, he should have gone to check.

And then it had been too late.

His commanding officer hadn't let him leave the embassy grounds. Helicopters had made dozens of trips into the compound, taking refugees and straggling Americans out to ships hovering off shore. And Matt had been run ragged keeping order. He'd been one of those Marines standing at the fence, denying entry to the panicked citizens outside.

So why all this guilt so many years later? Matt hadn't been responsible for Mai Ly. She was an adult. She'd made her own decision. And Matt hadn't known Sam had gotten her pregnant. He had nothing to feel guilty for. But all the logic in the world didn't dislodge the gut-deep feeling that he'd messed up.

~ * ~

"Is Steele trying to mess up his own campaign?" Blair Cabot asked as he flung a newspaper onto the floor.

TJ Smith paced from one window to the next, then back to the table where he'd spread out the series of op-ed clippings offering opinions on the recent debate. As Blair's campaign manager, he'd already wondered the same thing.

"Not if Rick Winfield has any to say about it. Doesn't look as if he has a handle on his own candidate at the moment, though, and we need him to get Steele back on track." TJ adjusted himself with crude informality, and then dropped onto the opposite couch. He shoved several clippings to the side and snatched up one that had offended him the most. "The only way we're going to win this thing is to convince the American public that we are the only party with responsible answers to our current fiscal crisis."

"And debunk Steele's," Blair added.

"Yeah, but that *Post* columnist makes it sound as if Steele's promoting the same things you are." TJ slammed the paper back onto the table. "Christ! His party is the author of all these damned entitlements. How the hell does he get off making himself out to be the savior?"

"Maybe he thinks he is," Blair offered in a thoughtful tone. "What we really need is someone in his camp to find out what's going through his mind. See if there really is a growing divide between Steele and Rick Winfield and the party faithful. Or if it's something more insidious."

TJ had a sudden revelation. He pressed his lips together and nodded slowly. "I might just have the answer to that possibility."

"Who?" Blair perked up.

"Let me work it first. I'll let you know if I get a nibble. Now about Miller..." He reached for another clipping and passed it across the table.

~ * ~

Rolly's phone vibrated in his pocket. He ignored it. He knew who was calling. She'd left two messages already. He'd already told her no, and he'd already explained why. He forced himself to pay attention to the young man who was speaking, preparing the audience for his introduction. The vibrating stopped.

When it began again less than a minute later to let him know he had a text message, he slid his hand into his pocket. Perhaps it wasn't her, and the message was important. As surreptitiously as possible, he slipped the phone far enough out of his pocket to read the screen. It was her! Damn. He shoved the phone back into his pocket.

Rolly couldn't put Ashley off indefinitely in spite of the effect giving in would have on his reputation if it became public knowledge. But now was the worst possible time. She should know that and cut him some slack. Give him the time he'd begged for. But here she was, nagging him again, and she seemed impervious to his repeated pleas about the inappropriate timing of her calls.

Fifteen years earlier, Roland Miller had successfully defended Ashley Lauder against a lawsuit claiming complicity in an investment scam. She'd been at least partly guilty of the charges leveled at her, but he'd managed to blur the lines of proof far enough to leave doubt in the minds of the jurors. It had not been one of his finer moments. Nor had what followed.

Ashley had not been above flashing the judge, the opposing attorney and himself generous and frequent glimpses of her voluptuous cleavage, nor of wearing obscenely short skirts that provided a view even the openly gay clerk had had trouble ignoring. Before the verdict was in, Rolly had allowed himself to follow her siren's call in a desperate attempt to prove something to himself. The affair had been messy, inappropriate and deeply disturbing. Had anyone ever found out, things would have gotten really nasty. Didn't Ashley understand that giving anyone even the vaguest of reasons to dig into their past connection could still ruin them both?

Ashley was a beautiful, sensual woman. He blushed to recall how shamelessly he had used her. Then reminded himself that she had used him as well. They'd used each other. But she'd been faithful to the deal they'd made back then and never said a word about it to anyone. She was generous and caring in her own way. And until now, circumspect.

~ * ~

Annie resisted the urge to yank her hands away when Thanh reached across the table to cover them with his slender fingers. Not because the feeling of his cool smooth skin was repugnant, but because his touch made her jumpy with desires she didn't want to acknowledge. She only wanted a friendship she could trust.

It had been almost a month since Thanh had first introduced himself in the basement of the Methodist church where the Vietnamese refugees gathered. Almost a month of meeting Thanh at her favorite diner to grab a bite to eat a couple times a week. She refused to call them dates because that implied the kind of relationship she wasn't planning on pursuing.

She needed a friend, and she liked Thanh. Why did he have to complicate things by filling her with unwanted urges? It was just lust. That's what it was always about with men. She should know.

"What are you doing this Saturday? Would you like to go to a movie?" Thanh asked. He rubbed his thumbs lightly over the backs of her hands.

"I promised to work at the campaign office."

Thanh let go of her hands and sat back. Good, the hot feeling swirling in her gut could go away now. Maybe. Except she felt bereft, rather than relieved.

Thanh looked at her with a pained expression clouding his handsome features. "How can you work for such a man?"

"He stands for everything I believe in," Annie defended her candidate.

"He is a ruthless man. He crushes people who get in his way. Is that the kind of man you feel would make the best leader?"

"He's not my ideal candidate, I admit, but Roland Miller is a puppet, and I just can't vote for a Democrat in spite of the fact that Mathew Steele is a friend of yours. Blair Cabot will bring the kind of change this country needs. He won't be tied to all the old entitlements he had nothing to do with enacting. He's not in the pocket of all the lobbyists either."

"He is only one man, Annie." Thanh picked up his fork and shoveled the last piece of his pie into his mouth, chewed and swallowed, then pushed his plate away. "He will have congress to contend with. Unless the voters put most of the current members out and elect an entirely new group of independents who think as Mr. Cabot does, nothing will really change."

"How come you know so much about American politics? You some kind of expert?" Annie hated the curt edge to her voice, but he'd irritated her by pointing out the unpleasant realities she tried to ignore most of the time.

"I have studied a great deal about the American government, but no, I am not an expert." He shrugged lightly. "I just think Mr. Steele is the better man. And it has nothing to do with being his friend. He would have a good portion of congress behind him. Besides, he is thinking more like your Mr. Cabot every day. Did you watch the debate the other night?"

"I—No, I didn't. I meant to, but I, I forgot."

Thanh's eyebrows shot up. "You forgot?"

"I stopped by my mother's, and we got into an argument. When I left, I was pissed off with her, and I drove around for a while to cool off. I didn't remember the debate until it was over."

"Why were you so angry with your mother?"

Annie couldn't tell Thanh the argument had been about her relationship with him, so she lied. "My father called me on my cell, and she guessed who it was."

Immediately Thanh's face grew concerned, and an unpleasant feeling of guilt flooded Annie. The feeling began to manifest itself as a flush creeping up her neck, so she slid from the booth and grabbed her jacket. "I've got to get going." She glanced at her watch. "I didn't realize what time it was."

"I thought you had the evening free?" Thanh stood with that lanky grace Annie found so appealing and shoved his arms into his own coat.

"I—I have a thing I need to write tonight," she blustered, trying to ignore the renewed awareness of him, but he was standing too close. The heat in her cheeks began to turn into heat in other places. She turned toward the door.

"I will walk you home, then." Thanh took three tens from his wallet and dropped them on the table.

The chilly air outside did little to cool Annie's flush so she began to walk rapidly away from the diner in the direction of her apartment. Thanh had to hurry to keep up.

"How about Sunday afternoon?" He put a hand under her elbow, forcing her to slow her pace.

"Sunday afternoon for what?"

"You can take me to the Air and Space Museum. Did you not tell me that was your favorite? I have not yet been there."

Relieved that he'd given up the movie idea, Annie agreed. An afternoon at the noisy museum filled with shouting kids and their distracted parents was a lot safer than the dark confines of a movie theater.

She relaxed. "That sounds like fun."

"And then I can take you to dinner afterward." Thanh pushed his luck.

"You just took me to dinner," Annie pointed out, removing her arm from his grasp to push the *walk* button on the light pole.

"Is there a limit to the number of times I can take you to dinner in a week?" The light changed, and they stepped into the street. Thanh grabbed her hand and pulled it into the crook of his elbow.

For all that he appeared slight at first glance, there was a rock-solidness to his arm. A decidedly masculine play of muscles that felt way too alluring. She'd felt the same hard muscular tension when he'd put an arm about her waist to usher her into the cab. They'd dashed for it when they'd got caught too far from home when the rain began. And then there'd been that time she'd tripped and kept herself from falling with both hands planted firmly against his abdomen. There had been no ignoring that ripped and sexy wall of muscles.

In spite of her best intentions, she'd caught herself watching the way his slacks pulled taut over the outline of his thighs when he walked, and had noted on more than one occasion the well-built spread of shoulders beneath the crisp dress shirt whenever he removed his jacket. Thanh had a body that was just way too tempting for her libido. Or for the high-minded plan to keep him at arm's length. What had happened to her sense of self-preservation?

Maybe I should just give in and jump into bed with him and get it over with. Maybe once the mystery is gone, the heat will go away. But then what? Could we go back to being just friends once we've slept together?

"Well, is there?" Thanh prompted.

"No. I guess not. Dinner would be nice, but nothing fancy. Okay?"

"Okay!" Thanh echoed her with his singsong lilt. Then he dropped her hand and put his arm about her waist.

The idea of succumbing was growing more appealing by the moment. Then she looked up and saw her father sitting on her doorstep.

Eight

After another night of restless sleep and disturbing dreams, Matt got up before it was fully light, careful not to disturb Eve. Feeling uncomfortably edgy, he decided to push his luck with Joe and see if they'd let him go rowing. Figuring a good offense was half the battle, he loaded his one-man shell onto the roof rack on his car before he opened the garage door.

But it wasn't Joe sitting out front sipping his usual mega-sized paper cup of coffee while his observant eyes kept watch. Two younger agents lounged against the bumper of their black SUV. The taller of the two, black-haired and looking very much like one would expect of a man named Bharat Sahir, pushed himself to his feet and strode in Matt's direction.

"Where are you planning to row, sir?"

"The Potomac."

"You got another boat?" Bharat didn't even try to dissuade him.

So much for being on the water alone! "Yeah. I'll get it." Matt headed back into the garage and hauled down his other boat, then tossed it on the empty half of the boat rack and lashed it down. He'd wanted to be alone on the water to get rid of the lingering cobwebs of sleep and erase the guilt inspired by his dreams. He'd have to settle for turning the predawn exercise into a two-man race.

Bharat climbed into the passenger seat and Matt tossed him a life vest. He supposed he should consider himself fortunate that the young agent was willing to go the extra mile and get out on the water at all. Joe had probably read them the riot act the last time Matt had eluded them and gone rowing unguarded.

"Are we racing today?" Bharat asked as he buckled his seat belt.

"I'm always racing when I get in my boat," Matt responded. He put his car in gear and backed out of the garage, then hit the gadget on his visor to close the garage door. "It's how I get the kinks out."

"A gym would be safer."

"Yeah, I suppose it would, but I can't think why anyone would be gunning for me anyway. You ever wonder what our founding fathers would think about all this protection stuff?"

Bharat shrugged. "If we didn't have it, I'd be out of a job."

"You're smart. You've got a college education. You'd find something else. Something your wife would probably like a whole lot better than wondering *if* rather than *when* you're coming home from work every day."

"She's okay with what I do," Bharat assured him, scanning their surroundings vigilantly as Matt pulled off the road into the boat ramp parking lot.

Matt parked at the far end of the almost empty lot next to his other agent's car and got out. He and Bharat had the boats off the roof and pushed halfway into the water when Bharat's partner showed up. Terry Muir had beaten them to the spot they knew Matt liked to launch from and had already cased the shore in both directions. Terry was Bharat's total opposite. A full foot shorter with pale blond hair and a dusting of freckles he probably hated. He barely looked old enough to shave. But looks were deceiving. Matt knew this man had thrown himself in harm's way more than once, been shot twice and saved at least one life under his protection.

Matt waited while Terry and Bharat consulted in brief urgent sentences. Then they allowed him to settle into his boat and Terry shoved him into the current.

With Bharat keeping pace, Matt dug the long sweeps into the murky brown water and leaned into the action, enjoying the quick responsive leap of the light boat. His hands, soft from weeks crammed with campaigning that left little time for physical exercise, began to sting, but he ignored them. His shoulders and back soon felt the ache of unaccustomed exercise as well, but he continued to push himself. It felt good to be out on the river again, pitting his strength against the current. He didn't slacken his pace until the bridge came in sight.

Then he turned the shell and returned the way he'd come. The drugged feeling had gone, but he still couldn't shake the vague sense of guilt. As if there were something he should have done and hadn't. He could think of nothing to bring on such a feeling, except, perhaps his dreams, since they'd been getting more persistent of late, robbing him of sleep he desperately needed. He shrugged and gazed across the river.

The sun rose from the hazy horizon, splashing glints of platinum and pink across the water. Ducks paddled along at the fringes, upending now and then to search for their breakfasts. The echo of a skiff with a single cycle engine putting noisily echoed from the far side of the river.

Time to get the boats out and get home. Too many people on the river made his security detail's job that much more difficult. Terry and Bharat were uneasy enough already.

Matt coasted the last hundred yards back to the landing. A light breeze played with his hair and sent a shiver across his sweat-slicked flesh. His muscles ached but he felt good. And glad he'd come.

~ * ~

As Matt pulled into his driveway a short time later, a familiar green van turned the corner. His good humor faltered, but he climbed out of his car, thanked Bharat, and forced a smile onto his face as the newcomer pulled into the drive and erupted from his car.

"Morning, Rick. I thought I gave you the day off."

"We've got to talk," Winfield began without preamble.

Rick was probably the best campaign manager in the business. He, along with Don Yates, consultant and fundraiser, and Jack Holland were the core of Matt's campaign team.

In sharp contrast to Matt's generally unflappable calm, Rick was in constant motion and easily riled. It was due entirely to Rick's talent and effectiveness that his quick temper was just as swiftly forgiven. This morning, however, Matt didn't feel like dealing with either Rick or his temper.

"Have you had breakfast?"

"Coffee," Rick answered impatiently. "Where have you been?"

Matt glanced at his watch. It wasn't yet seven "I've been rowing."

"You must drive the Secret Service nuts." Rick glanced toward the bulky black SUV parked at the curb.

"They take it in stride." Matt felt in no mood for a lecture about the men whose job it was to protect him. "Look, you might be able to survive on caffeine, but I can't and I haven't eaten yet. If we really need to talk business this early on a Sunday morning, at least come into the kitchen while I get myself some breakfast." Without waiting for a reply, he turned on his heel and headed for the house with Bharat still covering his six.

Rick stopped long enough to grab his briefcase from the car. Slamming the door shut again, he trailed Matt up the stairs, nodded at the agent, then stepped into the house.

"Have you got any idea how the press is interpreting the speech you gave last night?" Rick thrust one hip against the counter. He waved a folded newspaper in Matt's face, jabbing at it with an impatient finger. Matt ignored the paper and reached for a box of corn flakes.

"They're having a goddam field day."

"I don't think..." Matt began and was ruthlessly cut off.

"You didn't think. That's just it." Rick flung himself toward the window, then spun back. "This campaign has been going just the way we want it. Partly, I admit, because the opposition hasn't been able to find a shred of scandal to throw at you, and you've managed to distance yourself from the folly of the current administration. But mostly because you support family and kids and programs people have come to depend on when the rest of the field wants to cut everything."

Matt went into the pantry. For a few merciful moments, Rick's voice faded away. Matt filled a glass with milk and then poured some over his cereal. He sliced a banana on top. When he returned to the kitchen and slid into the breakfast nook, Rick still fumed.

"...believe you will take away their safety net. They're afraid they're going to find themselves out on the street. How do you suppose they're going to interpret last night's little lecture?"

"I wish you'd sit down." Matt stifled an urge to tell Rick to shut up.

"Are you listening, for Christ's sake?" Rick slid onto the opposite bench.

"You know, Rick, if I hadn't been there, you'd have me convinced I'd suggested putting an end to the entire welfare system. All I said..."

"All you said was that America has always been a land of opportunity, and should not let itself become another Europe. And the media has decided to translate that statement as the wealthy get wealthier and the poor get poorer. It's not the first time you've suggested that, either. I'd like to know where the hell you're coming from." He slammed his fist down on the table, upsetting Matt's milk glass. Rick grabbed for the glass and set it upright again but not before half the contents spilled across the table and into Matt's lap. "Jesus, Matt, I'm sorry. Here." Rick grabbed a handful of napkins out of the holder in the center of the table.

Matt blotted his clothing while Rick mopped the table and repeated his apology.

"It's only milk. Don't worry about it."

Rick hushed finally, and sat back, subdued.

Matt stared at his campaign manager while he pondered how to explain himself. Or even if he should try. He didn't doubt for a minute that the press, to say nothing of Blair Cabot, were gleefully dissecting the possible ramifications of his remarks.

"I recall quoting JFK. It certainly seemed to appeal to the masses when I did so during the debate, as I'm sure you'll agree." Matt scooped up a spoonful of already soggy cereal and studied Rick over it.

Rick made a clearly visible effort to speak carefully and hold on to his temper. "Creating opportunities is one thing. Tearing apart the welfare system to fulfill this quixotic dream of yours is vastly and far less popularly different."

"Our welfare system was meant to be a safety net, not a way of life. It's time it was overhauled." Matt gave up on his cereal, which had lost all its appeal. "You really ought to relax, Rick. You're going to have a heart attack at the rate you're going. How long since you took a day off?"

"Time enough for a vacation come November," Rick answered, waving a dismissive hand. "Right now, we have some serious fence-mending to see to and a week's worth of stumping to go over. Or had you forgotten?"

"As if I could." Matt got up to empty the remains of his breakfast into the disposal and stack the bowl in the dishwasher.

Rick had been left out of the loop on Matt and Hal's new deal for a reason. He was a dynamite organizer, brilliant at planning campaign strategy, and he'd never lost a campaign. But he was also totally wedded to the hard-line, far-left policies of the traditional Democratic doctrine.

Admittedly, it wasn't just the Democrats who'd written all the blank checks over the last half century, but the reality was that the checks were about to bounce. Something had to be done, even if shooting the messenger was easier than accepting reform.

Several months ago, Matt and Hal had put together the plan they intended as a blueprint for their four years in charge. But since then, it had become clear that not sharing the plan before the election was, in essence, misleading the voters just to get into the White House. That was something Matt had never done and didn't intend to start doing now. So they'd begun a careful campaign of slipping in pieces of the plan whenever appropriate and answering questions about the country's financial future as honestly as possible. But the overall plan and the details were on a need to know basis, and Rick didn't need to know. Rick didn't need to be sidetracked, or so Matt insisted whenever a scene like this erupted. Maybe that was the source of Matt's vague sense of guilt?

Rick swung his briefcase onto the table with a heavy thud, snapped it open and began to rifle through it. Resigned, Matt glanced at his watch. "You've got an hour. Then I have to get ready for church."

~ * ~

Four days later, having made appearances in several dozen places including a $1000-a plate fundraiser, a city still struggling to pull itself together after a devastating flood, an innovative microchip plant, the dedication of a new library, and a hand-shaking session outside an auto plant at closing time, Matt was back in Virginia. When he slipped, unannounced, through his front door, and it appeared that his wife and daughter were both out, he sagged thankfully into his comfortable recliner.

"May I get you something, Senator?" Thanh appeared out of nowhere.

Matt started. He'd thought he was alone in the house. Alone for the first time in days, in fact.

"Where did you come from? And where's everyone else? By the way, I've been 'Senatored' to death. Couldn't you bring yourself to call me Matt?"

"Certainly, Matt, sir. My computer crashed and your lovely wife, who is at a dinner for the DAR, gave me permission to use hers."

"And drop the *sir* if you want to remain on my good side."

"Your good side, sir?"

Matt snorted. "It's an expression. It means it would please me if you left off the *sir* and the *Senator.* Do you know how to make a highball?"

"Of course!" Thanh looked surprised at the question.

"I'll have a gin and tonic, then."

Thanh disappeared for a few minutes, then returned and handed Matt a squat frosted glass with ice clinking in the clear contents and a slice of lime perched on its rim. Then he settled himself into the chair opposite Matt's. "Megan is upstairs getting ready to go to a movie with her new man friend."

"It's *boyfriend*," Matt corrected. "I'm surprised your students haven't brought your idiomatic vocabulary up to speed."

"I learn a great deal from my students, except much of it is not fit for repeating." Thanh grinned. "But I am most often confused by the contradictions."

"Like?"

"Like how cool and hot can mean the same thing? Or how a fat chance and a slim chance are the same size."

Matt laughed out loud. "English is a contrary language."

"Yes, and believe me, Megan's new friend is not a boy. He is very much a man, and I am not so sure you will approve."

Before Matt could ask what Thanh meant, he heard Megan's footsteps descending to the hall. Then she emerged into the living room and bent to hug her father. "If I'd known you were going to be home this early, I'd have stayed in. Except I didn't and…" she broke off shrugging.

"So, do I get to meet your new beau?" What had Thanh meant by his assumption that Matt wouldn't approve? Did the guy have tattoos covering half his body and collect unemployment? Something that outrageous didn't sound like Megan's usual style. She had good taste, and he'd come to respect her choices. But he was coming to respect Thanh's opinions, as well.

"Oh, Daddy, don't be so Gothic," Megan said over her shoulder as she returned to the hall to retrieve her jacket from the closet. "Gotta go, Randy's waiting. Love you." The front door opened then closed, and she was gone.

"What is Gothic?" Thanh asked, frowning.

"She means that I'm getting old, and that I've completely forgotten she is a liberated woman in charge of her own life." Matt took a sip of his drink. "It also means we won't be introduced to Randy whatever-his-last-name-is."

"It is Robinson," Thanh supplied. "I have already met him."

"So, tell me what you know of this Randy Robinson, and I'll tell you how to get a great deal on a new computer."

Nine

TJ strode into Blair's office, shut the door behind him with a tap of his heel and dumped a pile of computer printouts he'd brought with him on the desk. He knew where his boss was going with this quest, but he didn't think it would make any difference. Matt Steele's voting record was already out there, and the man himself made no effort to disguise or explain away his earlier choices. But Blair had insisted.

"This is just the beginning. Where do you want me to start?"

"How is it organized?" Blair glanced up at him and pulled several pages off the top of the pile.

"By date, unfortunately." TJ grabbed a chair, pulled it up to the front of the desk and settled into it. "We'll have to scan through it to find the specific issues you were after."

"Well, take notes on everything else and mark important stuff." Blair yanked out a side drawer, pawed through its contents and tossed a pad of stickie notes across the desk. "Right now I'm mostly concerned with education and Obamacare, but it won't hurt to be prepared for defense and taxes."

"What about Social Security?"

Blair shrugged. "I doubt even Miller would verbalize any serious changes to Social Security. It would be political suicide. Steele definitely won't."

"Welfare and unemployment insurance are equally sacred cows, but he's had quite a bit to say about those."

"Which is why we are here at this ungodly hour digging through all this stuff before my first appearance of the day. Did you see the poll numbers pop yesterday? We've got to undermine this incipient swell of popular approval before it gets out of hand."

"Attacking his voting record isn't going to be enough," TJ warned. "He's got some bee in his bonnet that so far is finding willing ears, and he's always been such a straight arrow, people appear willing to believe he's having an honest change of heart. We're going to have to find something far more damaging to dent his image."

"Well, I'll leave the mud to you. In the meantime, I need to throw his past votes out there every time he sounds like he's on the same page I am. And I want accurate quotes. As many as I can dig up." Blair grabbed another fistful of paper and began to thumb through it.

"Derailing Miller would be your best chance to move a significant block of voters into our column. I think chasing Steele's voting record is a waste of time. Rumors and innuendos are far more damaging. And I heard an interesting rumor about Ashley Lauder."

"Lauder?" Blair shot TJ a frowning look.

"And a possibly awkward connection to Roland Miller," TJ added, enjoying his boss' sudden interest.

"Really?" Blair dropped his hands into his lap and pursed his lips.

"One of my informants told me Rolly received a text message from her in the middle of a campaign stop yesterday. A liaison with a woman whose reputation doesn't bear a lot of close scrutiny could do the man some serious damage."

"Receiving a text message doesn't mean he's having an affair with the woman. Didn't he represent her in a lawsuit some years back?" Blair asked.

"If he did, I'll dig up the particulars. I'd love to shove a spoke in Rolly's wheel. Just think of all the ultra-conservative voters who'd be looking for a new star to hitch their wagon to. And you can bet your next paycheck they won't go so far to the left as to vote for Steele."

"Well, stay on it," Blair hissed, "...and keep me in the loop."

"You bet, boss." TJ saluted and did a snappy about-face before striding toward the door.

~ * ~

Matt spent Saturday morning alone in the house following up on fundraising calls.

"Win or lose," he muttered to himself, "...I'll need my head examined if I ever consider another run for the oval office." He absolutely hated the endless phone calls begging for money. All his previous campaigns had demanded serious amounts of cash too, but this, the biggest race of all, was obscene in its demand for funds.

As he ticked off names, congratulating himself on an unusual run of success, he began to wonder where Eve was. He looked at his watch. Half past eleven. Nearly lunchtime, and he could have sworn she'd said she was coming straight home from her dentist appointment. Just when he began to be seriously concerned, he heard her voice in the hall along with that of his advance man, Reuben Murdoch.

Matt went out to meet them, wondering what brought Murdoch over.

"He followed me home," Eve spoke as if she were talking about a puppy. "He looked hungry so I figured we ought to feed him."

"You've come to the right place." Matt clapped Murdoch on the shoulder. "Eve's got a soft spot for strays."

After lunch, Megan challenged her father to a game of basketball, which immediately swelled to include Murdoch and Thanh, who'd also showed up in time for lunch. While Megan argued about who should be on whose team, Matt sat on the bottom step tying his sneakers, and Murdoch limbered up his shooting arm.

"Youth against the experience," Murdock suggested.

"But..." Megan glanced at Thanh. "You ever played before?"

"Just a little," Thanh confessed.

"You afraid of a couple old men?" Matt teased.

"You're on, old man!" Megan grabbed the ball from Murdock's unsuspecting grasp and tossed it to her father.

Stiff from a lack of practice, Matt missed his first shot.

"Better hustle, Daddy. Wouldn't want a little girl to beat the old hoopster." Megan dribbled past him and laid one up that slipped neatly through the net.

"Pride goes before a fall," he warned her in return, then took a pass from Murdoch and dropped a long shot.

Thanh might not have played much, but he showed a natural grace and aptitude. He stole the ball from Murdoch and passed it off to Megan, cheered on by Eve who'd come out to watch. As the afternoon wore on, and Thanh gained confidence, he and Megan began to pull ahead in spite of Matt's unerring long shot and Murdoch's murderous charges.

"Just wait 'til Ben comes home and finds out I've got a new teammate who's almost as good as he is," Megan announced, as Thanh left the ground and sank a jump shot over Murdock's head that put them ahead. Thanh crowed with pleasure.

"Just you keep your mind on the game," Matt huffed as he fielded the return from Murdoch and dropped another long ball that caught his daughter flat-footed and off balance.

"Maybe you should call it a draw." Eve suggested from her perch on the top step.

Sweaty and tired, but determined not to let the younger players outlast him, Matt shook his head.

"Next team to make a shot wins it," he managed to get out between gasps for breath and went in for a layup. Thanh blocked it, tried to copy Matt's hook and failed. Then Murdoch suffered a rare miss, and Megan had the ball again.

"Come and get me, Daddy," she teased, dribbling around Matt. He lunged and she shot past under his arm, but he'd anticipated her.

As he stole the ball, Megan jerked around in amazement. It left his hand in a long arcing shot and fell through the basket without a whisper.

"Nothing but air." He took a flourishing bow. Thanh's jaw hung open with amazement, and Murdoch slapped him on the back.

"You're incredible, Daddy." Megan gave Matt a hug. "But my day is coming, just you wait."

"I know, kitten. I know." He tousled her hair, happy to remain her hero for a little longer.

Getting old was hell. "But I'm not decrepit yet!"

~ * ~

TJ Smith hunched on his stool, nursing a beer, unfazed by the fact that he was as isolated as a leper in this den of Democratic politics. It hadn't always been that way. In fact, he and his college roommate had cut their political eyeteeth in this bar.

He thought back to those days of youthful exuberance and naïve belief. Back when he and Rick Winfield had been on the same page, pulling for the same guy and driven by similar convictions. When had that changed? Or had it changed at all?

Maybe he'd always been this cynical. Maybe he'd always been driven by the desire to win at any cost, and the convictions had always belonged to Rick. He remembered their first Democratic convention and the euphoria when their candidate had won the nomination. He also remembered the disillusionment when Dukakis failed to measure up in the general campaign.

Perhaps that's when their mutual coalition had begun to fray and the true nature of their personalities had driven them in different directions. Rick, ever the believer, following without question, the teaching and dogma of the party, while TJ jumped ship as often as need be to stay on the winning side.

TJ was counting on Rick's faithfulness. It was why he'd come to this bar in the first place. He and Rick had remained friends in spite of the divergent tracks their careers had taken, so Rick hadn't been suspicious when TJ called to suggest getting together over a few beers. Both had been in and out of Washington and every other major city in the country over the last few months, often crossing paths but never with the time to sit down and talk. So, TJ had called, and here he was waiting for Rick to show up.

Blair wanted to know what was going on with Steele's sudden shift in policy, because they needed to craft their own message to trump anything Steele offered that struck a note with the voters. And TJ knew that with enough beers under his belt, Rick would forget to be circumspect, especially with someone he trusted.

TJ drew a finger through the sweat on his glass and contemplated the breach of friendship he was planning. He really was a bastard. Just like his ex-wife had told him and anyone else who would listen before she washed her hands of him completely and moved to the other side of the country.

"Hey, TJ!" Rick slid onto the stool beside him and slapped him on the back. "How're they hanging?"

"About the same as always," TJ responded. He ran a hand over his own bald head, envying Rick his still-full head of dark curls and the flat stomach, so unlike his own that tended to droop farther over his belt with each passing year. "I heard you rejoined the singles scene."

A cloud passed over Rick's face. He was newly divorced. It hadn't been Rick's idea, and he was still very much in love with his ex. TJ knew it, but brought it up anyway to encourage any tendency Rick might have to drown his sorrows.

"Been too busy to join any scene," Rick said after a pause. "Haven't even seen my boys on my court-assigned nights lately. Things have gotten kind of crazy."

TJ caught the bartender's eye and signaled for another beer. "What'll you have?" he asked Rick.

Rick checked out the bottle TJ had just emptied. "Same."

TJ held up two fingers, then pointed at an empty table in the corner. "I think I'm getting old." He chuckled as he slid off his stool. "I can't sit on these things with my feet on the rungs for more than a few minutes before my legs go to sleep."

Rick gave him a quizzical look as if that had never happened to him, but shrugged good-naturedly and headed toward the table.

"So, did you call just to taunt me about Ellen, or have you really missed me?" Rick asked after two bottles of cold Heineken had been delivered, and he'd taken a long swallow.

~ * ~

Rolly Miller stepped into the gallery trying to ignore the claustrophobic feeling his security detail engendered. He shouldn't have come here, but he'd felt like walking from the early morning meeting to the luncheon where he was speaking. He'd known the gallery was on the way. He should have known he wouldn't be able to pass by without going in.

"Governor!" A tall, elegant woman greeted him with surprise in her voice. She hastened toward the door and extended her hand. "My brother didn't tell me you were coming."

Rolly took the extended hand and drew the woman close enough to brush air kisses near both rouged cheeks. "Please don't blame him. I didn't know I was coming. But I was on my way to a luncheon and there was a little extra time. So I decided to step in for a few moments."

"Just window shopping?" she asked, a puzzled note to her question.

"Perhaps," Rolly said glancing around the gallery. "You know how much I love Milner's work, and you always have such wonderful pieces. Has your brother acquired any new ones? Is he here?"

Barbara Miller looked uncomfortably at the men who'd entered the gallery with Rolly, pursed her lips as if she wasn't sure how to answer, and then turned toward the far end of the gallery they'd been moving through. "I'll get him."

She hastened toward an arch leading into another gallery and disappeared. A moment later a man appeared. He was clearly related to the woman, with the same slender elegance and red hair.

"Roland. It is good to see you," the man said. He did not offer his hand, but folded them behind his back instead. "Barbara says you are perhaps interested in a new Milner?"

"I...ah, yes," Rolly finally replied. He shouldn't have come after all. He'd known he shouldn't come, but the desire had been too strong. The temptation too much. Barbara stood in the archway looking at him reproachfully. He should just leave. This was all about Ash, not Barbara, and he was putting her on the spot.

"Come," the man said, putting a hand on Rolly's elbow and leading the way toward a free-standing display in the middle of the room. Soft light came from both the floor and ceiling, illuminating a large canvas depicting a sunlit garden in an ornate frame.

Rolly pretended to admire the painting. He could feel Barbara's eyes on him as well as those of her brother. After several uncomfortable minutes, he stepped back.

"It's delightful, but perhaps not precisely what I'm looking for. I need something lighter. Brighter, maybe. I...I must be going, but thank you for your time."

Before the dealer could reply, Rolly turned on his heel and headed for the door. His detail hustled to check the sidewalk before he stepped out. He overheard Deb Malden, the female agent, mutter something to her male counterpart about the painting being rather too bright in her opinion. Lew Tripp laughed, but Rolly didn't hear his reply. He was in too much of a hurry to put distance between himself and the gallery.

I'm sorry, Ash. I shouldn't have done that to you.

Ten

At ten to five on Monday morning, Matt found his seat in first class and dropped into it. Even after a hard run before the sun was up and a hot shower and two cups of coffee, his mirror had revealed dark shadows beneath his eyes and a haunted expression that left him appearing as tired and tortured as he felt. It was going to be a difficult week.

Jack preempted the seat next to Matt, saving him from Rick's Monday morning pep talk. Matt was less grateful for Jack's sarcastic comment about women and their unfailing talent for ruining a man's sleep. When he didn't respond, Jack gave up and opened his briefcase, leaving Matt to his own thoughts.

Thoughts he couldn't leave behind, no matter how hard he ran.

The confusing nightmares had become persistently regular and he didn't understand why. The dreams were a kaleidoscope of images from his hellish tours of duty in Vietnam, some distorted but real. Most like nothing he could recall. And when he woke, it was always with a haunting sense of guilt. As if there was something he should have done but hadn't. Or perhaps something he *had* done and didn't want to recall.

If he had more time for quiet self-analysis, perhaps he could dig his way to the bottom of the dreams, but he'd been too busy. And now he was too tired. The nightmares had robbed him of desperately needed sleep, and he needed to stay focused on the campaign. Only five weeks to go. He didn't have time for this. He and Hal had a lot to get accomplished in five weeks.

As he watched the preparations for takeoff, he tried to push the problem to the back of his mind. He mentally reviewed the densely packed schedule ahead of him.

"Would you care for a paper, sir?"

Matt turned back to the steward, who held out a copy of the morning *Post*. Matt thanked him, took the paper, and glanced at the front page. He forgot all about the nightmares.

"Steele's Love Child?" screamed the headline. Below it, a full-color photo of Matt and Thanh taken Saturday in Matt's driveway took up most of the space above the fold. Matt had been caught in midair, the ball just leaving his fingertips. Thanh had one arm up to block the shot. Their faces were only inches apart and the remarkably similar blue of their eyes struck Matt like an indictment.

"But he's Sam's son," Matt muttered in a stunned whisper. He skimmed the article. Who had written this? And why? Matt looked for the byline.

"Jack?" Shaken, Matt thrust the article toward his press secretary.

"Good God!" Jack exclaimed, sitting up abruptly. "Jesus, Matt. Why didn't you warn me?"

"Warn you about what? You knew about Thanh," Matt answered, still too shocked to be hurt that Jack apparently accepted the suggestion as fact. "But he's not *my* son."

Jack's piercing black gaze probed Matt's for a long appraising minute. "All right, but that doesn't change the damage this could do." Jack's dark eyes flickered intently as he raced through the article. "How close have you two become anyway? This makes it sound as if you've pretty much adopted him."

"May I bring you something for breakfast, gentlemen?"

"No!" Jack snapped, startling the solicitously hovering flight attendant. "Nothing just now, thank you," he amended, softening his voice with an apologetic smile. When the man moved on, Jack hunched his shoulder and turned back to Matt.

"Start at the beginning."

"He's way past being young enough to adopt, but if I'd known about him sooner, I would have," Matt began defiantly. He traced Thanh's face with one finger. "His father was my best friend. The kid was abandoned. That's unfortunately true. Except, Sam didn't do it on purpose. He got killed before he knew about Thanh."

"That doesn't explain how you got involved. I have to tell you, Matt, it doesn't look good."

"Sam was my cousin, as well as my best friend. So that makes Thanh family. Would you have me disown him just because it might be inconvenient to be seen with him?"

"I'd hardly call this accusation inconvenient." Jack slapped the article with his knuckles.

"He's a decent man who's already lived with a lot of narrow-minded intolerance in his own country. He's family and the world is going to have to come to terms with that. Sam would have done the same if it had been my son."

"Except Sam probably wouldn't have been running for president," Jack muttered. "Is there any proof?"

"Proof of what? That Sam's his father?" Matt asked, realizing all he'd based his original conviction on was an old photo. "You know there's not."

"Then how do you know?"

"I know. All right?" Matt was getting irritated with Jack's persistence. "Besides, my believing his story didn't give him any claim on me, so what did he have to gain by lying? All he wanted was information about his father."

"The press isn't going to be satisfied with your gut feeling, Matt."

"I know, dammit!"

"People love dirt. It's an unfortunate fact of life, which you should damn well know by now. Maybe you haven't sunk to mud flinging, but the rest of us have."

Jack sighed and began again. "For the first time since Ike, the public thinks they've got a squeaky clean, all-American hero to admire. You know, decorated war veteran, family man, dedicated public servant and all that shit. Believe me, even if Rolly Miller doesn't stoop to it, Blair Cabot won't hesitate a minute to use this to yank you off your pedestal if he can, whether it's true or not. And I can tell you, that rat TJ won't be able to scramble fast enough to jump all over this."

"Jesus H. Roosevelt Christ!" Rick erupted, appearing at Jack's elbow. His face mirrored the shock Matt still felt. A vein throbbed in his neck above the starched collar of his shirt.

"We've seen it," Jack said with resigned calm as Rick slammed his copy of the *Post* down on Jack's small table. "And more than likely, anyone with even a passing interest is listening. I suggest you get a grip."

"It can't be true. Tell me it isn't true," Rick begged.

"It's not," Jack answered. "But this isn't the time or place to discuss it. Take yourself off, and try to at least look like you aren't worried. We'll talk damage control when we get to Dallas."

Rick hung uncertainly over Jack's seat, clearly unwilling to exercise patience. Then, with enormous effort, nodded and went back to his seat.

"I wish I knew how to keep a rein on Winfield." Jack laughed, but there was no humor in it.

~ * ~

Not having foreseen a need to avoid the press, Matt and his entourage made their way up the air-conditioned jetway directly into the terminal and were met by a clamoring crowd of reporters in the main concourse. Doing his best to ignore the barrage of questions being fired at him, Matt strode along in Joe Venuto's wake, glad for once of the agent's broad protective shoulders.

"Is it true, Senator, that the young man photographed playing basketball with you is your son?" A younger, more agile reporter, managed to shove a microphone into their path as they neared the escalator.

"No, it's not true," Jack answered, putting himself between Matt and the microphone.

"Then who is he, and why is he spending so much time with the Senator's family if he's not his bastard?" another voice demanded.

"Senator, if you're innocent, why are you hiding behind Jack Holland?"

"The American public has a right to know the truth about people they elect to office."

Until now, Matt had generally viewed the press as his ally. This aggressive and hostile mob felt decidedly threatening. He didn't like the feeling.

Yet, out of the intimidating belligerence, one accusation struck him as fair. Americans did have the right to know the man they elected to lead them was what he claimed to be. Matt had frequently said so, arguing at times with his own staff, in favor of being completely candid.

"Let me talk to them, Jack."

"You don't want to do it, Matt," Jack said under his breath.

"They don't play by your rules."

"I have nothing to hide," Matt answered, making eye contact with the most vocal of the reporters.

"Who is he, Senator?"

A phalanx of microphones was immediately thrust in Matt's direction. He blinked in the blaze of flashing cameras and tried to gather his wits.

"Mr. Davis came to me a few weeks ago seeking my assistance. He is the son of an American serviceman. That much is true. However, he is not my son."

"Then, why has he been seen in your company so much?"

Joe stepped in front of a heavy-set reporter who poked a finger at Matt's chest for emphasis.

"Mr. Davis came to me looking for information about his father, who was killed in Vietnam."

"Is it also true that your staff created a job for him?" The same harsh accuser continued the attack.

"Mr. Davis has been in this country for more than two years and has been teaching school in Virginia since before I became aware of his existence," Matt answered, his patience beginning to give way to irritation.

"Why did Mr. Davis seek *you* out, Senator? And why are you so sure he is who he says he is? Aren't you being just a bit gullible? What else is he expecting from you?"

"He expected nothing from me except to learn what he could about his father." Matt tried to answer with composure in spite of an increasing sense of vulnerability.

"How well did you know this man he claims is his father? And why you?"

"His father was my cousin and closest friend. Why not me?" Matt countered, his words clipped.

"What was his name, Senator?" A strident female voice called out. "Why are you protecting a dead man?"

Matt fought to control his growing anger. "I didn't think this was public business and if I'm protecting anyone, it's the young man in question."

"Are you refusing to reveal the soldier's identity?"

"I'm not refusing anything. The soldier's name was Sam Davis. Sergeant Samuel Davis. He was also my cousin, which makes Thanh Davis my family." Matt's habitual calm deserted him, leaving a steel hard desire to hurt someone.

The unexpected hunger for physical violence would have appalled him at any other time. Just now, it filled him with righteous energy and a burning determination to set these yapping puppies straight.

He glared at them. The rage that roiled inside him, he suddenly realized, had been there for years, unacknowledged and festering.

They were young, all of them. Far too young to remember. But the men this country had sent to fight and die in a war they couldn't win and didn't understand had been young, too. Too young to be wasted. And it had been self-righteous mobs just like this one that had helped to demoralize those young soldiers so far from home and so alone.

"*The bastards should be shot for treason*," Sam had declared angrily when he'd discovered some of the things that were being reported stateside. Matt felt the full force of that anger now.

"Sam Davis was an outstanding soldier. He died a senseless death in a senseless war while you were all still wearing diapers." Video cameras whirred. Matt no longer cared. "Talk to your older colleagues who were there. Ask them what it was like. War is suffering and terror and loss. It's an atrocity you can't begin to imagine.

"Sam Davis was a decent man. He was no different from any of you except that he was asked to do unspeakable things for a cause he thought was just. He lived with carnage and anguish and inhumanity. He lost his innocence, his friends and his life.

"And his son, a son he never had the chance to know, suffered as well, through no fault of his own. Thanh lost one member of his family after another as a result of American involvement in his country. I cannot replace all he has lost, but I will do everything I can to make his future better. My cousin would have expected no less. You are free to believe what you will, but that is all I have to say."

Journalists gaped, pens poised and unmoving over forgotten notepads. Matt turned on his heel and stalked away so abruptly his staff had to scurry to catch up.

"Jesus, I've never seen him so worked up," Rick muttered, his voice just audible above the roar in Matt's ears.

He *was* worked up. How had he let his emotions get so out of control? He heard Jack say, "Something's bothering him, and I wish I knew what," and cringed.

"A headline like that would bother any one, for Christ's sake," Rick swore. "But I don't think I've ever seen him lose his temper, even when he'd have liked nothing better than to kick my sorry butt."

Aggravated with himself, Matt knew Jack had been right to caution him against talking to the press unprepared. Where the hell had all that anger come from? And what was happening to his lack of self-control?

"You're the expert, Jack. What's your take?" Rick asked, climbing into the waiting town car and settling onto the jump seat.

Jack shot Matt a measuring look, then finally returned his gaze to Rick. "Matt might have succeeded in putting a new spin on the story, but it won't stop the speculation, or the rapacious desire for scandal. And here's another thought. Matt's a man with a reputation for being cool under fire. This outburst might be interpreted as a sign of guilt."

Matt stared grimly out the window. Jack was right. He'd overreacted. He'd acted totally out of character, and he'd made the problem worse.

~ * ~

Jack's instinct proved unerringly and unpleasantly accurate.

Later in the day, when Matt found a moment to relax, he turned on the television only to hear a provocative talk-show host point out that heated reactions often masked things men didn't want to admit.

"Senator Steele saw action in two tours in Vietnam. I say his anger this morning is justified by the way he and all the rest of us got treated when we came home." A stocky man in the studio audience leapt to his feet to defend Matt's outburst.

This comment met with applause, and a younger woman stood to add, "It's a sorry state of affairs when a man can't do something generous for someone else without getting shot down."

The host moved about his audience, soliciting opinions. Surprisingly, in spite of the host's repeated attempts to stir up scandal, most of the comments seemed to support Matt.

Matt listened with half an ear while he tried calling home again. As he listened, he realized the argument had gone beyond his own innocence or guilt and now centered around animosities between a public avid for scandal and veterans still bitter about having gone when asked and been welcomed home with scorn. He realized the anger he'd allowed to color his words that morning had triggered this outpouring of emotion. Wounds that hadn't healed had found another opportunity to be voiced.

"Matt," Rick stuck his head in the door. "We've got to be downstairs in ten minutes."

"I'll be there," Matt promised. "I want to try home one more time. I have to know how Eve and Thanh are taking all of this."

Before he had time to dial the number, the phone rang. He snatched it up and answered personally.

"Hi, Daddy."

"Kitten!" He felt a jolt of apprehension. What was Megan doing home at this time of day? "What's up?"

"We've got a big powwow going on here, and we thought you'd want to know what's been going on."

"I've been trying to reach you. Can I speak to your mother?"

"Daddy, don't you remember? She's at that affair over in Georgetown with Murdoch. Mr. Elliot, I think he's the press guy from your senatorial office? Anyway, he's here. He said Jack called and told him to get over here and head off the press. Only he was too late. Mom had already talked to them. So now it's just Thanh and me and Ben here."

"Ben!"

"Yeah. He drove down this afternoon as soon as he heard. He came to see if Mom was okay. She was very cool. You'd have been proud of her. Ben was pretty impressed with how she handled the reporters."

"Tell me what happened." Matt settled back onto the bed. Rick would just have to manage without him for a few minutes longer.

"Well, Mom picked me up after lunch 'cause I had a dentist appointment I'd forgotten about. Anyway, when we got home afterwards, Ben was already here, and the reporters and curiosity seekers were camped all over the lawn."

Matt could tell by the excitement in her voice that she relished the drama.

"What did your mother say?"

"Oh, she told them she knew all about Sam Davis. She even dragged out a photograph of the two of you. You and Sam, I mean. She was very regal. She looked down her nose at them all and said that Sam's son would always be welcome in her home, but that they should take themselves away immediately, because they were not. She marched back into the house and left Mr. Elliot to say all the politically correct stuff." Megan giggled, and Matt heard Ben demanding the phone.

"Dad," Ben's voice came over the line. "I know you're probably worried about us, but we're fine. All except for Thanh, that is. He's really upset. He thinks he should just disappear from your life. You have to talk to him. He won't listen to us or even Mr. Elliot."

"Thanks for being there, Ben. It was good of you to drive all the way from Philly."

"Dad, I...well, never mind that. Will you talk to Thanh?"

"Put him on the line. And Ben? Thanks."

There was a muffled conversation, and then Thanh spoke. "Senator, I am so sorry for all this trouble I bring to you and your family."

"Cut the senator crap, Thanh. This is Matt you're talking to, remember."

"You should not be hurt by..."

"The only thing that will make me angrier than those jerks this morning is you if you persist in thinking that disappearing from our lives is going to make things better. It won't." Matt took a deep breath. "Look, Thanh, changing anything about our relationship will only give them what they will consider to be evidence of my guilt, which I'm sure Dave Elliot has already pointed out. Besides, Eve wouldn't forgive me if you aren't with us when we make that trip to Maine in a couple weeks."

"If you are sure, I will go, of course," Thanh answered hesitantly.

"I'm sure. Now, I'm supposed to be somewhere, like ten minutes ago, and Rick is probably having a stroke, so I've got to hang up. Please, tell Eve when she gets in that I won't call again tonight because it will be around two a.m. your time before I get back to my room, but I'll call first thing in the morning. Of course, she's free to call me if she's still up and wants to talk."

"I will be sure to tell her," Thanh said with precise inflection.

"Thanks. And Thanh? Stop acting like the world is on your shoulders. This isn't your fault."

"I will try."

"Get Megan to fix you guys some supper. That ought to give you something else to worry about."

He heard Thanh snicker as he hung up the receiver. Megan's cooking could easily challenge a fire-breathing dragon. Between gulping huge quantities of water and mopping his eyes, Thanh wouldn't be able to think about anything else. Matt wished he could get through the evening with nothing more to worry about than how long it would take his insides to recover from Megan's culinary skills.

"Senator Steele?" Joe knocked on the door.

"I'm coming," Matt answered, reaching for his jacket. He shrugged into it, stooped in front of the mirror to run his fingers through his hair and straighten his tie.

Before he stepped into the hall, he paused, girding himself for the night ahead of him. He had expected it to be a confrontational evening before the business of Thanh came up.

"Just suck it up, Steele," he told himself, squaring his shoulders as he opened the door. "You've lived through worse."

Eleven

"Too bad this damning headline is nothing more than some idiot's idea of a real story." TJ tossed his half-read copy of the *Washington Post* aside with a click of his tongue and picked up the *New York Times*.

"How do we know there's nothing to it?" Blair took a sip from his steaming cup of coffee.

"None of the facts back it up. It's just an inflammatory photo and a lot of wild conjecture. If this guy was really Steele's bastard, you think our hero-with-the-spotless-reputation would have paraded the kid around under everyone's nose? He's too smart for that. He'd have hidden Davis away as soon as he showed up."

"Thanh Davis is not exactly a kid. Not like Steele has any control over where he goes and what he does."

TJ grabbed his briefcase, plopped it down on his knees and lifted the lid. He rummaged through it and drew out a thin manila file. Snapping the case shut, he dropped it back on the floor by his feet, then opened the file and began reading.

"He's thirty-six to be exact. Born on January 22, 1976 in a re-education camp somewhere outside Ho Chi Minh City to a woman called Ly Linh Mai. She named the father as an American Marine, one Sergeant Samuel Gray Davis. Sgt. Davis served in Vietnam twice, nineteen seventy and seventy-one in the field, and again in seventy-four and five on the embassy detail. He was killed by a freak shelling at the DAO outside Saigon in April of nineteen seventy-five. The DAO was the only military presence we had in Vietnam at the time and they were just processing refugees. Anyway, Davis had requested and received permission to marry the Ly woman, but his death intervened. He apparently anticipated his honeymoon by a couple weeks. Unlucky bastard.

"The son, Thanh Davis, has been teaching at George Mason High School in Falls Church for just over a year. Started there last September. Before that, he was in San Diego for a year and did some substitute teaching at Cal Coast Academy. He emigrated in twenty-oh-nine. May eighteenth, direct from Ho Chi Minh City. But between his birth and the date he entered the US, I have only scanty information, and that mainly outlining his education. He has a university degree in liberal arts at the master's level, and he taught for several years at an orphanage before seeking a visa to immigrate to the US.

"Only contacts outside his employment I can find since the younger Davis hit the east coast are his landlord, one Burt Hogan, who says he never heard of any connection to Senator Steele before a month ago, and a Jeff Cuthbert, who recently moved to the Philadelphia area, but who also claims to have no knowledge of any connection Davis might have to the senator. Davis has apparently been dating another mix-breed war bastard named Annie Santos, but so far that relationship does not appear serious and didn't begin until after Davis and Steele claim to have first met.

"Davis' first contact with Steele appears to be at a rally in Virginia on September fifth of this year. He approached him and was allowed to board his bus after handing him something. My source thinks it was a photograph. It would appear he is who Steele claims he is."

"Where'd you get all this information?"

"I'm a very resourceful guy, and you did ask me to find out, if you'll recall."

Blair ran a hand over his close-cropped hair. "Yeah, I did. You think we can make anything of it?"

"No, I don't. But let the newshounds play with their bone. If there's any mileage in it, they'll do our work for us. But here's a twist. You'll never guess where Miss Annie Santos spends time as a volunteer."

Blair's eyebrows drew up in interest. "I hate guessing games, so just tell me."

"Your campaign office downtown." TJ felt a glow of satisfaction at the calculating look that came into Blair's eyes. He could almost see the wheels turning in his boss' mind. A mind almost as devious as his own. "I thought I might pay her a visit. Find out how much she knows about what goes on in the Steele household. Maybe I can recruit her as a mole."

"Can't hurt." Blair got up to refill his coffee cup. "Now, tell me what you've managed to dig up about Roland Miller and the Lauder woman."

~ * ~

Roland Miller felt the vibration of his phone and got up to move away from the conversation in the sitting room of his suite.

"Ash," he whispered. "I told you not to call me."

"I couldn't help myself," came the cheerful, unrepentant answer. "I need you."

Rolly glanced at the group, noticed no one was looking his way and drifted into the bedroom, then closed the door.

"You don't need anyone. You just want something."

"I can need you at the same time as wanting something," Ash replied petulantly.

"Look, I'm sorry I stopped by the other day. That wasn't fair to either of us."

"I enjoyed seeing you and having you close, even if it was only a few stolen moments in the middle of your busy campaign schedule."

"Well, it won't happen again. We can't change the status quo right now, and not being able to talk freely about...about things just frustrated me. I can't do anything until after the election. The party is trading on the faithful widower theme. I don't have to like it, but I don't really have a choice."

"What about Barbara?"

"That's different, and you know it."

"How is Barbara different?" Ash challenged.

"For Pete's sake! She was my wife's best friend, and she often played hostess when Jean Anne wasn't up to it. She's been doing it for years, and no one sees anything in it. Barbara likes her life just the way it is, and she doesn't have any inclination to tie herself down to anyone and everyone knows it. And you should know better than anyone that there is not now nor ever has been anything between Barbara and me."

"She might be willing to overlook a few things to be the wife of the president."

Rolly plopped down on the edge of the bed and ran his hand over his graying hair. Then he let himself tip back and lay looking up at the white ceiling. "Please, Ash. Don't fight me on this. I need you to be on my side. I need you in my life, just not in my public life. Not yet."

A long resigned sigh came from the other end of the connection. "Fine. Five weeks, then. But if you renege, I promise I'll find another lover."

A shot of pain lanced through Rolly's gut at the thought of Ash with another man. It was hard enough denying themselves the intimacy they so craved for the rest of the campaign, but the idea of Ash with another lover, even if it wasn't serious and only to make him jealous, would be more than he could bear.

"Please, Ash. Don't say things you don't mean."

"And what makes you think I don't mean it?"

"You wouldn't do that to me. To us." But of course Ash would. Rolly had always known there was a hard, selfish side to Ash. An unappealing willingness to use whatever means necessary to get the desired result, no matter who got hurt. But Rolly couldn't stop loving Ash in spite of it. Couldn't help the burning in his loins just thinking of their being together.

"I love you," Rolly said, desperate to put a stop to the hurtful conversation.

"I love you, too." Ash sighed. "I wish November was tomorrow."

"It will be here before you know it. Just promise me you won't call again. I'll call you. When I can."

"Will you let me be there on election night?"

"Can you be discreet?"

"I'll make sure I arrive in Barbara's party. Will that be discreet enough for you?"

Rolly considered the idea. "I wasn't talking about how you plan to arrive. More about how you plan to behave."

"Meaning I'm not allowed to kiss you to celebrate when you win."

Rolly swallowed. The shit would surely hit the fan if Ash gave him a hearty lip-lock on national TV. "A discreet kiss would be acceptable."

"Not to me," Ash grumbled, but it was clear from the tone of voice that while Rolly had conceded an inch, Ash had every intention of taking a mile. "I will have to go shopping and buy myself a wardrobe befitting the consort of a president."

"Ash!" Clearly, Rolly had not thought this through. He'd only been focused on keeping their relationship under wraps until after the election, when he'd been certain he would be in a position to indulge his desires without any sudden revelations to the world at large. God help him! Solving the problems of a troubled nation might just pale in comparison with living up to Ash's expectations.

"I can see me now," Ash purred. "Do you prefer me in navy or gray? With an occasional splurge of red perhaps. Of course I should have some basic black in my closet. But…"

"Ash, please. Can we discuss this at another time?"

"Of course. Just tell me one more time how much you love me, and I will go quietly into the night. For tonight anyway."

~*~

Matt tossed restlessly in the unfamiliar bed. He finally gave up trying to sleep and rolled onto his back. The drapes were drawn partially open and the glow of city nightlife winked and wavered across the ceiling. Hands clasped behind his head, he studied the shifting patterns and thought of Eve.

He wished Eve had been with him on this trip. If she'd been there, perhaps he wouldn't have over-reacted this morning. He might have taken Jack's warning more seriously if Eve had been there to second it. Instead, he'd created a fire where before there had only been smoke.

He couldn't take back his angry words and hadn't been home to take the blow of public outcry for his family. Guilt ate at him for things he'd done and things he should have done as well. He flipped onto his side, away from the flickering lights and tried to put Thanh and the furor surrounding his presence in Matt's life out of his head. He forcefully turned his mind toward The Plan instead.

Well before the night of the debate and Edna Jordan's condemning letter, Matt and Hal had set their controversial course of action. He'd felt the strength of their conviction when he'd quoted Jack Kennedy and offered the American people a challenge to pull together to restore the American Dream. He and Hal believed they had a mission, and Matt was determined not to back down, even when faced with misunderstanding from some of his strongest supporters.

"An interesting call to arms," his son had said with the first hint of approval Matt recalled hearing in a long time. His son's cautious encouragement had sparked the idea to ask total strangers to offer their ideas.

Not the people who ran his campaign and wrote his speeches. Matt knew where they stood, and it wasn't always where he thought it should be. Not politicians, and especially not journalists. Just ordinary people living ordinary lives.

This afternoon, he'd asked two women employed in the sprawling hotel complex. Their answers to the question, *"What does the American Dream mean to you?"* echoed the unsettling letter from the *Times*.

"The chance to make something of myself," the tiny Mexican-American woman named Juana had added confidently.

The elevator operator agreed. So did Matt's driver.

But Joe Venuto had said the American Dream was dead.

Over a beer in Matt's room, Jack hadn't even given the query a moment's consideration before answering flippantly, "A place where every mother's son can aspire to be president. Or daughter," he'd added, being politically correct.

94

"What about you?" Matt had turned to the surprised room service clerk who'd come to deliver a tray of sandwiches, and who'd obviously been listening in on Matt's question and Jack's sarcastic answer.

"I guess I don't think there is such a thing," the man admitted a little reluctantly. He was older, perhaps in his fifties and had the polished manner of a man who'd been at his job for years. He should have been a bell captain by now, but for some reason he was still working in a subordinate role. When Matt had given him his full attention, the man had elaborated.

"There is no dream. You just go to work every day, do the best you can and hope there'll be enough set aside so you can retire some day. Especially with the government changing the rules all the time. No one can count on anything anymore. My father used to talk about wanting us kids to have a better life than he did and he worked hard all his life trying to make it come true. But I don't think it happens like that anymore."

"Why doesn't it happen that way anymore? Is it because people don't work hard enough?"

"Oh, the average American works hard enough. I certainly work as hard as my father ever did, and my wife works, too. But we never seem able to make ends meet. The kids come home to an empty house every day, we fight all the time about who has to fix supper and do the housework, and we're still not sure how we'll put the kids through college. How is that better than what we had growing up?"

"So why do you think ordinary people have to struggle just to get by?"

"You tell me, Senator. The government keeps finding new ways to tax us and reduce how far what we do get to take home will go.

You're the one who makes the laws. *I* just live with them, so you tell me."

So you tell me. Matt rolled over to his other side, wrestled with the pillows and tried again to get comfortable. *So you tell me!* The bellhop's indictment rang in his head. The America Matt believed in, every dream and promise, every reason he had for being where he was now, had coalesced into a soul-searing conviction that he had to do something to change the direction in which his country was heading. Matt considered the option of sharing the sweeping scope of their plan over the next few weeks instead of just hinting at it. If only it wasn't so hard to let go of the familiar and jump into the unknown.

Just like 'Nam, he thought. Just like sitting in the open door of an assault helicopter screwing up the courage to jump. In his mind, he pictured a field of waving elephant grass obscuring the landing and hiding the enemy. In his gut, he felt the knot of fear tighten.

So you tell me. Matt knew he had to jump. The mission would require it. But obstructing his task was a populace that continually clamored for one thing and voted for another.

He turned his head to glance at the clock and wished Eve had called in spite of what he'd told Thanh.

~ * ~

Matt didn't recall dropping off to sleep, but he was gut-wrenchingly aware of the nightmare that had him in its grip as he shot up in the bed with the phone jangling in his ear. Tangled in damp bedclothes, he struggled to orient himself.

He managed to find the receiver and put it to his ear. "Lieutenant Steele here."

"Matt?" Eve's voice came softly into his disordered world. "Are you all right?"

"Of course," he answered automatically, then reached to switch on the light and banish the remnants of his private hell.

"I'm sorry I woke you. Were you having another nightmare?"

"No! Yes." He ignored the rushing in his head. "I'm sorry. I'm—What time is it?"

"It's a little past three."

"I fell asleep wishing you'd call, but figured you must have been in bed a long time ago."

"I wish!" Eve chuckled. "We got held up in an enormous traffic jam. Some drunk ran a red light and rammed a car full of college kids. We got trapped between the accident and the rescue trucks and couldn't leave 'til they got it cleaned up."

"Must have been a hell of a pile-up!"

"Well, we were already late when we ran into it. Murdoch and I stopped off for a cup of coffee after the meeting."

"I see." He didn't see. He'd wanted her to be home. Wanted her to call. Needing her gentle voice reassuring him at the end of a very difficult day. He'd been carrying a mountain of guilt around all day and he'd craved her absolution.

"Is something wrong, Matt?"

"You're there and I'm here."

"Are you worried about the flap over Thanh? Is that what's bothering you?"

She knew him too well. "I should have been there to take the heat instead of leaving you open to the newshounds."

"You can't be there every minute. And it wasn't your fault anyway."

"I could have kept myself from running at the mouth this morning. I'm sure that didn't help any."

"I thought you were magnificent. Sometimes the things you said need saying. People need to be reminded about the price of freedom once in awhile. You were only defending an innocent young man and the reputation of your friend."

"I was defending *my* reputation!"

"Matt? Where is all this guilt coming from? Is there something I don't know about that I should? Surely there's no truth to that outrageous headline?"

Twelve

Of course Matt had told Eve he had no idea where someone had gotten such an impossible idea, and did she really believe he'd lie to her about something that important? She'd immediately reassured him of her faith in him. Then they'd talked about the rest of his day and hers until he hadn't been able to keep his eyes open any longer.

But this morning, as Matt stared into his mirror carefully scraping away his stubble, an appalling realization lanced into his thoughts. His heart began to thud with painful intensity. He set the razor down and gripped the sink for support.

It *was* possible.

He studied the piercing blue of his own eyes and tried to recall Thanh's. His own cheekbones were not high, and Thanh didn't have a dimple. In fact, there was almost nothing similar about them except those haunting blue eyes. Unlikely, but possible.

Matt closed his eyes, shutting out his image. Suddenly he was back in Saigon, reeling with grief and boiling with anger as he told Mai Ly about Sam's death. He heard his own breathing, jerky and harsh, as memory flooded over him, and his knees felt like they might buckle.

~ * ~

Matt turned away from Mai Ly and hurried toward the shelf over his bed. He could live without his little transistor radio. His sister had sent it to him, but he'd be out of this cesspool of a country soon enough, and he wouldn't need to take it with him. He pulled it off the shelf and turned to find Mai Ly had followed him. She stood so close he could smell the scent of flowers in her hair and something else far more exotic. An enticing combination that ambushed his senses.

Matt shoved the little radio into her hands and began to explain how it worked. Anything to shut down the unwanted surge of desire her scent had unleashed. But Mai Ly began to shake. Her tears had stopped, but her body shuddered with pent-up emotion. "Mai Ly," he muttered pulling her into his arms. Hell! We both need to feel close to someone right now. "It'll be okay. I promise. I'll get your name on the list. You'll go to the US even without Sam. I'll help you. Somehow. I promise."

She melted into his embrace, her arms wrapped about the little radio, her head buried against his chest. Matt rocked her and made soothing sounds, and tried to ignore the growing awareness of her feminine curves pressed so intimately against his lean hardness. He knew he should put her away from him instantly and ask her to leave. This was all wrong. She was Sam's girl. Woman rather. She was Sam's woman and just because Sam was dead didn't mean the feelings leaping to life in him now were even remotely appropriate.

But damn! It had been so long. Too long. Too long since the last time he'd held a woman.

A surge of lust and hunger roared through him. She was soft where he was hard. And she seemed to need the searing contact as much as he. He indulged them both for a few moments longer, and then pulled himself together and resolutely pushed her away.

"You need to go, Mai Ly."

Mai Ly turned away and set the radio on a chair. Then she turned back in a disconcerting rush. She slid her arms around his middle and tightened her embrace before he could resist. "Please, you hold me. Only a little."

He closed his arms around her again and rested his chin on the top of her head. His body taut and humming with conflicting needs. "Okay, but in a minute you really have to go."

"You are late? You must go to embassy soon?"

Matt lifted one arm and peered at his watch in the growing gloom of the room. "Not for a few hours. But if you want me to start finding out how to get your name on the list, I should..." Mai Ly jerked the tails of his utility blouse from the waistband of his trousers. Matt gulped in alarm.

Mai Ly had never behaved this way with him. What did she want? Aching with confusion and need, he didn't stop her when the warmth of her hands skimmed over his bare skin, drowning out the remnants of his common sense. She tipped her face toward his, her brown eyes liquid pools of erotic enticement in the shadowy room. "Mai Ly?" he rasped in protest, but he was already lowering his mouth to hers.

The fire that ignited on contact blazed through him like a hundred volts of electric current, frying his brain and leaving only sizzling heat and unholy desire in its wake. Mai Ly shoved his trousers down past his hips, and he heard them hit the floor with a jangle of gear. Her hands were everywhere. On his buttocks, his hips, his stomach. Then his dick. All protest fled. Lost in a desperate need to take what she so clearly offered, he fell back onto his bed, pulling her with him.

When Matt woke, Mai Ly was gone. So was the radio and the paper with the official permission for a US Marine to marry an indigenous Vietnamese. The only ticket Mai Ly had left to get herself out of the country. Perhaps she thought Sam's name would not be recognized or his death not well known, and she'd get her seat on one of those flights in the confusion.

Then memory flooded back. Matt's stomach heaved. He *scrambled off the bed and groped for his trousers.* What have I done? *He wanted to throw up.* How could I even think it? And what about Mai Ly? *He liked and admired Mai Ly, and he knew she considered him a friend, but their connection had been Sam. And they had betrayed the man they both should have been grieving.*

Angrily, Matt buttoned his shirt and shoved it into trousers, his movements jumpy and uncoordinated at the unwanted memory of Mai Ly's hands yanking it free. "Never again," he shouted to the empty room. "I'll get you out of here for Sam's sake, but this can never happen again!" His mouth trembled. "Ever." This time, he didn't restrain his anger when the need to lash out overwhelmed him. His fist met a two by four square on. He yelped in pain as he pulled it back. Then, as he sank to his knees, his injured hand cradled against his chest, tears began pouring down his face.

~ * ~

"What have I done?" Matt opened his eyes and returned the accusing blue gaze in the mirror. "What if he's mine?"

Matt bolted from the bathroom and began dressing with hands as unsteady as they'd been over thirty years ago. Of course it wasn't possible. Mai Ly had not been a virgin. She and Sam had been having sex for months. She must have known she was pregnant. That had to be why she'd come onto him the way she had. Desperate to extricate herself from an untenable position, maybe she'd hoped Matt would believe he'd gotten her that way. She'd have only had to wait a couple weeks before telling him he'd gotten her pregnant, and he'd have married her even though he didn't love her. She'd known him well enough to be certain of that much.

Thanh is Sam's son. Thanh *has* to be Sam's son!

A little calmer, Matt stepped in front of the mirror to tie his tie and once again met his familiar blue gaze.

"But what if Thanh is my son?"

~ * ~

"Miss Santos?"

Annie looked up from the call list she'd been working her way through. Presidential candidate Blair Cabot's campaign manager, lounged casually against the corner of her desk as if it were something he did often. As much as she believed in Blair Cabot, she didn't trust this man. She'd heard stories about him and had kept her distance. The closeness and familiarity of his present position raised the hair on the back of her neck.

Annie knew TJ Smith considered himself a ladies' man, but the balding pate and the belly spilling over his belt didn't fit the picture. Nor did the ruthlessness habitually lurking in his eyes. At the moment, however, he was smiling at her. Which only made her more uncomfortable.

"Mr. Smith. What can I do for you?"

"Oh, it's not what you could do for me, although we might discuss that another day. It's what we'd like you to do for Mr. Cabot. Please, come into my office for a moment?"

Without waiting for an assent, he turned and returned to the glassed-in office at the back of the campaign headquarters tucked into a row of storefronts a short distance from the university campus. His step confident. He fully expected her to comply.

Slowly Annie got to her feet, exchanged a puzzled glance with the woman sitting across from her and reached for her purse. As she covered the distance to TJ's office and knocked on the half open door, she felt like every eye in the place was on her.

TJ nodded, studied the notes in front of him a moment longer, then looked up and gestured to a straight-backed chair in front of his desk. He waited until she'd seated herself in the chair, feeling like she'd been called into the principal's office for some offense.

"I believe you've been seeing a man named Thanh Davis. Is that correct?"

Annie's heart jumped. She had resolutely refused to think of Thanh as a boyfriend, and their frequent dinners out were not dates, but even so, hearing his name catapulted her heart into overdrive and put her on the defensive.

"Yes, I know him. Why?" Annie didn't like the calculating look in TJ's eyes.

"How well?" TJ's question was harsh and direct.

"He is a friend," Annie answered cautiously.

TJ smiled at this. Then his mouth pursed. "Mr. Davis would appear to desire more than a mere friendship. You had a date with him last night, and when he saw you to your door it appeared very friendly."

They had been spying on her? Annie felt renewed alarm slice through her. Someone had been watching her when Thanh took her home last night. Perspiration began to trickle between her breasts. Her armpits felt suddenly sodden and clammy.

They'd only gone to their regular diner and lingered over coffee. Then Thanh had walked her home, and she'd allowed him to hold her hand in the dark streets. But when she would have bid him a polite good night and slipped quickly into her house as she usually did, he'd backed her against the door. He hadn't been rough or even threatening. Just...amorous. And he'd claimed her mouth with his, sweetly gentle at first. Then with growing warmth. Until she had pushed him away, her breath coming in gasps at the startling response his kiss had brought to her own rebellious body. And all the while someone had been watching them. She felt violated. And afraid.

But afraid of what? So she was dating Thanh? How could this be of any interest to TJ? And what business was it of his? And why follow her? Why spy on her?

"Mr. Davis would like a—a more intimate relationship, perhaps?" TJ prompted.

"H-how do you know that?"

"It's my business to know things." TJ steepled his fingers and looked at her over their tips. "It's my business to know anything that might help to ensure that Blair Cabot is the next man to occupy the White House. And I've noticed your devotion to his campaign. You are committed to his winning, are you not?"

"Well, of course!" Annie felt on firmer ground now. "Why would I spend so many hours working here if I weren't?"

"Why indeed?" TJ purred. "And how far would you be willing to go, do you suppose?"

Alarm returned again. "I-I don't know what you mean."

"I would like you to allow this relationship with Mr. Davis to become something more than just mere friendship. We think it might be helpful to have a foot in the enemy camp, so to speak. If you were to become his girlfriend, Mr. Davis would take you with him when he visits Senator Steele's home perhaps. You might see or hear things that might be helpful to us."

"Y-you want me to spy on the senator?" Annie was shocked. "I couldn't do that. It's not right."

"*Spy* is such an unpleasant word. You would be merely observing. And reporting back to us what you learn." TJ's voice had taken on an oily tone that set Annie's teeth on edge.

She stood, preparing to leave. "I'm sorry. I can't do it. I do want Mr. Cabot to win, but I won't stoop to spying." She turned and headed for the door.

"You might want to consider what would happen to your mother, should her...er immigrant status be brought to the attention of the authorities."

Annie froze, her hand on the doorknob, and her heart caught in a vise. Slowly she turned back. TJ was on his feet as well, casually leaning one hip against the side of his desk with his arms folded across his chest.

"You wouldn't do that. Please, Mr. Smith. You can't punish my mother. She's done nothing wrong. She's sick. What would happen to her?" Annie's mind scrambled for a way out of the trap that had been sprung on her. She could become close to Thanh and spy on the family that had befriended him, or she could let her mother be deported.

Annie should have insisted that her mother seek permanent status in the US years ago. Back when it would have been easy to get. But with the current atmosphere surrounding illegals, her mother might not even get a chance to plead her case.

"But I *would* do that, Miss Santos. I would do a great deal more than that to ensure that Blair Cabot is elected. What is the fate of one illegal alien when the fate of the country is at stake?"

"B-but..."

"Think about it, Miss Santos. I'll give you a day or two to weigh your options." TJ looked past her, suddenly straightening his negligent pose. "Mr. Cabot, sir. We were just finished here." He looked back at Annie. "Thank you for all your hard work. I'm sure Mr. Cabot appreciates it. As do I."

Blair Cabot was an imposing man, not terribly tall, but solidly built, Yet he seemed quite harmless compared to his manager. He extended his hand and took hers in it, his fingers warm and gentle.

"I do thank you. Very much. Miss..." He glanced at his campaign manager.

"Miss Santos. Annie Santos, Mr. Cabot." TJ supplied in a formal tone.

Cabot stared at her with renewed interest and Annie's heart rate shot higher. Then he turned away, clearly dismissing her. Annie was free to leave.

Except she wasn't free. She was caught in a web from which she couldn't free herself without jeopardizing her mother.

A couple of days to weigh my options, she thought as she scurried from the building. *What options? I don't have any options.*

Thirteen

Thanh Davis followed Annie up the walk to her door, his hand resting lightly on the small of her back. Her heart raced with the same jumble of emotions that had beset her all day. Anger at TJ. Fear for her mother. Disgust with herself for allowing TJ's threats to buy her compliance. She was a coward, but she really didn't have a choice. To save her mother, she must deceive a really sweet man who didn't deserve to be so ill-used.

Yet, in spite of how contemptible what she was about to do was, she couldn't deny the tingle of giddy anticipation. More and more in recent weeks, her mind had wandered to daydreams about what it would be like to let the relationship with Thanh become more intimate. Keeping him at arm's length had gotten harder and harder. His kisses, when he became more persuasive and took the upper hand, had reduced her to damp, hungry need. She didn't want to love him, but she so wanted to make love with him.

"Huh?" Annie glanced at Thanh over her shoulder, her keys in her hand.

She hadn't paid the slightest attention to what he'd been saying. She'd been too busy pondering her next step. Should she just invite him to come in and let things go from there? Or, when he kissed her goodnight, should she return his passion with enough of her own to ignite a fire that would demand a great deal more?

"You have been very quiet tonight," Thanh said as she fit her keys into the lock. "Is something bothering you?"

"N-nothing." Annie tuned to face him. The intensity in his eyes flooded her with anguish. There was such honesty in his gaze. Desire, yes, but honest admiration as well. He liked her, and he let it show. And just now, he looked truly concerned. She desperately wanted to tell him, but she couldn't. If she did, she feared his liking would turn to disgust, and she would lose any hope of protecting her mother. "I was just..." Suddenly, her mouth was so dry she couldn't finish the invitation she'd been about to offer.

Thanh cupped her face with his slender fingers, tilting it toward his own. In spite of the poor lighting, Annie could see a parade of emotions flicker through his eyes as he closed the gap between their mouths. A question hovered somewhere in there beneath the unguarded ardor. A touch of hope. And vulnerability.

"Thanh." His name came out a husky whisper. She let herself lean into him.

His arms were strong, his chest firm, his lips soft. Gently, he explored the contours of her mouth with his own. Then he sprinkled a path of light kisses along her jaw and bent his head lower, ending with his lips pressed into the hollow of her throat. Annie arched into him. She wrapped her arms about his neck. Her head dropped back, inviting him to take more intimate liberties.

She felt his arousal pressed into her belly and moved against it. She slid her fingers into the silky strands of hair at the base of his skull and turned her face toward his.

Passion didn't flare as easily as she'd thought it would. Or as she'd counted on. Her own breath came in sharp, shallow gasps. Her body ached for him to take command, but when she whispered an invitation for him to come inside, Thanh pulled away. Now the only emotion she read in those amazing blue eyes was uncertainty.

"I do not wish to be teased." Thanh held her at arm's length.

"Who said I was teasing?" Annie tried to pull him close again, but he resisted.

"Before tonight, you have drawn a very clear line in the sand, and it has been equally clear which side you wished me to remain on. We talk so easily, and time passes so quickly. I enjoy being with you, and I think you enjoy being with me, but as soon as I wish to make something more of our relationship, you are quick to build a fence about yourself.

"Tonight you are silent. It has barely been an hour since we sat down to eat, but it feels like the minutes have gone on forever, and we are anything but easy with each other. Yet when I kiss you goodnight, it is you who invites more intimacy. I do not know what you want from me."

"I—I want..." Annie swallowed hard.

The lump in her throat felt like it was going to choke her. She could not tell him the truth, but she could not lie to him either. She would not tell him something she did not feel. Except, perhaps it was not lying to admit to wanting him. Physically, at least. But coming right out and asking him to take her to bed seemed so shameless. Letting him think she felt things she did not would be just as false. But did she have a choice?

"I am afraid." That at least, was the truth.

"Of me?" Thank held her shoulders with both hands and peered at her with confusion clouding his eyes.

"Of falling in love." Another truth. Thanh deserved that much.

"I would not hurt you. Is that why you are afraid?" A frown pressed a deep furrow between his brows.

She nodded slowly, agreeing with both his statement and his question, but in fact, her fear had now grown to include hurting him. She was caught between a rock and a hard place, and there was no way someone wasn't going to get hurt. Perhaps a lot of someones. Thanh. Herself. Matt Steele. If she didn't comply with TJ's demand, her mother. And God only knew who else.

To her relief, Thanh pulled her back into his embrace and rocked her against him. Unfortunately, the passion that had been in him a few moments before seemed to have evaporated. She was right back to square one.

"Do you truly wish for me to come in?" Thanh's question took her completely by surprise.

She'd been preparing herself for a chaste kiss on the forehead and watching him turn to walk down the path into the dark, knowing she'd just have to go through this night, all over again the next time they were together.

"Yes," she whispered breathlessly.

Another truth. She squeezed her eyes tight, wishing away all the other conflicting and unpleasant aspects of this arrangement. Instead, she concentrated on the prospect of an intimacy she suspected would be sweet beyond anything she'd experienced before. She opened her eyes again and gazed up at him with as little guile as she could manage.

"Yes. Very much."

~ * ~

Thanh whistled as he walked down the corridor to his classroom. He felt like he was on top of the world this morning. He'd had to tear himself away from Annie at an unhappily early hour and rush home to shower and change, but the euphoria of the night they had spent together had survived. He felt certain she still hid something from him, but the lovemaking had been genuine.

She had not been a virgin, but he had known that. Although she had left out a lot of the details, she had told him perhaps more than she realized about Alejandro. Thanh's first reaction had been to hunt the bastard down and do him serious injury. But knowing about her past had helped him understand her fear of loving anyone else, and he realized he should be thankful Alejandro was just part of her past and not still in her present.

In spite of her lack of innocence, there had been a fresh openness about her lovemaking. With a dozen candles flickering about her tidy, yet very femininely frilly bedroom, casting seductive shadows over their nakedness, she had explored his body with open admiration. And she had allowed him to do the same, relaxed and sure of her beauty, as he aroused her inch by inch.

When they had come together at last, it had felt as if he had come to the end of a very long journey. Annie was his other half in every way. He regretted only the condom, that last thin barrier separating them, but it was too soon to assume more. She would be his one day, and they would make babies together. But for now, what they had shared last night was enough. What they would share again tonight. And tomorrow, God willing.

His heart felt very full. What a difference the last six weeks had made in his life. He had met a man who felt more like a father to him than any man he had ever known. Acquired a family he thought never to have. And now he had possessed the woman he was meant to love for a lifetime. Life was very good.

~ * ~

On Tuesday, while waiting for a short flight that would take them from Detroit to Chicago, Matt along with Rick, Jack and Joe Venuto grabbed a quick supper in a private lounge at the airport. Over sandwiches and soda, Matt tried to explain the changes he'd made in Rick's carefully screened speech.

Rick was having a conniption.

"I'm trying to reach a huge and pretty much ignored minority," Matt explained. "Men and women, mostly women, who have been trapped in the relief system and can't or couldn't get out because government policy makes it impossible. People who want to get out. For years we've been blind to how the programs we consider indispensable keep them dependent. I want them to know I'm listening, and I'm willing to do something about it."

"You can't just wipe out fifty years of public assistance programs. How does that help these people?" Rick demanded.

"It can't," Matt answered patiently. "Not all at once, anyway. But I didn't propose wiping out welfare entirely anyway."

"Then exactly what the hell are you proposing?" Rick paced, smoking furiously.

Jack shook his head sadly from across the smoky room.

Matt shrugged and explained his idea once again, simplifying the economic concepts in an effort to make Rick see the wisdom and importance of it.

"Fine. I applaud your brilliance." Rick's voice dripped sarcasm. "But the party won't buy it. Congress won't buy it. And the voters won't buy it. So I suggest you shut up if you have any desire to get elected." Rick ground out the last of his cigarettes and reached for a new pack.

"You hired me to win this campaign and that's what I intend to do. After November eighth, I don't give a tinker's damn what you do. But right now, I'm in charge. Got it?"

Matt kept his mouth shut while Rick felt through his pockets and came up empty. Joe silently held out a pack with one lone smoke left in it. Rick nodded his thanks, lit up, then came back to perch on the arm of a sofa to make one final plea for Matt to see reason. He lowered his voice with obvious effort.

"You've been steadily gaining on Rolly, and you're still ahead of that upstart, Cabot. Any day I expect to see the numbers tip in our favor. Even the Thanh Davis fiasco doesn't appear to have hurt you."

Matt's heart jolted at the reminder of Thanh, and it must have shown on his face.

"Trust me. There's no truth in it, and it'll die a natural death."

But what if there *is* truth in it? Matt did his best to hide his fear. He'd never been very good at poker.

"You're this close." Rick held up his forefinger and thumb poised a half an inch apart. "If you don't rock the boat, Eve will be making up menus for White House dinners come January. Why put everything in jeopardy with this impossible notion of yours now?"

"It's not a notion, Rick. It's a mission statement." Back on solid ground, Matt felt his confidence returning.

"You're tilting at windmills, Matt, and it can't work. They'll scoff at you just like they did Quixote. Trust me." Rick launched himself off the sofa. "Save it for your inauguration speech."

Rick didn't wait for a reply. He'd left the room, more than likely, in search of another cigarette and saner conversation.

"I told you how he'd take it," Jack said, getting up to open the door and air out the room. "I'll admit, now that I've given it some serious thought, I'm inclined to think your plan might be the only real solution to a difficult and stubborn problem, but I'm not sure its time has come. Right, Joe?"

Joe Venuto looked up at Jack and lowered his book.

"What d'you think?"

"I already told the boss. I'm paid to keep him whole, not have opinions." Joe's tone didn't give any indication of either support or disdain. He went back to his book.

"What's Hal say?" Jack returned to take up the arm of the sofa vacated by Rick.

"This is a partnership. We're on board together."

"So, you've been..."

"United flight six-sixty-three to Chicago now boarding at gate E-four," a clipped English voice cut into Jack's question.

The announcement jerked both men to their feet. Matt scrambled to gather up his briefcase and scattered notes while Jack snatched his discarded jacket off a chair and pulled open the door. Joe stood with deceptive nonchalance and edged past Matt into the hall.

"Where the hell has Rick gone off to?" Jack asked.

"He never misses a flight," Matt tossed over his shoulder. "The man's got built-in timing."

Joe guided Matt past the inevitable members of the press hanging over the ropes in hopes of recording an exclusive comment or unguarded remark. Matt handed his boarding pass to the attendant and hurried down the tunnel to the plane.

Rick, already seated and in possession of a stiff martini, glowered at Matt as he moved past. He found his row and swung himself into the window seat. Jack dropped into the seat next to him.

They busied themselves with the usual pre-flight rituals of buckling their seat belts, ignoring the safety sermon and rifling through the airline magazine. When they were safely in the air and the flight attendant was up and taking drink orders again, Matt set his seat back as far as it would go. Exhausted from lack of sleep, he stretched out wearily.

"Wake me up sometime tomorrow," he told Jack and closed his eyes. He slipped almost at once into an uneasy sleep.

~ * ~

"Who the hell's on watch?" Sam hissed.

"Wasn't that supposed to be you?" Matt hissed back, dragging his eyelids open and gazing wearily into a pale gray dawn.

"But I thought you had my back." Sam was hovering over the cot, staring at Matt with shocked, sad eyes.

"I've always got your back." Matt looked around the familiar walls of the apartment they shared a few blocks from the embassy, wondering why Sam was in such a strange mood. He noticed his little radio was missing and wondered where it had gotten to. "Did you take the radio off for something?"

"You gave the damned thing to Mai Ly," Sam responded in a tone that implied the same shock and sadness his eyes held. "I thought you had my back," he repeated.

"What are you talking about?" Matt swung his feet over the side of the cot and stood up, realizing he was wearing only his uniform shirt. His trousers were in a heap on the floor beside the cot. It wasn't like him to leave his clothes in such an untidy heap. It wasn't like him to sleep in his uniform either. Not in the safety of their apartment anyway.

"I'm talking about Mai Ly." Sam was angry now. His tone accusing.

Suddenly Matt realized what he was talking about. He blushed hotly, shame sweeping over him in a fiery rush. "I'm sorry. Oh, God, Sam. I'm so sorry. I didn't mean for it to happen. I don't know what I was thinking."

"You were thinking with your fucking dick. That's what you were doing. Dammit. So, what are you going to do about it? About time you took responsibility, don't you think? You owe me that much at least. You owe Thanh even more." Sam turned away and Matt almost didn't hear the last angry accusation.

"Wait, Sam!" Matt reached out to grab Sam's shoulder. "I can explain."

~ * ~

"Sorry, I'm not Sam."
"I don't need excuses." Sam's voice faded.
"Sam…"

"Christ, Matt. It's Jack. You having a nightmare?"

Matt focused with difficulty. He swallowed and tried to master the sudden scrum of nausea in his belly.

"Man, you don't look too good. You aren't going to puke, are you?" Jack rustled through the seat pocket and came up with a barf bag.

"Don't need it. Thanks anyway." Matt's world began to right itself.

"You sure?" Jack looked dubious and left the bag between them on the corner of his drop-down table just in case.

"I'm okay." Matt slid the knot of his tie down and released his collar button. "I'm sorry. It was just a dream."

"This thing about Sam Davis and Thanh is really bothering you, isn't it?" Jack sat back, shaking his head. "Nobody who knows you believes it for an instant, you know."

Matt didn't answer. He didn't have an answer. At least not one he could share.

By the time the blue landing lights of O'Hare International came into view, Matt had wrestled his personal nightmare into submission and tried to focus on the evening that still lay ahead of him.

Jack pretended to read, but he glanced worriedly at Matt from time to time. Matt forced a smile he hoped was reassuring and brought his seat to the upright position.

The huge bird's wheels touched down with barely a whisper, and as the plane slowed and made the turn off the runway, passengers began to turn on their cell phones and touch base with their fast-moving worlds. The normalcy of it all filled Matt with a disquieting sense of detachment.

He stood with the rest when the door opened and the captain emerged from the cockpit to wish his passengers a pleasant evening.

With his jacket folded over one arm, Matt accepted the crew's good wishes and stepped off the plane.

Rick, completely focused on tonight's appearance, didn't notice Matt's remote quietness. On the way through the concourse, he gave Matt a thumbnail sketch of the VIPs they would be meeting. He rattled off a list of who might be expected to come up with much-needed contributions, who could be counted on to secure sizable blocks of votes and who it was essential for Matt to win over.

Matt listened, catalogued the information and tried to mentally prepare himself, but deep inside he couldn't banish the anguish his dream had left behind. Or the accusing sadness in Sam's eyes.

Fourteen

Ken McColl, Matt Steele's strategist, had cornered Matt and demanded to know what was going on, both regarding Thanh Davis and the bizarre turn Matt's message seemed to have taken. It was time and then some, Matt had decided, to have a come-to-Jesus meeting with his primary staff. So here they were, gathered in Matt's living room, to be brought into the loop on his and Hal's shake-up scheme and to plot out the remaining few weeks of the campaign.

At least most of them were here. Ken perched on a dining room chair in front of the fireplace, his dark blond head bent over his notebook while he scribbled notes in the margins of the computer printout Matt had handed him when he walked in. Matt's primary speech writer, Penny Dunlop, studied her copy of the plan, her slim legs gently pushing the rocker she sat in back and forth while she read. Ruben Murdock, Matt's campaign advance man, slouched at one end of the couch, a mug of coffee in one hand and the plan in the other as his black-eyed gaze raced across the page. Jack Holland, a speed-reader, had devoured his copy in just minutes and lounged next to Reuben eyeing Matt and Hal with a curiously amused light in his dark eyes.

Hal cradled the coffee Eve had served him in his big hands and settled into Eve's recliner, stretching his long legs out in front of him. "So, where's Rick? I'd have thought he'd be the first one here."

Penny lifted her head of unruly brown curls and looked first at Hal, then Matt. "He called me earlier. He's bursting with some bit of news, but wouldn't say what. He did say he was running late, but don't start without him."

"Why'd he call you? Not me?" Matt knew Rick was irritated with him, but he didn't think it had gone so far that he had to call Penny to beg for a few extra minutes.

"I'm bringing the birthday cake tonight. His son will be fifteen on Saturday, but of course, his ex didn't invite Rick to the party she's throwing. So Rick is going to celebrate it tonight since this is his night to have the kids."

"I'd forgotten." Matt felt a pang of guilt that his anxiety over Thanh had made him forget an important date in Rick's life. Matt had always made a point of remembering birthdays, anniversaries, pending babies and such, but somehow he'd overlooked it in his self-absorbed preoccupation.

"He's not going to like any of this!" Ken looked up, shaking the papers in his hand. "Can't say I'm all that happy about it, either." He glanced at Hal. "You don't look too surprised?"

"Half my idea," Hal drawled.

Ken's eyebrows shot up into his shaggy blond fringe. His intelligent hazel eyes widened. He jerked his gaze from Hal to Matt and back several times. "How long have you two been hatching this? And why wait so long to let us in on it? The party is going to be in an uproar, you know."

"Mostly, it's a strategy we planned to pursue after inauguration. At least, that's how it started out," Hal answered in his deep lazy voice. "But things sorta changed."

"I had an epiphany," Matt admitted, steepling his fingers. "And a twinge of conscience."

"An epiphany, I'll buy, but this is hardly a twinge." Ken scribbled another note on the bottom of the last page.

"That's our guy!" Ruben interjected. "Never do anything by half measures."

"I like it," Penny offered in her soft, thoughtful voice.

Jack jerked his head to one side and shrugged one shoulder. "On the whole, me too. We have a majorly serious economic problem that is not going to be solved with Band-Aids. It's going to take surgery to fix what's broke and this..." He held up his copy of the plan, "...is major surgery."

The doorbell rang, then Matt heard Eve's footsteps heading to the front door.

"I'll get it." Joe Venuto's tread joined Eve's. A moment later, Joe ushered Rick into the living room. Eve hovered behind him, offering coffee.

"No...okay, maybe I will take a cup. Thanks." Rick took in the assembled group, then headed toward the only remaining empty seat, which happened to be between Reuben and Jack on the couch. "I got caught up in checking something out. I hope I haven't missed too much."

Penny leaned across Reuben to hand Rick his copy of the plan. Matt had given her all the extras. Eve appeared again with a mug of coffee, which she crossed the room to place on a folding table beside Rick's chair. She smiled encouragingly at Matt then she retraced her steps to leave them to their meeting. As she passed his chair, she let her fingers touch the back of his hand for a moment. Then she was gone. Matt hadn't expected her to stay, but her brief touch had renewed his confidence. He and Hal were on the right track and before the afternoon was out, his team would be behind them.

"Why now?" Ken asked as Rick hurriedly scanned the copy Penny had handed him. "Why not wait until after the election? You can't do any of this if you don't get elected, and to be honest, I have serious reservations about you getting elected if you decide to go public with it now."

"He's got a point," Jack agreed. "Everyone wants the problem solved, but no one wants to give up their perks. You're asking *everyone* to give up something. Makes everyone more likely to check someone else's box come November seventh just so they don't lose what they have now."

Rick glanced up with a frown creasing his brow. "I don't like it."

"You don't have to like it," Matt answered as equably as he could. Rick obviously hadn't taken the time to think any of it through. He was just condemning it out of hand.

"Party faithful aren't going to like it, either."

"I am no longer trying to please the party faithful. I'm trying to reach out to the millions of voters who are desperately looking for someone with the courage to take the steps we need taken to save our country from ruin. We can't keep kicking the can down the road for the next generation to deal with."

"Perhaps you haven't noticed the recent bump in our numbers," Hal interjected. "Ever since Quixote here started leaking bits and pieces of this outline, he's gained daily on Miller and Cabot. Maybe that's what the American people have been looking for all along, someone with the *cajones* to tell it like it is and put his neck on the block to get it fixed." The vulgarity coming so carelessly from the mouth of a man known for his gentlemanly conduct and speech caught everyone by surprise.

Ken raised an eyebrow and studied Hal thoughtfully. Penny blushed.

"*Cajones* hell!" Rick shot out of his chair. "He's lost his mind."

"Sit down, Rick." Matt held his breath, waiting for his manager to comply.

Rick hesitated, then sank slowly back onto his chair. "You're burning your bridges, and you're going to lose."

"If I win, I want it to be a mandate, not based on a lie. I have never promised one thing to get elected and then done the opposite after I won. And I don't intend to start now."

"What's the lie? Everything we've done before this is not a lie. Why is it a lie now?"

"Because I no longer believe we can continue in the path we once thought righteous. If I lay out the sacrifices that will be needed to fix our economy and make America strong again, and I make the voters understand why their participation is necessary, and they elect me anyway, then I go into office in a position to make it happen. If I let them elect me based on the same old same old, then *that's* a lie. And Hal and I won't be in a position to make any serious changes. The economy won't get fixed, our military will go on being stretched to the limit, education will continue to shortchange our children and no one will be assured a comfortable retirement or reliable healthcare.

"I didn't run for this office so I can repeat the mistakes of my predecessors, and I don't want to spend my entire time in office scrambling to find a legacy. *This* is my legacy."

"You won't have to worry about a legacy if you don't get elected," Rick seethed.

"Anyone need a refill?" Eve stood in the doorway with a fresh pot of coffee. Everyone held up their cup, obviously needing a break to catch their breath. Matt felt as disappointed as Rick looked angry. Matt needed his manager on his side, not fighting him every step of the way. Rick had been with him since the beginning, almost twenty years ago, and Matt had counted on the friendship that had grown out of their shared vision. He was reasonable enough to realize that the change in vision was all his, but he'd hoped Rick could step aside from party dogma long enough to see the wisdom in it.

In the general hubbub of refilling coffee mugs, Matt got up and asked Rick to step out into the hall for a moment. In a quiet alcove, he told Rick about how he and Hal had gotten started with their ideas. He told him about the letter from Edna, and how that had prompted him to share some of his ideas in that second debate. He told him about his son's approbation. Rick knew how far apart Matt and Ben had drifted in the last ten years, and he also knew how much that distance had pained Matt.

"This just feels right, Rick. In my heart, I know this is the only course I can follow and still look myself in the mirror. I need you. I hope you can share my vision, but even if you can't, I still need you. Please give this a chance."

Rick studied Matt with his shrewd blue gaze for a long while. Matt couldn't guess what was going on in his friend's head, but he began to pray. He really did need Rick. More than the other man perhaps knew. Not just because he was the best campaign manager in the business, but because his enthusiasm had always kept Matt going when he felt more like quitting. Because Rick's energy fired Matt's own. And because he cared about this man and wanted him on his side.

"I'm scared shitless," Rick finally said.

"That makes two of us." Matt gave Rick a brief, hard hug.

~ * ~

The calendar that had been mostly blank spaces when they began had been filled, and everyone sat back with a satisfied groan. Rick lifted his head.

"Okay. Now it's my turn. You will never guess the dirt I've dug up on Roland Miller."

Jack perked up. "Well, don't keep us guessing."

Rick looked first at Matt, then around the circle of faces. "Rolly's gay."

Ken dropped his notebook on the carpet and bent to snatch it back. Hal sat up so abruptly he sloshed coffee in his lap. Penny stopped rocking. Jack just gaped.

"How did you come by this information?" Matt asked quietly.

"I don't think you want to know." Rick looked uncharacteristically ill at ease.

Matt decided he probably didn't want to know the lengths Rick had gone to. Or rather the muddy depths. "It doesn't change anything," he interjected before Jack could pursue the question. Jack's media antennae were up and wagging furiously.

"It doesn't change anything? Are you nuts? Man, if this gets out, the voting public is going to go mad. And just think of the media. You think piranhas are merciless!" Rick's normal enthusiasm was back. "This could break the campaign wide open."

"How does Roland Miller's sexual orientation change the way he'd govern if elected?" Matt sat back and crossed one foot over his knee.

"It doesn't matter a whit, but that's not the point. Every gay in the country will be in his camp in a heartbeat, but the rest of the country is going to take a giant step back and rethink their opinion. The pious little bastard's been playing the grieving widower to the hilt. Which means he's a fraud. He's probably been lying for years. Poor Jean Anne. How do you think that'll go over?" Rick demanded.

"All politicians are liars. At least that's the general consensus," Jack offered with a shrug.

Matt thought about the possibility that he was Thanh's father and about the assurances he'd made when the first accusation regarding Thanh's parentage had been voiced. Matt hadn't lied, at least not knowingly at the time. But by doing nothing to confirm or deny it, was he lying by omission?

"Most politicians bend the truth when it's convenient," Ken observed with a nod of his head.

"More often, we simply leave the truth out," Matt rejoined the discussion. "That's all Rolly is guilty of. No one ever asked him if he was gay. They did accuse him of having an affair with Ashley Lauder, which he denied. And that, most likely, is the truth of it."

"How is it you seem to know all about this and you never mentioned it?" Jack's probing gaze fixed on Matt.

"I came by the knowledge quite by accident and not all at once. Does it matter?"

"I'm just curious. You know me." Jack winked. "Avidly curious. It's a failing of mine."

"Some years ago, Eve and I were out celebrating our anniversary at a little out of the way restaurant in horse country. My face had been all over the news due to my opposition to going to war in Iraq, so we'd picked this place because I thought no one I knew would ever frequent it. You can imagine my astonishment when we ran into Roland Miller while waiting to be seated. Ironically, he was with Miss Lauder at the time. Anyway, he introduced her to me as Ashley Lauder, but when he turned to her, he said, Shelley, may I introduce Senator Steele?"

"Shelley? Who calls her that?"

"Rolly does. I believe her middle name is Michelle. I assumed that she preferred—"

"So, where are you going with this little story anyway?" Rick interrupted impatiently.

"At the time, thinking I'd happened on a clandestine tryst, I only thought it was pretty low of him to be dating this woman behind his wife's very ill back. Jean Anne died only a few months later. But by then, I'd dug up the information that Rolly was defending Miss Lauder in a lawsuit, so, while it might have looked questionable, it didn't prove he was cheating on Jean Anne."

"Get to the point!" Rick leapt to his feet and moved to lean an arm on the mantle.

"Okay," Matt took pity on the man. "Fast forward to two years ago. Megan dragged me to this gallery where a friend of hers had mounted a show. It's in Georgetown. Very pricey. And not my usual preference in art, but Megan had promised her friend we would come. So, she's busy chatting with her friend and I'm trying to look interested in the stuff hanging on the walls. But instead, I get drawn into listening to the owner who's on the phone. At first I thought it was just a business call and tried to ignore it. The man obviously had no idea anyone was close enough to overhear. So, I turn to make my escape, but not before I became aware that the call was far more personal. The owner, one Asher Elliott, was quarreling with his lover. And the lover's name was Rolly."

Jack rubbed his hands together in glee. "I'm lovin' the way this is turning out. Go on."

"A few days later, Eve tells me Megan dragged her to the same gallery, and while Megan's busy propping her friend's confidence up, Eve's chatting up the owner of the gallery. Then, in walks Roland Miller. Apparently the expression on Mr. Elliot's face gave away his involvement with Miller, according to Eve's feminine intuition. Anyway, Eve said the rest of the time she was there, the two men avoided each other like water and oil and it was obvious to anyone who wasn't blind that something was going on."

"So..." Rick's blue eyes burned with interest. "How are we best going to use this information?"

"We aren't," Matt stated flatly. *He who casts the first stone* went through his mind. Besides, he'd never once stooped to mud slinging, and he wasn't about to start now. "We're not using it."

"You have got to be kidding me. Matt, this is huge. *Huge!* How can we *not* use it?"

"To start with, Roland Miller's sex life is none of our business and it shouldn't be anyone else's either."

"To say nothing of the fact that Cabot is far more likely to gain any votes Miller loses than we would," Ken observed with a thoughtful expression.

"Good point," Jack mused. "But it sure goes against the grain not to share such a juicy tidbit with at least one or two of the newshounds who've done us favors in the past. Besides, I love a good scandal."

Matt shook his head at his press secretary. He suspected Jack would love nothing better than to drop a hint into a receptive ear and watch the wildfire spread. He also knew that Jack would honor the boss' wishes, however much it pained him to do so.

Matt just wished he could be as certain that Rick had come as fully on board with the more important element of today's meeting as he'd let on. Rick would be indispensable in pulling together all the most powerful of Matt's backers and, along with Ken and Jack, a principal in molding the message for the general voting public.

Timing would be everything. Hal and Matt would continue as they had, allowing themselves to be drawn into discussions that gave them opportunities to suggest some of the more radical fixes they felt were important. They would answer any direct question honestly, but with as few details as possible, but until much closer to the actual election, neither man would get pinned down to specifics. The longer the period of time between revealing the specific details and November seventh, the longer Cabot and Miller would have to distort Matt's goals and put their own spin on the discussion.

As he saw his staff to the door, thanking them for their time and efforts, Matt felt as though he should be excited and energized. It was all happening. Really happening. Where was the anticipation? The sense of rightness?

Then Thanh and his startlingly blue eyes thrust themselves into Matt's consciousness.

Fifteen

Thanh sat on the edge of Annie's bed watching her putter nervously about the room. He had not been home in four days except to dash into the silent apartment long enough to shower and change before school each morning. Knowing he would be seeing Annie again as soon as she left work made his days fly by, and the prospect of yet another night in her bed filled him with bubbling happiness. He had never realized falling in love would feel so wonderful.

Yet something about Annie's behavior right at the moment made him uneasy. Maybe she did not share his untroubled contentment. Rather than seeming less ill at ease than she had the first time she had invited him to stay, she acted more so. He wished he knew what bothered her. He wished she trusted him enough to tell him.

"Is something wrong, Annie? Would you rather I did not stay tonight?" He prayed she would not take him up on the offer. He was already aroused. Already anticipating another night of lovemaking. But that would be selfish. Annie meant so much more to him than just getting laid.

Annie turned from the dresser where she had been stowing her jewelry and braced her hands on the dresser's edge as she faced him. Her pose drew the flimsy material of her pajamas taut against her nipples, outlining their pert erectness. Thanh almost groaned with the stab of desire that shot through him.

"I don't want you to leave." A fleeting smile lifted the corner of her lips.

It would be easier to talk sensibly with her standing across the room from him, but the look of vulnerable uncertainty on her face trumped prudence. "Come here," he invited gently. Thanh patted his knee.

She crossed the room and stood before him, but did not sit. Thanh reached for her hands and drew her down onto his lap. So much for calm discussion! His body jumped with eager desire.

"Something bothers you."

"N-nothing is bothering me. I'm just—I'm glad you're here, and I want you to stay."

"Is it the morality of sleeping together without a commitment? Does it trouble your conscience?" If so, he was ready to marry her tomorrow. Or at the very least become engaged. He was in love. Completely, head over heels, in love.

He did not know for sure when it had happened. Perhaps that first night when he had seen her sitting at the table looking so alone and so bored. Maybe when he had drummed up the courage to approach her, it had been the sparkling smile of interest she had turned on him. But he thought it more likely that he had fallen in love as he had gotten to know her. Learned her history and her dreams. Sensed her strengths and seen her vulnerable side. Listened to the music of her laughter and found himself chucking at her unique brand of humor.

He loved the way she made him feel. Not just when she touched him intimately, but when she touched his mind and appreciated his humor and intellect. He loved her slanted Vietnamese eyes that teased him with hidden secrets and twinkled with amusement. He loved her warm Hispanic complexion and the thick luxurious fall of her hair. Loved the way if felt between his fingers and trailing over his naked skin. He loved everything about her. Except maybe the worry that she could not yet share with him.

He was so totally, hopelessly in love with her, he had trouble concentrating at school. Even his students had begun to notice his preoccupation and tease him about it. He did not care. He was ready to declare his love for the whole world to know.

Except something held Annie back. And that something kept a part of her locked away. She had been hurt before, so perhaps he just needed to be patient. Needed to wait for Annie to learn how trust him. He needed to wait for Annie to be ready to give her heart away again.

"Do you wish we had remained only friends and not become lovers?"

Annie slumped against him, burying her face in the crook of his neck. She wound her arms about his shoulders and shook her head. "No." Her voice was muffled, but definite.

"Are you sure? You act as if you are not certain."

"I act as if I can't believe you find me so attractive." Annie toyed with the hair on the back of his neck.

Thanh pushed her away, then let his gaze travel from her face down to her toes and back to her face with appreciative familiarity. "You are the most beautiful woman I have ever known."

"I am too short."

"I like being so much taller. It makes me feel like a superman."

"I've already begun to sag."

Thanh took another leisurely look at her delectable body. "Not that I have noticed. But even when you do, I promise I will love every wrinkle."

"I have an ugly scar."

"I love that you are daring enough to go snorkeling into a coral-rimmed cave to get such a scar." He eased the wide neck of her pajama top down over her shoulder and kissed the disputed scar. He thought it looked more like a flower than something ugly, but either way, it did not detract from her beauty in his eyes.

"You are a flatterer."

"Yes, but I mean every word of it." He widened his eyes to convince her of his sincerity.

She laughed, and the nervousness receded as it did every night when the lovemaking began. She flopped backward onto the bed in a flurry of graceful limbs and tugged at the waistband of his briefs. "Take me, I'm yours!"

~ * ~

"I'm all yours!" Megan Steele hurried down the stairs toward the man leaning against the fender of a souped-up pickup truck with chromed, dual-exhaust pipes, thick-treaded tires and a row of yellow lights arrayed across its roof.

Stylish jeans hung from narrow hips and a crisply ironed shirt, open at the throat, set off the young man's lean, wide-shouldered body with devastating effect. With raven black hair and shrewd black eyes, he exuded masculine sexuality.

Matt, from his vantage point on the veranda, saw immediately why Megan was so taken with Randy Robinson and, just as immediately, formed an acute dislike.

"Don't wait up," Megan called over her shoulder as she slowed her pace and approached the man, hips swaying provocatively.

Where had last year's hard-driving tomboy gone? Now that Matt had time to think about it, Megan's choice of clothing seemed a little more provocative than was her usual style, as well. Hell, a lot more provocative! Matt wanted to call her back.

Megan had been so wrapped up in sports in high school that she hadn't even gone to her senior prom. Always a diligent student, she'd spent her first year in college with her nose glued to her books. She'd never given her parents a moment's worry, but now she seemed to have suddenly, if belatedly, discovered the opposite sex and meant to make up for lost time. And Matt wasn't sure he liked the transformation.

Robinson hadn't made any move to introduce himself either to Matt or to Brenda Evans, the woman assigned to Megan's security detail for the evening. Randal J. Robinson had been vetted, of course, but that had been done by some staffer in an office somewhere downtown, who'd only seen the man on paper, not in person. As Megan approached, Robinson shoved himself away from the truck. He turned to open the door for her, sliding his free hand up under the hem of Megan's too-tight, too-short sweater with deliberate familiarity.

Keep your hands off my daughter. Matt bit back the words. He tried to reassure himself that the man was at least gentleman enough to open doors for his date. He supposed Ben behaved no differently, but somehow it was different when it was *your* daughter. Matt watched until the truck rumbled out of sight, its engine as potent and compelling as its owner. Reluctantly, Matt turned and went into the house.

The quiet emptiness of the place depressed him. He missed Eve, who was away on a two-day campaign jaunt with Hal Weymouth's wife. Skip, their aging Golden Retriever, greeted Matt's return to the house with a silently wagging tail, and then escorted him into his study. The dog promptly flopped down onto the braided rug beside the desk and closed his eyes.

"A lot of company you are," Matt commented as he tossed his briefcase onto the desk and removed his laptop.

Skip lifted one eyelid, thumped his tail twice, and shut his eye again.

After connecting the power adapter, and pressing the on button to boot the computer up, Matt headed to the kitchen. Skip got to his feet and followed, then sat patiently while Matt listened to a lengthy queue of messages on the answering machine.

"Sorry, sport." Matt ruffled the dog's furry head. "Megan forgot to feed you, huh?" He opened the cupboard, found a can of dog food and opened it. With the dog fed, Matt fixed himself a sandwich and took it back to his study to eat while he caught up on his email. Then he had an entire pile of stuff to wade through that his secretary had sent over from his senatorial office for his consideration.

At ten thirty, he went back to the kitchen to fix himself a cup of tea and let the dog out. Skip had just come in and settled himself in the corner when the front door banged open, then thumped shut with enough force to rattle Eve's china.

Matt hurried into the hall, heart rate accelerating.

Megan rushed past him without a word and flew up the stairs. He heard the crash of her door slamming shut and debated going after her. What could have happened to reduce his usually easy-going daughter to this level of fury? Should he go after her or not? Then, shrugging, he mounted the stairs.

He stood uneasily outside her door. Maybe it was none of his business. He wished Eve were home. Eve would know if he should butt in or leave her be. Megan didn't answer his knock. He hesitated. He probably should go away and give her the privacy she deserved. Another long moment of indecision ended with a muffled string of curses and something crashed against the door.

He knocked louder.

"What?" Megan responded with sharp incivility. Then Matt heard footsteps. Megan opened the door, but stood blocking entry.

"You okay?"

"I'm fine!" She glared at him, her body a study in righteous indignation. Then she wilted. "Okay, so I'm not fine. I'm pissed. Sorry, I'm angry."

"Want to talk about it?" Matt still wasn't sure he should have followed her, but she'd opened the door, perhaps she really did want to share what was bothering her in spite of all the attitude.

"Oh, Daddy! Why are men so crude?"

Alarmed, Matt pushed his way fully into the room. He noticed the shards of a broken figurine and looked at Megan in concern. "Care to tell me what happened?"

A number of unpleasant scenarios ran through Matt's mind, but were dismissed. Whatever had happened had been verbal, he assured himself. Brenda Evans would have stepped in if things had become physical.

"I don't know where to begin." Megan slumped onto the edge of her bed.

"Try the beginning." Matt sank into the comfortable rocker between Megan's bed and a bookshelf lined with Precious Moments figurines, one of which now lay behind the door, shattered beyond fixing.

"The beginning of tonight's fiasco? Or the beginning when I met the louse?"

"Start wherever you want." Matt forced himself to withhold judgment.

"It's probably all my fault." Megan's voice wobbled and tears replaced the angry glint.

"It's probably not your fault, but unless you tell me what happened, I really won't know." Megan's earlier anger had moved into *his* breast. Whatever that brash young man had done, had reduced his usually confident daughter to this. Matt wanted to strangle the guy.

"We went out for pizza first. Then to a movie. Only it was a lousy movie so Randy suggested going for a drive. And I agreed. I also agreed to sneak out a side door so Brenda wouldn't know we were leaving."

Alarm shot through Matt again. Perhaps things had gotten physical. His gut twisted.

"Randy drove us to this little place by the river. I suppose he thought if he took me somewhere nice and romantic that it would put me in the right mood. And it was kind of romantic with the moon shining on the water and all, but I wasn't in the mood. And I didn't want to get in the mood."

Matt had a feeling he knew where this was going, and he didn't like it. Only his daughter's matter-of-fact recital kept him from leaping to the conclusion that the bastard had forced himself on her, or tried to. "The mood for what?"

"I mean, I'm not a prude or anything, and it's not like I've never been kissed or anything. I like kissing."

He felt his blood pressure rising. That's normal, he reminded himself, and something she has every right to enjoy. She's an adult. In charge of her own life.

"I tried to make him understand we didn't know each other well enough for what he wanted, but he wouldn't listen. He called me a tease and—and something a lot worse. Then he got physical. And he was stronger than me." Megan's words began to tumble out with abandon, and tears trembled in the corners of her eyes before spilling down her cheeks. "I was scared, Daddy."

Matt flew off the chair and pulled his daughter into his arms. If Eve were here, Matt would have been out tearing the town apart, hunting the young man down. *And done what?* he asked himself. A vicious beating appealed to his need to punish the bastard and, unavoidably, he knew he was capable of it. He forced the desire from his mind and tried to concentrate on what Megan was telling him.

"Randy is so sexy, and it was exciting when he made me feel that way too, but when he started acting like a jerk, I just wanted to be anywhere else. Then he wouldn't take his hands off me, so I got out of the truck and ran.

"He shouted for me to get back in the truck, but I pretended I didn't hear and kept going. I got lucky. A police car came down the road almost as soon as I got to it. I flagged it down, and they brought me home." She shuddered against him and the hysterical flow of words stopped abruptly.

"Does Brenda know you're home?" Matt thought frantically about what he should say next. How he should react to her recital and the events themselves.

Megan shook her head.

"Okay, first things first. I'll call Brenda and tell her you're at home, with me." Matt set her away to look down into her troubled, tear-stained face. "You wash your face, then come downstairs, and we'll fix ourselves some hot chocolate. Maybe we need to talk about a few things."

~ * ~

Seated across the kitchen table from Matt, her hair now bundled into a clip and her slender body enfolded by an enormous fluffy pink robe, Megan cupped her hands about a warm mug. With her face free of makeup and tears, she looked like his little girl again. But a new wisdom colored her deep brown eyes.

"You were right about Randy. I didn't know him very well at all. Not as good as I thought I did, anyway." She paused, then, staring determinedly at the cocoa in her mug, asked in a rush, "Are men all like that? I mean, is sex all they really want from a woman?" Megan looked up again, her expression serious, trusting. "Were you like that?"

Matt felt as if she'd slapped him. What would she think if she knew about Mai Ly? Would the trust in his daughter's eyes turn to contempt?

Megan waited for his answer. He couldn't recall the last time she'd sought his advice on anything this personal, and he knew he couldn't fail her. He just had to keep her problems and his own separate in his head.

"It's not a yes or no question, exactly," he began, feeling his way cautiously. "Most of the time it's not the only thing a man wants from a woman, but sometimes it's all he can think about."

He swallowed and forced himself to look his daughter in the eye. Had he behaved any differently that fateful day in Saigon? Maybe he hadn't initiated it, but that was a poor excuse. He hadn't fought very hard either. Eve and the promises he'd made to her had been the last thing on his mind when Mai Ly's pliant and very willing body pressed itself against his, and her hands began tugging at his clothing. He hadn't given a lot of thought to Mai Ly or what she wanted either. It had been all about sex. It had been only about sex as he'd pulled Mai Ly down onto his bed.

Megan waited for him to go on, her gaze steady and interested.

"About the feelings," he began, almost overwhelmed with embarrassment and guilt. "You said you liked the way Randy made you feel. You told me you thought he was sexy. A hunk, is how you described him last week, I think. And to be honest, you were dressed to impress when you left here tonight. Right?"

She looked away. "Yes," she admitted faintly. A slow flush stole up her neck and into her hair.

"What kind of message do you think Randy got from that?" Matt continued in spite of the tumult battering his conscience. He'd gotten Mai Ly's message loud and clear. "It's pretty normal for a man, especially a young man, to want more than just a few kisses, if he's been led to believe his desire is reciprocated."

"But I didn't want more," Megan protested, her voice rising.

"Maybe not this time, or with this man, but someday you will. Randy should have stopped when you asked, but sometimes it's hard to stop, even when you know you should."

"Megan?" Matt reached across the table and touched her face, compelling her to look at him. "Randy did not behave as he should have, and you had every right to be angry and upset. But you have to accept some of the responsibility for having put yourself in the situation in the first place. You wore clothes calculated to turn him on. You flirted with him with both your behavior and the things you said. And you were willing to elude your secret service agent to be alone with him. Can you see how he might have gotten the wrong impression?"

She nodded slowly.

"Until you feel ready for that kind of a relationship, it's up to you not to let a man think that you are. Everyone goes parking, or whatever you guys call it nowadays. But you need to be aware of what might happen when you do. Both parties need to know just how far it's all right to go before you get to a point where you find you can no longer think clearly."

Kind of like the pot calling the kettle black. Matt's conscience cringed. There had been nothing right about what he'd let happen with Mai Ly. And no discussing it, either before or after. He'd just taken what she offered, spilled himself inside her with total irresponsibility, then abandoned her to bear a child that might very well be his and face the consequences alone.

Megan sniffed and a slow tear trickled its way down her cheek. "I feel so ashamed."

"Don't." Matt struggled to bury his own battle of conscience and deal with Megan's. He cupped her face with one hand. "Don't ever feel ashamed for making a mistake. No one is perfect. Everyone makes mistakes. Learn from your mistakes and grow from them. Let them make you a better person, but don't be ashamed of yourself because you're human and don't be afraid to try new things because you might fail. Success in life is a matter of picking yourself up one more time than you fall.

"Try to forgive your young man and definitely forgive yourself."

Megan lunged out of her chair and circled the table to throw her arms about Matt's neck. "You have to be the best father a woman could ever have. I don't deserve you."

"I'm glad you think so, kitten, but I'm far from perfect."

"Yeah, I know, you're getting flabby around the middle." She patted his stomach. "And tomorrow morning I'm getting the basketball out, and I'm going to beat you for once!"

"You're on."

Megan yawned. "Thanks, Daddy." She blew him a kiss and disappeared through the swinging door in a flurry of her pink robe.

He had his daughter back, at least for a little while longer. There would eventually come a day when he'd be expected to give her away with grace and composure to some other man who would take liberties with her that no father ever wanted to contemplate.

He shook his head and got up to put the mugs in the dishwasher. The arrogant, sex-on-the-brain Randy still made Matt's blood boil, but Megan had had the good sense to walk away before it was too late. All her life, Matt had protected her. But now, if he'd taught her well, he had to have faith that she could protect herself.

But who had been there to protect Mai Ly?

Sixteen

"Thanks, Joe." Megan's voice trilled along the hall, preceding her into the kitchen. She shouldered her way through the door and plopped two pizza boxes on the counter.

Matt hauled four beers from the fridge and set them next to the pizza, then rummaged in the drawer for a bottle opener. "Isn't Joe going to have any?"

"He says he's on duty, and he already ate."

Matt shrugged and put one beer away, then opened the others and passed them around. He should have guessed Joe would decline, but Matt always liked to invite the man to join them when he could.

Megan hiked her butt onto a stool next to Thanh and brought one of the bottles to her mouth. Then she set it back on the counter with a gusty sigh. "God, I needed that. I'm parched."

"Basketball does that to me, too." Thanh removed a wad of chewing gum from his mouth and perched it on the side of his plate. Then he grabbed one of the bottles and joined her.

"So, Daddy, are we still going to Maine for the long weekend? Please don't say you're cancelling because of the campaign."

Matt had been about to take a bite out of his slice of pizza, but returned it to his plate. "No, we're all still going. I'm just trying to work out the logistics." He'd been looking forward to the break in the grueling campaign schedule, and it wouldn't be the same if everyone couldn't get there. Besides, he'd promised Thanh a trip to his father's hometown the first day they'd met and had yet to make good on the promise.

"What's to work out?" Megan swallowed, wiped her mouth and grinned. "Aren't we going up in the bus?"

"Originally, I thought so. I figured we'd sleep while the driver got us there overnight. But now Rick and Murdock have scheduled a bunch of stops along the way. Your mother and I leave on Wednesday. You have classes on Thursday and Thanh has to work Friday, too. Ben's free both days so we can pick him up on the way. But I think I'll have to fly you and Thanh into Portland and pick you up at the airport."

"The bus is more fun, but I'm good with flying up." Megan grabbed a second slice of pizza. "How about you, Thanh?"

"What if someone could fly us up in a private plane?" Thanh suggested shyly.

Matt turned on his stool and studied Thanh, eyebrows lifted. "Who do you know with a private plane?"

"Annie's Dad."

"Ooooh! Sounds like this is getting serious." Megan poked Thanh in the ribs. "Time to meet the parents?"

"Yes." Thanh colored faintly, but looked happy in spite of his embarrassment. "I have already met both of Annie's parents but..." he paused and turned to Matt. "I know you are not my parents, but I would still very much like to introduce Annie to you and Eve."

"You're just trying to impress your girl with your connections to important people," Megan teased.

"That is not so," Thanh protested, coloring even more. "Besides, I am not certain how impressed she would be. She volunteers for

Blair Cabot." Thanh pulled his mouth into a disapproving grimace. "She is usually very smart, but everyone has their blind spots. I just want to introduce her to the only people I have who feel like family."

"How sweet." Megan leaned over and gave Thanh a hug. "How about that, Daddy? I have two brothers now.

Matt dropped his half-eaten slice of pizza, cheese side down and hastily fumbled it back onto his plate. Megan's innocent observation felt like an electronic blow to his heart. He'd never been on the receiving end of a taser, but perhaps this was what it felt like.

"Maybe we can change Annie's mind and turn her into a Democrat!" Megan grinned at her father, oblivious to his guilty reaction. Then she turned back to Thanh. "But I didn't think Annie's dad lived around here."

"He does not, but he is coming to visit Annie this week. Maybe he would be willing to fly us all to Maine? He would not have to go into Portland if another airport was more convenient. If he would not mind a trip to Maine, that is." Thanh looked anxiously at Matt.

Matt pulled himself together and considered Thanh's request. "Avgas isn't cheap, but I'd be willing to fill his tanks if he's willing to drive the plane." Matt lifted the lid of the pizza box and pulled another slice onto his plate. "How many passengers can he carry? Megan comes with a bodyguard, you know. Probably two of them."

"Five passengers," Thanh answered, then added, "but one of the secret service guys could ride in the copilot's seat." He held up his hand and began folding fingers down. "Megan, me, Annie, two agents and Tony."

"Tony?"

"Tony Santos. Annie's father."

"Well, why don't you find out how Annie and her father feel about a weekend in Maine? In the meantime, I'll have Annie and her father checked out so there won't be a problem with security. I'm looking forward to meeting your young lady."

"You're going to like her, Daddy." Megan hopped off her stool and began gathering up the used paper plates. "She's funny and smart. Well, most of the time she's smart." Megan winked at Thanh.

Matt raised his eyebrows at his daughter in surprise. "When did you get to meet her?"

"Daddy, if you were home more, you'd have met her by now, too. Thanh can hardly drag himself away long enough to meet me for a cup of coffee, so inviting myself over was the only way to see anything of him." Megan stopped talking abruptly and looked at Thanh. "Where is Annie tonight, anyway?"

"She is working late."

"Ahhh! That explains you showing up to challenge me to a game of hoops! Well, I gotta go get a paper written. I did the dishes." Megan nodded in the direction of the rubbish bin. "You guys get to clean the counter." Then she disappeared through the swinging door, and Matt heard her footsteps sprinting lightly up the stairs.

"I should be going." Thanh slid off his stool.

"So soon?" Matt had a ton of work to get done tonight, but he'd been away and hadn't seen Thanh in days.

"You probably have a lot to do, and I do not wish to be in the way."

"I do have a bunch of calls I need to make, but..." Calls he'd never get to if Thanh stayed and they got talking. Their conversations had a way of going on for hours. Especially when Thanh got Matt onto the subject of his boyhood and his hometown.

"But don't be a stranger. Come by more often and bring your young lady. I'm eager to meet her. I'll see you to the door."

"That is not necessary, sir. I know my way out."

"And knock off the sir!" Matt folded the pizza box in half, then moved to the rubbish bin to dispose of it. He hesitated, staring down at the pink gob of gum Thanh had been chewing earlier. But then he shoved the box in and crunched it down until the cover closed over it. "Let me know what Annie's dad has to say and we'll go from there."

"I will call him tonight." Thanh turned to go, then turned back. "Um, sir?"

Matt frowned at him in mock displeasure.

"Matt?"

"Yes?"

"Thank you."

"Thank you for what? I haven't—haven't done anything." *Except maybe gotten your mother pregnant.*

"For letting Annie come with us. It is presumptuous of me, but I love her and, and I want her to meet you."

Matt crossed the kitchen and wrapped an arm about Thanh's shoulders. The gesture seemed so easy. Easier than hugging Ben had been in recent years. "It's not presumptuous at all. I'm glad you suggested it. Things are going to get crazy as soon as we get back from Maine, and I won't have another free moment until sometime in November."

~ * ~

Matt studied the items from the DNA kit he'd laid out on the bathroom counter. Thanh's wad of gum Matt had retrieved from the kitchen rubbish bin, saved in a plastic baggie to avoid further contamination. The swab he'd rubbed around the inside of his own cheek and preserved in the tube that came in the kit. The mailing envelope. And the instructions.

For the thousandth time, he asked himself if he really wanted to do this. And for the thousandth time, he answered his own doubts in the affirmative. He needed to know. For sure. Even if he was the only one who would ever know. He needed to know the truth.

Quickly before dread and doubt could change his mind, he bundled everything up and shoved it into the envelope, then added the money order he'd obtained from the same discreet source from which he'd gotten the test kit. Three days. They promised a report in three days. If the result came back positive, then he'd know. Sam might have been his cousin and they'd grown up as close as brothers, but Matt had been adopted, which meant his and Sam's DNA would be completely different. One way or another, Matt wanted to know the truth.

~ * ~

"Back it up a bit," TJ Smith hunched closer to the big flat screen TV mounted on the wall in his boss' office. He needed to find something. *Anything!* Just one misstep that might give him a purchase point for tearing into the Steele/Weymouth surge in approval ratings. With Miller's demise in the works, Steele was the only thing left standing in the way of his candidate's success.

Blair pressed rewind on the remote, then started the clip again. They were watching a videotape of Hal Weymouth's recent address to a NAACP audience in California. It had been a very controversial speech, according to all the reviews.

"It troubles me that right from the start of this campaign, some factions have assumed I'd use my influence to enlarge on benefits for black Americans and, frankly, many of the questions I've heard today just reaffirm that." Weymouth shook his head as if saddened by this fact.

"The belief that I will use my position as Matt Steele's running mate to broaden the scope of affirmative action is misplaced. I'm not sure I even agree that affirmative action is constitutional."

"Well, how convenient is that?" TJ bit out contemptuously. "A product of the ghetto doesn't get to where Weymouth is today without someone cutting him breaks along the way. And now he wonders if it's constitutional?"

"Hush," Blair hissed.

"The courts think so," someone in the audience shouted.

"I'd rather see educational opportunities expanded. I'd rather see young black Americans qualify on an even playing field for the things they want rather than lowering the standards. Lowering the standards just puts all of us behind the rest of the world. Other industrialized nations are already outscoring our kids in math and science. Their educational standards are already producing better results, and if we continue as we have been, they'll leave us in the dust."

"I thought that's what Matt Steele's Senate bill was all about." Another disembodied voice asked.

Weymouth ignored the taunt. *"I am convinced black people have been more oppressed in the past twenty years by what has been done for them than by everything done to them in the previous hundred.*

"I'm not claiming nothing has been gained. Thousands of black men and women have gotten educations and secured positions few could have obtained fifty years ago. But there are far too many others who've let themselves be helped right back into dependence. It's a destructive cycle to families and to self-esteem and above all, to our youth."

Weymouth turned his head, apparently listening to a question that had not been picked up by the audio feed.

148

"Yes," Weymouth nodded thoughtfully. "I did grow up in a slum, but I do not have affirmative action to thank for my success. There was a cop on the beat in the gang-ruled neighborhood where I lived. A big, black cop, who bucked all the odds to graduate from the academy and become a policeman. For some reason that officer took an interest in a skinny punk with no father and no goals in life beyond looking cool. Some of his methods would not be considered politically correct today, but they were effective.

"Officer Griffin is the single biggest reason I'm even alive today, never mind running for vice president. He never once cut me any slack. When he caught me straying into trouble, he hauled my butt down to the station and made me sit in the middle of the squad room while he lectured me on the likely end I would come to if I didn't start using the brains God had given me. Then he put a basketball in my hand and introduced me to a different bunch of guys. And he never let up on the need for a high school diploma.

"My choice of colleges expanded significantly due to my skill with a basketball. And once I was in, I used that opportunity to get the best education that school could give me. Studying didn't come easy to me and neither did the grades, in spite of everything Officer Griffin had pounded into my head. I had to work hard to keep up my grades at the same time I was keeping up on the court, but I was determined to make my shot at a decent education count. I couldn't let the only human being who'd ever taken an interest in me down.

"What we need today is not more entitlements, but more Officer Griffins. More people who care enough to kick a few lazy butts around until they wise up. America has become a land of takers. We've gotten so used to thinking of the government's largesse as our birthright that we've lost sight of what the word opportunity *means. I'm not talking just about blacks, but all of us, you, me,*

everyone. We've all got our pet gimmies, and we all scream when they're threatened.

"What started out as a safety net for the least among us has become a way of life. Too many poor black families have let themselves fall right back into subservience and dependency. They need incentives to get out of the rut, not reasons to stay in it. We need to give the underprivileged youth of America—black, white, Hispanic, all of our young people—the motivation to challenge themselves and then find ways to ensure their success."

Weymouth's soft southern drawl didn't match the fiery zeal in his eyes. He'd done a good job of keeping unpopular theories to himself. Until now! Who would have guessed he was such a revolutionary? TJ felt a smug sense of anticipation filling his breast.

"Where do you suppose Weymouth means to go with this line of rhetoric?" Blair brought a sweating can of cola to his mouth and drank.

TJ pursed his lips considering the possibilities. "A couple months ago, I'd have said he was a ringer hired by Miller to sabotage Steele's platform, but Steele's been on a similar tangent lately. I thought they were trying to play the middle of the road to take the wind out of our sails at first. But now, they've gone even farther to the right. They might just give us enough rope for a lynching if we're lucky."

"Now wouldn't that be a pleasant thought," Blair agreed with an unpleasant snort.

TJ and Blair turned their attention back to the television screen.

A short woman with an enormous hat stood up in the front row, her hand demanding attention. "Mr. Weymouth, when you first got into politics, what did you plan to accomplish?"

The vehemence drained from Hal Weymouth's face "My first public office?" He laughed. "You mean on the local planning

*board? I was just mad at the guy who gave out building permits."
Weymouth snorted derisively. "I figured anyone could do a better
job than he did, but to tell the truth, I didn't know anything about
it."*

*Weymouth stopped, then sobered. "I think, mostly, it was a
thorough disgust of corruption and graft. That's how my running
mate, Matt Steele, began, too. He had a pretty successful law
practice, and he never had any intention of getting into politics. But
he didn't hesitate to get up at town meetings and voice his opinion.
His friends were always pushing him to run for office, but he didn't
take them seriously until the year when the choices were between an
inept incumbent and an outright cheat.*

*"It wasn't much of a race. People were tired of business as
usual. They knew Matt Steele as an honest man with a reputation
for spending as much time and effort defending people who could
not afford his services as he did the ones who could. Matt didn't
make a lot of grandiose promises. His pitch wasn't filled with spin
and rhetoric. He just promised that every decision he made would
be based on what was best for the state and its citizens. He would
listen to all sides of the argument and was willing to sit down with
the opposition to make a deal that worked for everyone.*

*"Like me, it didn't take Matt long to realize how well-greased
the wheels of the political machine were and how hard it would be
to buck the system. If I had known when I got into this business
what I know now, I probably wouldn't be standing here, and you
never would have even heard of me unless you followed college
basketball thirty years ago. If I'd known how many of my ideals I
would have to shed, how many compromises I'd be required to
make, and how many unpalatable programs I'd be forced to put my
name on, I would have quit before I started. But I stuck it out and
here I am, as unlikely as that might seem.*

"Matt Steele has given me a chance to right all those wrongs. To reclaim my soul and make a real difference. I guarantee if you vote the Democratic ticket in November, you will be voting for solutions, not just fancy words. We live in a country with unprecedented wealth, unsurpassed educational opportunities and the best healthcare resources in the world. Capitalism does work, but not if we keep thwarting it. It's been said that socialism only works until you run out of other people's money. Well, we're about to run out, and it's time to revolutionize our thinking."

As the video came to a stop and the room went silent, Blair turned to his campaign manager. "Time to remind the voters how many times these guys have voted against the very reforms they are touting now."

Seventeen

Roland Miller sank onto the edge of the luxurious, king-sized bed in his downtown penthouse suite. He felt as if he'd been battered with pummeling, hate-filled fists and wasn't sure he didn't wish the beating had been physical. He glanced at the glaring headline on the discarded copy of the *Post* and the beloved features below the indictment.

He closed his eyes, but the bold, condemning words swam against the inside of his eyelids. *The love of Roland Miller's life is not the scandalous Ms Ashley Michelle "Shelley" Lauder as the gossips have been suggesting, but rather Mr. Asher Leighton Elliot, the openly gay art dealer and owner of a prominent downtown gallery.*

Bitterly angry representatives of the Republican National Committee had just left after nearly an hour of hurling abusive allegations and nasty reproaches at his head. His own campaign manager had been just as vitriolic, and there hadn't been a single sympathetic or understanding supporter in the room. The people he'd relied on the most had turned on him just as surely as the voting public would. Just three weeks away from the election. He'd needed only three more weeks.

A knock sounded on his door.

"Go away." Rolly couldn't bear one more word of recrimination. "I'm sorry." The voice outside his door sounded close to tears.

Rolly hurtled himself off the bed and flung the door open. Ash fell into the room and swallowed him in his embrace.

"I'm so sorry," Ash repeated, now openly weeping. "I didn't say anything. I don't know how they found out. I was frustrated, but I would never have done this to you. Never!"

Rolly found himself oddly dry-eyed. In spite of the verbal beating and the almost sure loss of his bid for the presidency, he felt curiously light. Free at last of all the constraints that had made his life a straight jacket. He patted his lover's shoulders and made soothing noises. It felt good to be crushed against that broad muscular chest. Even better to feel the love and acceptance of who he really was. Who he'd always been.

Rolly freed one hand and fished in his pocket for his handkerchief. "Here. Dry your eyes and let's go out to dinner."

Ash jerked free of Rolly's embrace and gazed at him with stunned, disbelieving eyes. "You don't mean that."

"The fat's in the fire. Why not?" Rolly turned toward the closet and reached for his jacket. "I can't think of a better way to stifle the wagging tongues than to brazen it out. My campaign might be lost, but I'm going out with dignity. Not with my tail between my legs." He shoved his arms into his suit jacket, took a quick peek into the mirror then straightened his shoulders. "You going to stand there gaping at me all night?"

Ash shut his mouth. "Let me wash my face first." He headed toward the bathroom. Then turned and came back. He took Rolly's face in his hands and lowered his mouth to Rolly's. His kiss was gentle and filled with love and...promise.

"You're a bigger man than I am, Rolly, and I love you for it."

Now Rolly felt like weeping! But he didn't. He had a public to face, and he planned to do so with courage and style.

~ * ~

Matt Steele sat back in astonishment, *The Washington Post* dropping onto his lap. "Tell me Rick Winfield didn't have anything to do with this."

Jack Holland shook his head, his expression a mixture of reproof and rapid calculation. "He promised he didn't. He seemed as stunned as you are. And I believe him. He might have been angry that day, but he'd never go behind your back like that. And I doubt anyone else in the room would have either."

"TJ Smith!" It had to have been Blair Cabot's ruthless campaign manager. If there was dirt to be dug up, TJ would be the one to find it. If Rick had ferreted out the truth, Matt wondered why he ever thought TJ wouldn't.

"We're sunk." Jack dropped into the chair on the other side of Matt's desk. He put his head in his hands and moved it back and forth.

"We're not sunk," Matt insisted firmly. "We have as much chance of winning Rolly's lost votes as Blair Cabot." Matt wished he believed the assurances as unflaggingly as his voice had uttered them. He and Hal had a platform as promising, more promising, than the Independent's. That much he did believe in. But, if TJ could scour up the damning evidence that would sink Rolly's campaign, he'd be sure to pounce on any proof of misconduct in Matt's past.

He thought of the DNA kit he'd shipped out. His source had been discreet. And the lab promised discretion. But Roland Smith had lived with utter discretion for years, and he'd been outed. What was to stop TJ from digging deep enough to discover the samples Matt had sent off for examination?

Matt felt suddenly light-headed. He'd wanted incontrovertible proof. He'd wanted exoneration. Or so he told himself every time the dispatch of the kit returned to haunt his thoughts. But did he really want acquittal? Or was he hoping in some secret place in his heart that Thanh would turn out to be his son and not Sam's?

In spite of the war going on in his soul, Matt dreaded the result. What if the world knew before he did? Before he could put things right with the important people in his life? With Eve? And with Thanh? Or Megan and Ben? He remembered the shock of seeing that photo of himself and Thanh on the front page of *The Washington Post*. Remembered his angry denial and the unquestioning support of his family. Did it all go back to a sin he'd committed over thirty years ago and all but forgotten until that day Thanh had sat across from him in the campaign bus with the tattered old photo between them?

Matt realized Jack was talking. Had been talking for some time. "What?"

"I said we need to sit down with Ken and Rick and decide what to do with this," Jack repeated. "We're leaving early in the morning, and we'll be on the bus for a couple hours before our first stop. We can run through all the possibilities then."

"We're picking Ben up in Philadelphia," Matt reminded him.

"So?"

Matt shrugged. "Yeah, right. Not a problem." Matt felt like the guilt that sat so heavy in his heart must show for anyone to see. He was afraid of the things Ben would say if he could read his thoughts. But Ben couldn't. And that wasn't what Jack was talking about anyway.

Jack pulled himself out of the chair and headed for the door. "See you tomorrow, Boss. Early." He saluted and disappeared down the hall.

Tomorrow, Matt echoed in his head. *And by tomorrow, maybe I'll know the truth about myself.*

~ * ~

Matt dropped his briefcase on the floor and began sorting through the mail. He started a pile for Eve, one for Megan, one to hand over to his secretary and tossed junk mail into the basket on the floor.

Then he saw the logo of the lab. His heart jumped even though that's what he'd been looking for.

He balanced the envelope on his palm as if weighing its merits. His heart shot into overdrive, and he sucked in a ragged breath. His head roared like a waterfall. He pressed his lips together hard and tried to quell the turmoil. Then he closed his fingers around the envelope and headed for his study.

Matt stepped into the darkened room and flicked on the lights. Then after pausing for a moment, he carefully closed the door behind him. He set the letter from the lab with the rest of his mail in the middle of his desk, and went to gaze out at Eve's garden, or what he could see of it illuminated by the light from his study window. Finally, after many long minutes, he returned to his desk and sat in the massive leather chair. Resting his head against the back of the chair, he gazed up at the paneled ceiling. Then, in a rush, he sat up, grabbed his letter opener and slit the envelope from the lab. He pulled out the single sheet inside and unfolded it. He swallowed as he digested its contents.

Thanh is my son.

For a moment, he thought he might faint. It seemed as if his heart had stopped beating entirely, and his blood had ceased to circulate.

Thanh is my *son. Not Sam's.*

He closed his eyes and sank back into the chair again.

Thanh is my son. All these years I had a son. How could I not have known?

He rocked his head back and forth as the memories bludgeoned his conscience. Memories of the day he'd committed the most contemptible of betrayals against the man who'd meant more to him than anyone other than his adoptive father.

Matt flung himself out of the chair. He paced angrily back to the window, then not happy looking at his own reflection in the glass, he returned to the switch and turned the light off. Back at the window, he ran reasons to justify what had happened between himself and Mai Ly through his head. People did things in wartime they'd not do otherwise. It was natural to cling to expressions of life while living in the midst of death. But the only death they had been experiencing was Sam's. Which brought Matt right back to the sick feeling of having betrayed his friend.

He'd puked back when it happened. After he'd woken to find Mai Ly gone, along with the radio and the marriage license. He'd put his fist through the wall, and then he'd been sick. He'd wretched until there was nothing left in his stomach. Until he ached with it. Proof, if any was needed, at how unacceptable his behavior had been.

Mai Ly started it, his demon reminded him. She'd wept when Matt told her Sam was dead, but almost immediately her concern had been for getting herself out of Vietnam. Had that been all Sam had meant to her? Mai Ly wouldn't have been the first nor the last woman to entice a man into her bed to buy her way to a new life. Plenty of Vietnamese women had done just that. And before them, the Koreans and the Filipinos, the French, Germans, even British women had used the loneliness and homesickness of American GIs to buy their ticket to the USA. But if that had been Mai Ly's only reason, why had she not come to the embassy afterward?

He had promised to get her out, but she'd never come. It had been too easy to let himself believe she'd changed her mind and didn't want to face a life in a totally new world, away from everything she knew. So, he'd turned his back on his promises. On Sam's promises. He'd focused on his job and been swept up in the hectic evacuation of thousands of Americans as well as Vietnamese who were more afraid of the advancing Communists than the hardships of a new life. He hadn't even thought of her as he sat in the door of the helicopter on its last run, staring back at the abandoned embassy and the people his country had turned its back on.

"Matt?"

Matt jerked around. A band of light from the hallway shafted across the carpet, then grew bigger, and Eve entered his study.

"What on earth are you doing in here in the dark?" She crossed the room toward him. "Are you okay?"

Matt didn't answer. He felt nauseous, and he had a raging headache. His emotions were as confused and battered as a shuttlecock. Eve bent to turn the desk light on and peered at him with a look of concern furrowing her brow.

"What's wrong, Matt?"

How could he tell her? He had betrayed her as much as he'd betrayed Sam. He had to say something. She reached to grasp his hands in hers, waiting. Patient. Supportive. Always supportive. He could trust her. He *had* to trust her.

"Tha—" Matt's voice broke. He cleared his throat and began again. "Thanh is my son."

Eve's fingers tightened on his, but she didn't say anything. Her gaze never left his, and it hadn't changed from the selfless concern for whatever was bothering him.

"He's my son, Eve. Not Sam's." Matt let out a ragged breath he hadn't known he'd been holding.

"I wondered when you were going to figure that out." Eve released his hands. She moved closer, her arms encircling his waist.

"H-how?" Matt was having a really difficult time making his voice work. "How did you know?"

"He's so like you, Matt. More like you than Ben. Or Megan. Physically, it's his eyes... mostly."

Those incredibly blue eyes! Matt closed his eyes and saw them, bright and very blue in the bathroom mirror. Then he saw Thanh's eyes watching him intently that day on the bus. Equally blue. Bluer than Sam's had ever been.

"It's not just the fact that they're blue," Eve went on, her voice gently analytical. "It's the way he looks at a person. It's the soul inside him shining out of those blue eyes. And it's other things, too." She tipped her head to the side as she did when she was contemplating something seriously. "He rakes his fingers through his hair when he's anxious and leaves it standing on end the same way you've always done. And he winks just like you do. He walks like you, too. And," she lifted one hand to the back of Matt's head and traced a curl of hair with her finger. "He's got the same little whorl in his hair in the very same spot."

"How come you aren't as disgusted with me as I am?"

Eve leaned away and gaped up at him, disbelief clear in her expression. "Why should I be disgusted?"

"I left a bastard behind in Vietnam, and I didn't even have the decency to do anything about it."

"Did you have a choice?"

"A choice?" he parroted, an edge to his voice. "What do you mean by choice? I could have *chosen* to keep my fly zipped. And when I didn't manage that, I could have *chosen* to consider the possibility that I might have knocked her up and found the courage to make sure I hadn't."

"And when would you have done that? I got the impression from Thanh that by the time his mother knew she was pregnant, you would have been long since gone."

"Don't you even care *how* I managed to get Sam's fiancée pregnant?" Matt pulled free of Eve's embrace and slumped down onto the window seat."

"Only if you need to tell me." Eve followed and sat next to him, pulling a small, embroidered pillow onto her lap and hugging it against her belly.

Eve was the only woman Matt had ever loved, but that love hadn't stopped him from giving in to temptation when it was thrown at him. Even though there had been a part of him that wanted Thanh to be his son, the part he was dealing with right now had committed an awful betrayal of two people he cared about and admitting it was burning a hole in his gut.

"I love you." Matt couldn't look her in the eye.

"I know you do. And I'm betting this confession is just about killing you."

"While you were back in Maine, writing faithfully every day, I was screwing someone else. What about the promises I made to you?" The nausea roiled alarmingly close to revolt.

"It wasn't right," Eve conceded, a pained look crossing her face. "But it was a long time ago. You were a long way from home and— things happen…"

"Shit happens!" Matt spat out angrily.

"Did you love her?"

Matt jerked in response to Eve's question. "No," he answered at last. "I can't even claim that as an excuse."

Eve let the pillow slide to the floor and put her hands on the sides of Matt's face, forcing him to look at her. "I didn't think so."

His eyes watered, and he thought he might cry. He tried to look away.

Eve held his face firmly, and didn't let him retreat. "I've never been in a place like you were then, so I don't know first hand. But if your nightmares told me anything, I know it was pretty awful. If you somehow found a moment of—a bit of relief from the ugliness with this woman..." Eve swallowed, then went on in a defensive rush. "And I'm betting she was as willing as you were."

"More willing," Matt blurted without thinking. Then he began to understand the truth of it. He *had* made an effort to put a stop to Mai Ly's advances. Not that it excused his fall from grace.

"If you had known she was pregnant. If you had known it was your baby, would you have married her?" Eve's dark eyes peered at him intently. Now there was more than just a hint of pain in their depths. She looked almost haunted. As if considering a fate she couldn't bear.

"Probably. Yeah, I would have. I'd have had to," Matt answered reluctantly and suddenly saw the yawning gap between his life as it was and as it might have been.

"And then there would have been no *us*." Eve put the awful possibility she'd perceived into words. "And no Ben. And no Megan. Would you give them back? Never mind all the years you and I have shared. Would you change all that if you could?"

Matt's heart contracted in anguish. "Of course not."

"Then maybe everything was meant to happen the way it did. Things happen for a reason. Ben and Megan were meant to be born, and for that to happen, you and I had to happen. And none of that would be true if you'd brought that poor girl home from Vietnam and married her."

Matt closed his eyes. Her absolution was too much to absorb all at once. Deep down, he wanted her to be right. If there was no meaning to their lives then nothing made sense. Not the things he was trying to bring to the table for his country. Not the sacrifice Sam had made all those years ago. Or the one Mai Ly had made. There must be a reason for things and just because the reasons eluded him, didn't mean they weren't there.

He thought about Thanh. His son. His son, who's growing up he'd missed. The boy who'd so desperately wanted to know his father and hadn't because Matt hadn't known he existed.

"What do I tell Thanh?" Matt asked, his voice barely more than a whisper.

"What do you want to tell him? He's happy right now having you as a friend and thinking his father was Sam. Will it make him any happier knowing the truth?"

"I don't know," Matt answered honestly. "But I don't know if I can go on living a lie." Now that he knew. "The guilt was eating me up even before I guessed the truth. It's been distracting me from the things I need to pay attention to."

"Then perhaps you should tell him." Eve argued reasonably. She let her hands release his face and slide down to rest on his shoulders.

"What if he rejects me?" Matt's eyes ached with another press of tears.

Eve reached up to touch Matt's face. Her fingers were cool and light as they brushed away a tear that had leaked out and trickled down to his chin. "Thanh loves you. He won't reject you. Maybe he'll be shocked. He might be hurt. But in the end, he'll still love you. Most likely he will love you more. For your honesty. For acknowledging him. Maybe just because you are his father and knowing that will make all the difference in his world." Then she cupped the back of Matt's head and pulled his face into her shoulder. "If he's half the man his father is, he will forgive you for all of it.

Eighteen

Matt Steele heard the grandfather clock in the hall downstairs chime midnight. Eve slept peacefully, but he lay awake, reliving his confession and Eve's response. He hadn't actually thought about how she would feel when she found out. He'd been far too focused on his own sense of guilt. He'd worried more about Sam, who'd been beyond caring even at the time. And about Thanh. And how it might change a relationship Matt had come to cherish.

But if he had thought about it, he'd have expected a far different reaction. When he left for his second tour in Vietnam, he and Eve had been engaged. Plain and simple, he'd cheated on her. Even without Thanh, the belated revelation of that long-ago infidelity must have hurt. He suspected that if it had been Eve who'd fallen into bed with another man and kept it from him, he would not have been so magnanimous.

Matt rolled onto his side facing Eve. Not quite touching, but close enough to feel her warmth and catch the seductive scent of her. They'd been married so long he took her presence in his life for granted far too often. He took her utter trust in him as his due. And her fidelity.

Moonlight shone softly on the curve of her cheek. Matt ran his finger gently along the line of her jaw. She smiled in her sleep, and his heart swelled with emotion. The lyrics of a song from the musical *The Sound of Music* drifted into his head. He could almost hear the captain's voice marveling that Maria could love him in spite of his miserable past and wondering what he'd done to deserve her love.

Matt felt like that now. What had he ever done to deserve Eve? Either her love or her forgiveness? He wrapped his arm about her and pulled her into the curve of his body. She snuggled against him in her sleep.

"Everything happens for a reason, Matt. Everything!" Eve's assurance settled into his heart. *Even the begetting of Thanh.*

~ * ~

The airport hummed with activity. Sam looked handsome in his uniform, sharply creased and adorned with a remarkable array of decorations. He balanced his duffle over one shoulder and hugged Eve with his free arm. She returned his smacking kiss.

He pinched her cheek. "Don't worry about Matt. He's too ornery to die. Besides, I promise to keep an eye on his stubborn butt and see it gets home in one piece."

Eve tried to smile. Matt knew it was hard for her not to smile at Sam's nonsense, but he could see the struggle going on behind her swimming eyes.

"Please don't cry, honey." He dropped his own duffle and took her into his embrace. She pressed her face into his chest, sobbing soundlessly.

Matt's eyes stung, and he fought for composure. When the men around them began to move, he had to pry her away.

"I told you how it would be if you let her bring us to the airport," Sam muttered shaking his head sadly. Good-naturedly, he hefted Matt's duffle onto his other shoulder and headed down the ramp to give them a few moments of privacy.

Matt tried to ignore the jostling as he memorized Eve's features, the way her hair fell about her face in a silky curtain, the warm honey brown of her eyes. Even red with weeping, they were the prettiest eyes he'd ever seen. When they were a world apart, he wanted her image vivid in his memory.

I love you. His lips formed the words, but no sound came out.

Eve bit her lip to stop the wobble. She touched her thumb to her breast, then pressed the thumb against his uniform jacket. His heart beat painfully beneath her gentle touch.

"I'll write. I'll write every day." What else could he tell her? He wouldn't make promises he might not be able to keep.

Eve shook her head, trying to deny what neither had the power to change.

"Honey, we've got to say goodbye. I've got to go."

"God go with you, Matt." Tears continued to spill over and run down her face. Then, abruptly she turned and fled.

Eve bumped blindly into an elderly gentleman who steadied her for a brief second before she ran on. Matt watched her run, unable to follow, unable to turn away.

As he followed her progress, the busy airport terminal faded away. Eve seemed to be running into a field. Her bare legs flashed through tall grass. Alien grass. Grass that kept getting taller until it swallowed her up.

Another woman's hands tugged at Matt's shoulders, tearing his attention away from the swaying grass. Another woman, not Eve, clung to him weeping. Molding her body to his. Murmuring forbidden things. Matt forgot about Eve. The vortex of sexual desire tugged him down into its depths.

Abruptly the other woman began running. She ran into a milling mob of clamoring people. The woman was carrying a baby. His baby. He called after her, but she didn't turn back. Shouting came from all sides. The heavy beat of helicopter blades sounded overhead.

He needed to go after her, but hands held him back. Marines like himself. He tried to make them understand, but they didn't seem to notice the woman and the baby disappearing into the mob.

"Eve is waiting for you," one of the Marines shouted at him, his voice pitched to be heard above the thwop *of helicopters and the chaos of the mob. "You're out of here on the next bird."*

"But my son," Matt protested trying to pull away again.

"Get your gear, and move it out."

Matt finally tore free of the other man's grip and flung himself toward the fence. Men clung to the fence, trying to climb over, but the Marines pushed them back. Women screamed in panic.

But Mai Ly and the baby were gone.

~ * ~

Matt woke with a start. The moon had drifted to the far side of the house and the room was in near total darkness. He let his eyes adjust and tried to figure out what had woken him. Then he realized he'd been dreaming. More nightmare than dream. A nightmare filled with tears and anguish. He tried to recall details, but already they were fading. An enormous sense of remorse filled his heart.

His eyes ached with exhaustion. He shut them and tried to return to sleep, but they popped open. The ache in his breast intensified. Accepting the fact that sleep wasn't likely to return any time soon, Matt slipped from the bed, careful not to disturb Eve, and crept silently from the room.

He wandered through the dark house and ended up in his study. The light on the answering machine blinked. When he'd hurried to his study earlier in the evening, he'd been so completely focused on the DNA report, he hadn't even remembered to check the machine for messages. He pressed the button.

Beep.

"Hey, Jarhead! Where the hell are you? We held up the meeting for half an hour, but you never showed. Give me a call."

Beep.

"Jesus, Matt, two nights in a row? Don't you ever listen to your machine anymore? I know you're not in hiding. I keep seeing your goddamn face in the papers."

Beep.

Matt flipped open his calendar, keeping half an ear cocked for the rest of his messages. He didn't have a clue what meeting Lance was talking about. Lance was his sister's husband and a close friend, but Matt hadn't seen him in several weeks and couldn't recall promising to attend any meeting.

"Hi Matt. Sorry I missed you." Eve's lilting voice caught his attention. "The do this evening went well, I think. I've got a couple stops to make. Then I'll be home. Love ya."

Beep.

She'd come home to find him still reeling with the knowledge he'd sought but had trouble digesting. In her gentle, sympathetic way she had done her best to ease his raging sense of guilt at what cost to her, he couldn't begin to guess. The ache he'd woken with morphed into thankfulness. How could he have ever managed his life without Eve and her unstinting, bottomless love? He pressed erase, then play.

Beep.

"You better pick up your messages soon, or I'm going to send out a rescue team. Anyway, what's with this disgraceful story about you and some Vietnamese babe? You better have a good excuse!"

Beep.

"Hey, Dad. Ben here. I decided to drive up to Maine on Friday so no need to pick me up tomorrow. I'll meet you and Mom at

Grandma's. Leave Skip at the house. I'll pick him up on my way. He can keep me company on the drive and I'm sure he'd prefer me to the kennel. Later."

Beep.

"Matt. It's Dillon. Give me a call."

Beep.

"The bus will be out front at ten sharp. I already spoke to Joe. He's sending Terri Muir and Bharat Sahir on this trip. Catch you on the flip side."

Beep.

Matt pressed the *erase all* button. The machine cycled, and the blinking light went out. He wondered how anyone had managed to keep their lives on track before the advent of answering machines and cell phones. He'd located the notation about the meeting. He'd promised to attend the youth basketball organizational meeting. Sort of a change-of-command performance since he would not be free to run the league this winter. Lance would do fine, though, and Matt could send over the stuff he had by courier before they left in the morning.

In case he didn't see Megan in the morning, he scribbled a note to let her know Ben would be coming to get the dog.

Matt wondered what his buddy Dillon wanted. He and Dillon had gone through OCS together, shared the misery of training and the pride of succeeding, and had stayed in touch ever since. After his discharge from the Marines, Dillon had become a reporter, then moved on to television where he'd eventually landed a job producing the popular political talk show, *The Scoop with Jeff Hall.* Last Matt knew, Dillon had been on leave, recovering from a dirt bike injury. Matt shrugged, picked up the note for Megan and headed to the kitchen.

~ * ~

When Matt's alarm dragged him into wakefulness, his eyes felt like sandpaper. Eve, as usual, was already up, and just emerging from the bathroom with her makeup on and her hair done. He took himself to the shower and prayed hot water would wash away the evidence of his wakeful night. It helped, he decided, surveying his face in the mirror as he scraped at his beard. But not much.

"Dammit!"

"You okay?" Eve called from the other side of the door.

"I cut myself shaving, but I'll live." If only he could stick a bit of tissue on the bags under his eyes and make them go away.

"I laid out your blue suit. Okay?"

Matt walked into the bedroom with a finger pressed against his jaw. "The blue is fine."

"Here, let me look." Eve pried his finger up and looked intently at the wound. "You're right, no stitches this time." She captured his face between her palms and frowned. "A bad night?"

"Not good," he admitted, looking into her concerned eyes.

"It'll be okay, Matt. We'll all be okay. Try not to brood about it between here and Maine."

"Easy for you to say." Even as he said it, he realized it wasn't any easier for her than it was for him. She just coped better. He pulled her into his arms and bent his head to rest his cheek against the top of her head. "Sorry. That wasn't fair."

"Don't be sorry, Matt." Eve slid her arms about his waist and hugged him. "You've repented. As far as I'm concerned, we only look forward now. I know you love me, and I know you feel like you let me down. But you've given me so much. My life is so good and so full." She squeezed him hard, then leaned back to look up at him. "I love Thanh, too, and I don't wish anything undone."

171

He definitely had not done anything in his entire life worthy of this woman's love and generosity. "I don't deserve you."

"And don't you forget it," Eve said with mock severity. "Now get dressed or the bus will be here, and you'll still be wearing nothing more than a pair of briefs." Then she gave him a smacking kiss and turned away to finish dressing.

He pulled his trousers off the hanger and stepped into them, then grabbed his shirt off the bed. While he stood, tucking his shirttails in, he watched Eve wriggle into a pair of pantyhose and thought about last night.

Thought about how she'd known all along about Thanh, yet let him figure it out for himself. Even more, she forgave him the infidelity that had brought Thanh into the world in the first place, and accepted Thanh into the family without reservation.

"I'm serious, you know."

"Serious about what?" Eve looked up from tugging on her heels.

"I don't deserve you."

Her eyes softened. "Yeah, you do. Now get dressed. We've got a campaign to win, a road trip to get started on and a weekend respite to enjoy." Then she touched her thumb to her breast and wagged it in his direction before ducking out of the room and heading downstairs.

~ * ~

Two mornings later, at a hotel outside of Boston, Matt stepped into the scuffed interior of the service elevator and pushed a button. The advantage of using the less elegant service elevator was in arriving at the bottom and not finding a crowd of journalists and cameramen waiting.

It was early yet and the restaurant was still nearly empty. A waiter stepped forward immediately and ushered Matt toward the rear dining room. Eve, always up before Matt, sat alone at a large corner table reading a newspaper, while her Secret Service agent sat watchfully at the next table.

"Morning, Eve." Matt bent to kiss the back of Eve's neck before he took the seat next to hers.

"Matt!" She looked up, surprised.

"Don't let me interrupt." He'd surprised himself with the uncharacteristic public display as well. He took the menu from the waiter and turned his attention to ordering breakfast.

"Senator Steele, may I speak with you a moment?" A slender, sandy-haired woman who looked young enough to be Matt's daughter, had approached the table on sneaker-clad feet.

"I don't think…" Terry stepped between the young woman and Matt.

"Dillon sent me," the young woman said in a rushed and urgent tone.

"Dillon?" Matt rose, wondering if this had anything to do with the message Dillon had left on his answering machine. "It's okay. Dillon's a friend of mine," he told the agent.

"Dillon said to give you this." The woman reached past Teri and slipped a business card into Matt's hand.

Matt glanced at the familiar scrawl on the back, turned it over to see Dillon McGuire's information on the front, then turned it back again to read the message.

"That would depend. When did you have in mind?" Matt asked when he looked up at her again.

"Next week?" The young woman took immediate advantage, sliding into the seat next to Matt. "Dillon said if I could get to you instead of your manager, I might get lucky."

"I'll have to think about it. Can I get back to you?" Matt subsided back into his chair. A wave of anxious guilt swept through him. Out of the corner of his eye, he caught Eve's quick glance in his direction.

Before she'd drifted off to sleep, she had asked Matt if he would tell the voters the truth about Thanh, and he'd decided he had to. In keeping with his promise of total honestly, he really couldn't continue to let the lie live on. But they'd both agreed, Thanh, Megan and Ben must know first. That confession wouldn't happen until they had some private family time. This weekend, in Maine.

"I'd need to know pretty soon. The slot opened up unexpectedly, and I've gotta fill it quickly." The woman tapped her slender fingers on the table and narrowed her eyes appraisingly.

Two weeks ago, if this young woman had approached him, Matt would have jumped at the chance to showcase his economic plan. But now, with the truth about Thanh hanging heavy on his soul, the idea of being questioned on live television by a man of Jeff Hall's caliber scared the hell out of him.

Coming into the room at his usual breakneck pace, Jack took exception to the interloper's presence immediately. Before Matt could clue him in, Jack curled his hand around the woman's upper arm and lifted her from her chair.

"This is a private room, I believe."

"Yes, sir, but the senator and I were discussing an opportunity he really should accept." The young woman held her ground.

"His schedule's booked. Now get out before I have you thrown out." Jack released her arm and glanced at Teri Muir.

"Sorry to have disturbed you, Senator." The woman flashed Matt an insouciant grin. "I look forward to hearing from you in the next day or so. Here's where you can find me." Placing a second business card next to Matt's plate, she winked audaciously and took herself off, smoothing the rumples Jack's hand had left in her jacket sleeve as she went.

"I wonder what school paper she's reporting for?" Jack asked as he slipped into the vacated seat.

"*The Scoop*," Matt read off the card. "And she's not a reporter."

"What scoop?"

"The talk show with Jeff Hall, Jack. The program Blair Cabot appeared on the week before last."

"No way!" Jack reached for the card.

Matt slipped it into his pocket, then added the one with Dillon's message. "Trust me. She's legit. She's filling in for Dillon McGuire."

"Christ, she didn't look older than sixteen," Jack muttered.

"Nice way to treat a young woman," Teri observed sardonically.

"I thought she was a boy until I grabbed her." Jack tried to defend himself. "How come you didn't send her packing?" He glanced first at Teri, then at Matt.

"She came highly recommended," Matt answered.

Nineteen

Annie Santos heaved a big sigh. She drew a line through the last call she'd made, shut the enormous computer-generated list of registered Republican voters and shoved it to the edge of the table. Then she tidied the workspace, dropped the pen she'd been using into a mug bearing Blair Cabot's likeness and began gathering up her personal belongings. She couldn't wait to get out of the Cabot campaign headquarters.

It was her fervent hope that she'd be able to escape for the upcoming weekend without running into anyone she knew. Especially not TJ Smith. For two reasons. TJ hadn't rescinded his threat to her mother, and he was getting impatient with her inability to provide the kind of information he sought. Secondly, the dirty politics that triggered this latest push to win over disenchanted voters from the Republican Party turned her stomach.

Annie's dislike and distrust of TJ had grown after the outing of Roland Miller, which she knew beyond doubt TJ had engineered because of the smug expression he'd been wearing ever since the information became public knowledge. She found the whole thing repugnant, and if she could figure out how to extricate herself from her entire involvement with Blair Cabot's campaign, she would.

Annie reached under the table and grabbed her suitcase. She'd told her dad she would pick him up at his hotel as soon as she finished work. They'd swing by Thanh's apartment next, then head directly to College Park Airport north of DC where her Dad always left his plane when he was visiting the city. Megan would be meeting them at the plane for the flight to Maine. Not only was Annie finally going to meet Matthew Steele and his wife, Eve, she would be a guest in their home for three days.

If Megan was anything like her parents, Annie could expect to be welcomed into the family circle with grace and warmth. The fact that she would be the Steele's guest made it even more important that she get out of here without being stopped. If TJ found out where she was going, he was sure to increase the pressure on her to ferret out some scandalous tidbit of family history.

She hustled to the door, her suitcase rolling along in her wake. She kept her head down and didn't make eye contact with any of her fellow volunteers.

"Miss Santos."

Annie's heart rammed itself against her ribcage. She kept walking, hoping she could get away with pretending she hadn't heard TJ calling after her.

"Why the big hurry?" A dark suit-clad arm thrust itself in her path, barring Annie's exit.

Reluctantly, Annie looked up. TJ stood with his hand braced against the doorjamb, a sharp, calculating look in his black eyes and a broad grin on his lips.

"I'm p-picking my father up." Annie tilted the suitcase back onto its legs. She glanced pointedly at her watch. "And I'm late."

"Just your father?" TJ didn't remove his arm from her path.

Annie didn't know how much he knew so she kept her mouth shut.

"I heard your father is flying you and Loverboy along with Matt Steele's daughter to the family home in Maine for the long weekend."

Annie swallowed. How could he know all that? "Thanh is not…"

"Not what? Not your lover?" TJ snorted. "I know better." The smile disappeared from TJ's face, and a hard implacable look took its place. He removed his arm from the doorjamb and stepped back. "Have a nice weekend, Miss Santos. I look forward to chatting with you on Tuesday."

Annie burst through the door, gulping steadying breaths of cool fresh air. Her heart raced so hard it felt like a bird trying to get out of her chest. What did that man expect from her? What dirt did he expect her to dig up? Even if she wanted to find something incriminating, what did TJ think a weekend in Maine would elicit?

She didn't want to be doing this at all. Allowing the relationship with Thanh to blossom into an outright affair had been easy. Easy, because she really liked Thanh. And because he turned her on like no man ever had before. The fact that TJ knew how far their relationship had gone meant he must have someone spying on her. That made her feel sick and more than a little afraid.

Thanh was everything Alejandro was not. He was caring, thoughtful, considerate, and in love with her. Annie had done the one thing she'd promised herself she wasn't going to do. She'd fallen in love with Thanh. Betraying him by helping to ruin a man he so admired would be beyond contemptible. Thanh might never forgive her. And then she'd get her heart broken all over again.

Why, Mama? Why didn't you get your citizenship when it would have been so easy? Why did you let your anger at Daddy stop you?

If only her mother were not so frail. Annie doubted her mother could survive being sent back to Vietnam, even if she could locate her family again and even if they would take her in.

Annie hustled into the parking garage, punched the button for the elevator, then waited impatiently for the door to open. She rode the elevator down to the level where she'd left her car. The shining walls reflected a wavy imitation of herself. Her father's thick brown hair and her mother's eyes. Eyes that had watched over her when she was small, and now looked to Annie for support. She simply couldn't turn her back on her mother. Not with the INS so intractable in recent years.

The door opened again, and Annie stepped out and hurried to her car. She retracted the handle and stowed her suitcase in the trunk. Then she climbed into the driver's seat where she sat, hands wound tightly together in her lap, trying to think of a way out of the bind she was in.

~ * ~

As the campaign bus hurtled north on I-95, Matt Steele mentally reviewed his weekend agenda and tried to think where and how he would find time to talk to Thanh and then his son and daughter. He needed this brief respite before the final weeks of the campaign. Especially in light of the surge Blair Cabot had made in the polls after the scandal of Roland Miller's sexual preferences had hit the news. Matt and Hal would have to scramble to make up the lost ground.

The young woman sent by Dillon McGuire had offered Matt an opportunity he really needed to accept. He could kill two birds with one stone. Get the business of confessing Thanh's parentage off his chest and behind him, then launch his own economic plan to rival the vague outline Blair Cabot had touted two weeks previously.

Jeff Hall could rip him a new one, that was a given. He was a dynamite interviewer and usually managed to dig out information no one else even knew to look for. But he was also fair and even-handed. He'd given Cabot a chance to showcase his program, had even delved for specifics in the face of Cabot's deliberate ambiguity. Hall would certainly do the same for Matt once they got past the scandal of Thanh.

The idea scared the shit out of him, but he'd been under fire before and lived. Thanh was the only skeleton in his closet, so he really didn't have anything else to fear. Matt knew he was going to call that woman back, but that didn't stop the hyperventilation just thinking about a forty-five minute interview with Jeff Hall induced.

Matt forced himself to stop dwelling on the fear factor and focused on how to bring the subject up with his campaign manager. But at the moment, he just didn't have the energy. Fatigue was to be expected in a campaign of this magnitude, of course. Just a normal result of the jam-packed busyness of the final weeks of a hotly contested political race. But it was more than that. The sleepless, dream-filled nights had worn Matt down. The escalating sense of guilt had become a distraction, and the conviction that he was living a lie was beginning to compromise everything. He needed to get this behind him and damn what Rick thought or didn't think.

Eve sat in one corner of the comfortably large sofa, her legs tucked under her with the light from her Kindle illuminating her face as she read. They'd had little chance to share notes during the day, but she'd mingled energetically at the reception following his speech, seeking out nearly every major economic don present. When they were alone tonight, she'd be full of tidbits she'd gleaned from here and there.

They sped past the familiar billboard with its Downeast greeting, *Maine, the way life should be*. And, as always happened, he began to feel his city self slide away. Although he suspected it was not a physical fact, he felt as if his pulse slowed as well. But then again, maybe it did. He was going home. The tension drained out of his muscles.

He must have dozed because the next thing he noticed was the sudden crunch of the bus' big tires on the gravel drive of his home in Levitt, Maine.

Apparently, Megan had been watching from the windows. Even before the bus pulled to a halt, she bounded down the wide porch steps. Skip ambled after her, his plumed tail waving happily. Ben had arrived ahead of them as well. His little Subaru was parked in front of the garage.

"Daddy, you'll never guess who's here!" Megan stepped into the bus, grinning mischievously.

"Not offhand, but I know you'll tell me, kitten." Matt stood and stretched.

"No, guess." Megan teased.

"My brain's fried." He grabbed her around the shoulders with one arm and gave her a squeeze, before stepping off the bus and realizing his home was lit up like a Christmas tree.

"All right," Megan relented. "Gramma's here. And Grampa. And there's a party going on. Everyone's here!"

Good God, what had his mother been up to?

"Who's everyone?" Eve asked joining them in the driveway.

"You're not going to believe it, Mom."

Matt could. He knew his mother.

"Grampa Ira's here, but that's easy." Megan skipped along next to them. "But then there's Uncle Greg and Aunt Kelly and Uncle Lance and Andrew and Aunt Jojo and all the cousins. And Great-aunt Nissie, Great-Grampa Taggart and Bill Welland and Miss Everson and…"

Matt only thought he knew his mother. So far Megan's litany hadn't left out a single relative, and she'd just begun on the neighbors. What had happened to his quiet weekend?

The wide front door stood open and light streamed across the porch. Ben's tall, broad-shouldered form was outlined in the doorway. He watched the little party approach, his lips turned up in a good-humored grin.

"Was this all planned behind my back?" Matt asked. Megan's earlier concern that he might back out of the weekend trip began to look suspect.

Ben confirmed Matt's hunch. "For weeks, Dad. This is in the way of a pep rally. You know, hometown-supports-local-boy sort of thing." Ben hugged his mother, his grin widening at her look of astonishment.

"But the town had a rally right after the convention," Matt protested.

"Well, Gramma decided that was ancient history. Besides, she says you've been looking downright haggard lately, and she figured you needed a little perking up. Might as well come in and get it over with. Then we can get down to some serious partying."

~ * ~

Perhaps his mother had been right, Matt mused as he perched on the wide flat railing along the front of his porch, listening to the sound of the sea, after all the friends and relatives had gone home. He couldn't remember the last time he'd so thoroughly enjoyed himself or his family without the thought in the back of his head that he had things he needed to do or a public persona to protect.

Ellen Steele's guest list had been a bit more discerning than Megan or Ben knew. All were old and comfortable friends, many of whom, Matt reflected wryly, had probably dandled him on their knees once upon a time. It was hard to take yourself too seriously with people who kept calling you son and telling stories you wished had been forgotten.

"What are you doing all alone out here in the dark?" Ben asked as the screen door slapped shut behind him.

"I thought you'd gone to bed already."

"You've got to be kidding. It's only midnight." Ben hiked himself up onto the railing next to Matt.

"Well, that's the middle of the night for a town that rolls up its sidewalks after dark."

Ben gazed out across the yard toward the dunes that bordered the beach. "I forgot how black it gets around here. Like the inside of a bag."

"Wait a minute. The moon will come out again."

"It'll still be blacker than Philly ever gets." Ben drew his knees up into the circle of his arms and leaned back against the upright post. "I guess I was born to be a city boy. I like the hustle and bustle. There's always something to do, places to go, people to see."

"You'd like my life lately, then," Matt rebutted wearily. "Sometimes, I think if I should win this race, I won't get a decent night's sleep for another four years. At least."

"If you feel that way, why did you run?"

"Because I believed I could make a difference."

"You know, Dad," Ben began thoughtfully. "A month ago I would have disagreed with you, but lately…"

"Lately, what?" Matt heard a hint of uncertainty in Ben's tone.

"Lately, I've been hearing things I never thought I'd hear from you. I think I could count on one hand the number of times we ever agreed on anything political. But lately you're beginning to sound like me. What I can't figure is, if I've changed or you have."

"I'm flattered you've been following my campaign that closely," Matt replied, stunned by Ben's admission and warmed by his approval.

"It's hard to ignore on campus. Everything you, Cabot and Miller say is examined, debated and rebutted *ad nauseam*." He dropped his feet back to the porch deck and leaned toward Matt. "And this latest bombshell about Miller. My God, who would have guessed? How big a difference do you think it will make? For your chances of beating Cabot, that is?"

"It shouldn't make any difference in my opinion, but that's naïve of me, I guess."

"I heard Cabot jumped a good ten points in just two days. Most of the fourteen points Miller lost. Puts you and Cabot in a dead heat, unless that bump hasn't finished happening."

"Yeah, well…" Matt thought about the revelations to come.

It would be equally naïve of him to think his own confession wouldn't have a profound effect as well. But a man had to draw a line somewhere, and he'd drawn his a long time ago. Honesty was his line in the sand. Both personally and politically. He either went into this election with all his cards on the table and came out a winner with a mandate, or he might as well return to private life and do his best to make a difference on a much smaller scale.

The moon came out at that moment, glistening across the surface of the ocean like a river of platinum. Waves grew up out of the dark sea like ghosts then broke in a rush of eerie bright foam before surging up the sandy slope of the beach. It was a sight Matt would never tire of nor fail to find peace in.

"I'll admit it sure is pretty when it's like this." Ben echoed Matt's thoughts.

Suddenly, it occurred to Matt that his son Ben was as astute and as unrelenting as Jeff Hall. If he shared the economic recovery plan he and Hal had formulated with Ben, perhaps his reaction would help in preparing for a debut on television. "Ben? If I asked you to read something, would you be willing to give me your unvarnished opinion?"

"Well, jeeze, Dad. When have I *not* told you exactly what I think? What the hell is it, anyway?"

"I'd rather you read it first before I say anything."

"I hope you've got it with you. I have a mountain of reading waiting for me when I get back to school."

"You want it tonight?" Matt slid off the railing.

"Might as well. I'll never get to sleep this early." Ben followed Matt into the house, this time being quieter with the door.

They snuck up the stairs, careful not to step on the loose third tread that had squeaked for as long as Matt could remember. Ben waited in the hall while Matt went to retrieve his proposal.

"I'm open to all your thoughts. Pro and con," Matt said placing the document into Ben's hand.

"Really?" Ben lifted one eyebrow as if he couldn't quite believe his father was really asking for his input. Politically, they hadn't agreed on much of anything for years.

"Really."

"Well, good night, Dad." Ben hesitated.

Matt wanted to reach out and hug Ben as easily has he had when Ben was a boy. He gripped his shoulder instead. "Good night, Ben. And thanks."

"Don't thank me 'til you hear what I have to say," Ben warned with a chuckle. Then he turned and moved down the hall to the tiny room he still called his. Not much more than a sitting room perched above the front entry, but he said he liked the view and he didn't need more room than that.

~ * ~

Annie laid in the dark listening to Megan's soft breathing. Megan had been telling Annie a story about the dog they'd had before Skip, but she'd drifted off to sleep in the middle of a sentence. Now all Annie could think about was Thanh, alone on the pull-out bed in the den. That and the threat that awaited her return to DC.

Mostly she wanted to be with Thanh so she could forget about the threat. If they'd been in the same bed, they'd be making love and she wouldn't be thinking about how kind and wonderful the Steeles were or what she'd been blackmailed into doing to them.

Her mind skittered away from the memory of Matt Steele's warm grip when his hand swallowed hers in a welcome as sincere as the crinkles at the corners of his eyes. Or the same crinkles on the face of the woman who was his mother. When presented with extra guests for the party she'd planned for Matt Steele's oldest friends and family, Ellen Steele hadn't batted an eye. She'd just handed Annie a platter and a stack of plastic containers filled with cut vegetables and asked her to *arrange them, please*. Just as she'd done with Megan and the cold cuts.

How could Annie do anything so despicable as launder their dirty linen in TJ's sink? She had prayed that nothing would come up to relate. During the course of the evening, she'd heard one elderly gentleman telling a tale about Matt stealing corn from his field one summer. It had been an amusing story, actually. How Matt and his cousin Sam had built a fire in the middle of the cornfield, brought a pot of water to boil, then cooked the cobs and ate them right there in the field, dripping with butter, no doubt filched from his mother's refrigerator.

Another man, Annie thought he was Matt's uncle, told an equally innocuous story about catching Matt and his cousin on the beach at one a.m., making out with two girls they'd promised to take directly home after the movie let out. An elegantly-dressed woman, who had to be in her nineties, had laughed about the time she'd caught the mischievous cousins playing cowboys and Indians and running across the roofs of the old chicken houses they'd been told to stay away from. Kid stuff.

Annie hoped she didn't have to tell TJ any of it. It was just kid stuff. The kind of escapades everyone had in their past. Except TJ would find a way make it sound much worse. Theft, assault, trespassing. That's how TJ would make the stories come out.

Megan lurched onto her side facing the wall, let out a drowsy sigh and settled into sleep again. Annie couldn't stand it.

She slipped from the bed and let herself out of the room. Carefully, she crept down the stairs. But when she let her weight come down on the third stair from the bottom, it creaked with a snap so loud it sounded like a gun going off. Annie froze, expecting half a dozen doors to pop open and curious faces to peer down at her. But none did.

With her heart pounding, she dashed down the last two stairs and bolted for the den.

Thanh sat on the edge of the bed that folded out of the sofa clad only in his boxers. "Was that you?"

Annie nodded. "I thought the whole house must have heard that stair creak."

"What are you doing here?" He stood, the covers falling askew onto the floor.

"I—I couldn't sleep." She hovered in the doorway, uncertain if he wished her gone or welcomed her unexpected arrival.

He stretched a hand toward her, and she hurried toward him. "I probably should not let you stay." His arms enclosed her in a solid embrace.

"I promise I won't stay all night, and no one will ever know I was here." Annie hugged him gratefully. "It's—I just feel so strange here. Like I don't belong."

Thanh didn't say anything for a long while. He just hugged her, rocking their bodies back and forth. Then finally he set her away and sat down again. "You are getting cold." He swung his feet onto the bed and lifted the blankets invitingly.

Quickly, Annie slid between the sheets and into his embrace again. "I never thought about where I'd be sleeping when I agreed to come with you," Annie murmured, pressing her chilled body against the muscled length of him and absorbing his warmth.

"Why, does Megan snore?" Thanh chuckled, and the familiar sound rumbled through his chest.

"No. But she's not you." Annie tipped her face toward Thanh's and slipped her arms about his neck. "I hope the Steeles won't think less of me if they find out we've been sleeping together."

"Let us hope." Thanh lowered his mouth to hers and slid his hands up under her pajama top.

Twenty

Matt scanned the throng of people crowding against the fence pleading to be let in. He searched for Mai Li, desperate to find her familiar face in the mob. He hunted for any woman grown plump with pregnancy. The helicopters grew louder, and his fellow Marines more insistent as they urged him away from the fence and the clamoring would-be refugees.

Why hadn't she come? Surely she knew he would save her? Surely she trusted him that much. He would never turn his back on his son. He wasn't that kind of man.

He thought of Eve. Thought how hurt she was going to be when he had to tell her he couldn't marry her. But she'd understand. She wouldn't ask him to leave his son behind. She'd cry, but probably not where he would see. And she'd know it was something he had to do.

He didn't love Mai Ly, but she was carrying his child. He'd fucked up. He loved Eve, but he'd messed that up, too. His heart ached as if it had been kicked, and his eyes hurt with tears he couldn't shed.

"Why?" The words ripped from somewhere deep inside him. "Why?" His voice strangled in a throat tight with guilt and pain and loss.

~ * ~

Wakened by the sound of his own voice, Matt opened his eyes and stared into the darkness. His face was wet, and it took several minutes before he realized he'd been dreaming again, and apparently crying. He was coming apart at the seams.

He rolled off the bed and padded over to the window. Pushing the drapes back, he stared out at the dark limitless sea. The moon had continued on its course and shone now from behind the house, leaving mysterious shadows stretching away from the house and down to the shore.

Like an accident you don't want to see, but can't look away from, Matt sorted through the fragmented remnants of the dream, feeling the heavy weight of guilt. Hurting Eve had added a whole new level to his shame. He wiped his face with the back of his hand and shivered in the chill air.

"Come back to bed, Matt." Eve spoke gently.

Matt startled. "I thought you were asleep."

"Well, I can't sleep with you over there brooding and me over here feeling like I'm losing you to a ghost from the past."

He took one last glance at the inky sea then returned and sat on the side of the bed.

"You were dreaming about her, weren't you?"

"Yes."

"You were at that fence again. Beating yourself up because you didn't get her out. But you couldn't have known about Thanh."

Matt nodded reluctantly.

Eve rubbed his back.

After a while, he lay back down and took her hand in his. "I was beating myself up about you, too. I dreamt I'd screwed my chances with you, and my heart ached like hell." Matt touched his heart, exploring it gingerly as if it really had been kicked. "I dreamt you would cry when you found out, but you wouldn't let me know how much I hurt you."

Eve was silent for a while. Then she squeezed his hand. "I probably would have cried back then. And I'd have been too proud to let you know how hurt I was. I'd have been angry instead."

"But you're not angry now?"

"Not really. Certainly not enough to let it come between us. We have a good life, Matt. And a good marriage. Do you think I'd toss all that away because of a mistake you made more than thirty years ago before we were even married? You could have just kept all this to yourself and told yourself I'd never know, but that's not the kind of man I fell in love with. I love you because of who you are, not because you're some knight on a white horse who never screwed up."

Matt rolled over and pulled Eve into his arms. "I don't tell you nearly often enough how much I love you. I am one lucky sonofabitch."

"Shall I remind you next time you're on a tear about something?"

He chuckled and held her closer. The last of the nagging dregs of his dream had gone. "You do that."

"Or, you could show me," Eve purred, nibbling his ear.

A bubble of desire surged to life in his gut, replacing the regret that had been lodged there for days. "In the middle of the night?" he teased with mock disapproval.

Eve wriggled out of his embrace and sat up. "We're way too young for you to be turning into an old fogey!" She grinned down at him. Then with a flourish, she yanked her flannel nightgown over her head and tossed it off the bed.

Where would he be without this incredible woman in his life? "Good point!" With a laugh, he pulled her back under the covers.

Then he began a methodical exploration of smooth, warm skin and still very sexy curves.

~ * ~

Matt slept dreamlessly and woke with the first faint rays of a spectacular sunrise shafting across the room. Eve was up ahead of him, of course. The flannel nightgown now hung over the bedpost on her side of the bed and his pajamas had been folded into a neat pile on the chair beside the bed. He got up and headed to the bathroom.

Downstairs twenty minutes later, in the familiar old kitchen, he puttered silently, filling the coffeemaker and finding a mug. Eve must have gone out. Probably for a walk on the beach. He considered going after her. If it had been earlier, they could have snuggled in the chilly dawn air and watched the sun come up together. But now it was too late, the sun was already up. And she could be a mile down the beach already, probably deep into a discussion on the latest book both she and the agent on her protection detail were reading.

He poured himself a cup of coffee and offered one to Terry Muir, who'd just come into the kitchen pulling a sweatshirt over his head and muttering about the early hour.

"I'm taking mine out on the porch," Matt told the agent, as he pulled a jacket off the hook. Terry hurried ahead to the porch, then nodded his okay for Matt to follow.

Matt sat down on the top step and thought about his dad.

Without being aware of it, he'd been counting on unburdening his soul to his father, and last night that hope had been dashed. The distressing truth was that Douglas Steele had begun to slip quickly into a world that paid little attention to reality. He was placidly cheerful, smiling approval for first one idea, then only moments later, for its opposite. When Matt had asked how long the nightmares about Korea had lasted, Douglas Steele had seemed confused for a moment, then recounted a fairly lucid tale of a bridge he'd helped to destroy. But the recital had lacked emotion or regret.

Matt sipped from his mug. The coffee had cooled already.

"Morning, Dad."

Matt jerked around, slopping coffee on the steps between his feet at the sound of Ben's voice.

"Christ, Ben! Do you sneak up on your roommates like that?" Matt's heart pounded furiously. He envied Terry Muir who apparently saw everything three steps ahead of happening and hadn't been caught unaware. "What are you doing up so early, anyway?"

"I heard you come down, and I wanted to tell you what I thought about your manifesto."

"My manifesto?" Matt fought to drag his thoughts back from his father's mental deterioration.

"Are you sure you wrote this?"

"Not in my usual style, is it?" Matt asked. He really needed a fresh cup of coffee, but here was Ben settling in beside him with an eager look on his face. He set the mug aside.

"Not even close. You need a refill? I'm going to need a cup myself with the short night I had." Ben scrambled to his feet again and reached for Matt's mug.

A few moments later, he reappeared with two steaming mugs and resettled himself on the top step. He handed Matt one of the mugs and took a sip from the other.

"I'm still having a hard time believing this is your work. It flies in the face of everything you've ever done. And I doubt it makes the people who got you on the ticket happy, either. How are you going to justify such an about-face?"

"If I get elected, it will be because of that plan." Matt balanced his mug on one bent knee and looked sideways at his son. "This country is in serious financial trouble. It won't be easy or painless to fix and talking about it but doing nothing is no longer an option."

"I never thought you had the balls to support something this drastic." Ben said succinctly, his eyes conveying his disbelief.

"Thanks for the vote of confidence." Matt felt like he'd been slapped. One thing no one had ever questioned was his courage. He'd always stood up for what he believed in, often against formidable foes.

"Wouldn't it be easier to win the election, then start introducing this stuff?"

"That's what Rick Winfield feels I should do." Matt couldn't keep the hint of resentment from coloring his words.

"Winfield's a pretty savvy campaign manager."

Matt sensed another negative judgment on its way and felt immediately defensive. "It's a matter of public trust. How many times have you told me you wish politicians could be believed? If I were to wait, knowing this is the direction I want my presidency to take, wouldn't that just be business as usual?"

"I suppose," Ben conceded thoughtfully. "But think of the unbelievably big chance you're taking. There's not much time left for you to sell it. A lot of people probably don't understand enough about economics to see the point anyway. And Blair Cabot won't hesitate to put his spin on it. He'll be out there convincing people that whatever margin they've managed to put between themselves and poverty will disappear overnight if they elect you. It won't matter that he's even more radical than you, because he isn't handing out details anyone can relate to themselves."

"That's a chance I have to take. If I make my case, honestly and without gimmicks, in a way people can understand, and if they elect me anyway, then I go into office with the support of the electorate, and that will be hard for Congress to ignore."

"And if they don't?"

"Then I go back to the Senate and work at it from there."

"Well, if you do go through with it," Ben said with heavy emphasis on the *if,* "I'll be impressed." He finished his coffee and stood up. "By the way, on the whole, I would have to say, I think your plan is the fairest, most workable and most impressive agenda I've ever seen to fix what's wrong with our government. I'm amazed."

Matt stared up at his son, torn between pleasure and pique. He'd expected Ben to agree in principle. After all, it answered every challenge he'd thrown in Matt's face for years, and more.

"Thank you, Ben. For being honest." Matt said, forcing himself to ignore the hurtful assessment of his courage and resolve.

Ben rolled his eyes. "Whatever. Have you eaten yet? I've got a couple more thoughts I could offer. Except, I'm starved. I'd rather do it over some eggs and bacon."

Matt got to his feet and followed his son into the house.

~ * ~

After lunch Eve went off to a Christmas Bazaar at Matt's old church with Matt's mother and sister. Matt and everyone else left at the house with the exception of Tony Santos, who was watching a Dallas Cowboys game on television, went out for a walk. As Matt stepped off the back porch and crossed the leaf-strewn lawn toward the woods, he reflected that any other year and he'd be looking forward to hunting season right about now. But not this year and hopefully not for the next four. But today was about enjoying the moment. Savoring the contentment of being with his kids away from the demands of politics.

Startled, he realized he'd unthinkingly included Thanh. He watched Thanh striving to keep up with Ben's long loping gait along the familiar path and marveled at how quickly Thanh had fit in. Both Megan and Ben eagerly shared stories from their collective past, but somehow, the telling only drew Thanh closer into the circle, rather than shutting him out.

"And here's where *your* father shot himself in the foot," Megan observed with relish as she halted in a small clearing and turned to grin at Thanh.

That was Sam. Not me. Matt thought with a guilty start. *I've got to tell Thanh the truth. I've got to tell them all. Before it gets any more complicated.*

"He shot his own foot?" Thanh raised skeptical eyebrows.

"Right, and Daddy had to carry him piggyback all the way to Grampa's house."

"But I thought you said he was a crack shot?" Thanh looked doubtfully at Matt.

"We were only eleven at the time." Matt shrugged his shoulders uncomfortably. "Our first time hunting on our own, too. It was his dad's twenty-two and somehow, Sam managed to pull the trigger before he raised the gun. After I got over being scared, I was so angry, I swore I wasn't ever going hunting with Sam again."

"Dumb-assed kids," Terry Muir muttered, only half listening to the story as his eyes scanned the woods for threats.

"You never forgave him?" Thanh glanced back with lifted brows.

"'Course he did!" Megan snorted. "Daddy doesn't hold grudges. Besides, a long time before that, your dad saved Daddy's hide, so they were even."

Annie hunched her shoulders and looked as if she wished she hadn't come.

"This is my favorite story," Ben cut in. "Mostly because, whenever Dad caught me doing something stupid, I got to remind him he'd done some pretty dumb things."

About a mile from the house, the trees thinned and the path ended abruptly at the top of a ridge. Halfway down the slope an eight-foot chain link fence barred the way between the woods and a broad, swiftly running river. Ben jumped down over a tangle of briars and headed east along the perimeter of the fence. Megan, Annie and Thanh followed. Matt hung back, remembering the bizarre dream he'd had about this fence a few weeks back. The dream that had begun in a scramble out of a half-frozen river in Maine and ended outside the embassy in war-torn Saigon. The nightmare he'd had even before he knew the truth about Thanh.

Matt only half heard Megan telling her new friends about two young boys' brush with an icy drowning. Instead of a rusted fence with red and orange leaves gathered in its lee, he was seeing an angry, panicked mob trying to scale the gate in front of the embassy. And he was suddenly swamped yet again with guilt.

"Sir?" Terry had stopped as well. He looked at Matt with a question in his eyes.

Matt shook his head and moved out without answering. He hurried his steps to catch up to the young people. He had to stop this second-guessing the actions he did or didn't take more than thirty years ago. He couldn't change it now, and he really hadn't had a lot of choice at the time. As Eve had reminded him more than once, he'd just followed orders, and he'd had no way of knowing about Thanh.

Matt caught up to them just as Megan finished describing the wintery scene.

"The ice is large enough to ride on?" Thanh eyed the river incredulously.

"In the winter the river freezes over. Or it used to when we were kids, anyway. Then in the spring, when it starts to warm up, the ice breaks up into huge chunks. Some of them are really big." Ben made an expansive gesture with his arms.

"Only, Dad forgot about the tide rapids a couple hundred yards downstream," Megan added pointing to her temple. "Duh!"

"I didn't forget," Matt defended himself. "I just didn't think about the problem of getting ashore again before we got to the rapids."

"So, how did you get off?" Thanh's eyes were round with wonder.

"We jumped," Matt said, keeping the terror he'd felt to himself.

"But it was really stupid to try riding the ice in the first place. Dad would have fallen in if your father hadn't grabbed him. Dad could have drowned or gotten hypothermia," Ben added with relish.

"We were lucky," Matt agreed sheepishly. "We were lucky a lot." Then Sam's luck had run out at an airfield on the other side of the world.

"Like the time you went swimming in the water tower," Megan immediately launched into another of her favorite tales.

Matt smiled faintly at his daughter's recitation, told with such glee. It was less painful to remember the peccadilloes of his youth than let himself dwell on his failures with Thanh's mother.

By the time Megan had recreated the picture of two skinny, shivering, dripping, and chastened boys, the small party had passed the place where the tide fought the river for dominance. The fence had rusted away in the salty air, and they were able to step over the beaten down remnants onto a narrow stony beach. Then they were on the main beach. A wide sandy stretch with waves swinging in from the open ocean and breaking in an endless rote.

"It's a wonder you lived to grow up," Terry observed wryly.

"I suppose you never did anything dumb?" Matt glanced at his security agent.

"It's nothing short of a miracle I lived to adulthood," Terry admitted with a grin. "I come from the bad side of DC, don't forget."

Matt chuckled as he made his way through soft sand to the firm damp shoreline. Ben and Thanh jogged ahead while Megan twirled about, arms outstretched. Only Annie looked as if she wished she were anywhere but at the edge of the sea.

"Don't you like the beach?" Matt asked her. She jumped at the sound of his voice and looked at him oddly. To Matt, it looked as if she felt guilty about something. But maybe he was projecting.

"No! I love the beach. I just—I'm cold. I guess I didn't wear a warm enough jacket."

"Don't you just love the smell of the ocean?" Megan asked of no one in particular.

"Yeah, right! Mud flats and rotting seaweed. The next hot seller at the cosmetics counter," Ben scoffed and rolled his eyes at Thanh.

"You can be a real jerk sometimes, Ben." Megan scowled at him then bent to pick up a bit of purple shell and pretended to ignore him altogether.

"It is very different from the Eastern Sea," Thanh said, his voice wistful and soft.

The nearly clear skies of the night before had given way to heavy menacing clouds that scudded in from the southwest leaving the ocean slate gray and forbidding. It was as different from Matt's recollection of the South China Sea as their cultures. The sea that bordered Vietnam was warm and tropically blue with white sandy beaches that sometimes, Matt suddenly recalled, had been mined. As Matt stared out over the chilly white-capped waves trying to banish that unbidden recollection, a pair of military helicopters from the nearby Navy base appeared abruptly above the forest behind them and buzzed low over the beach.

Matt hit the sand hard.

"Daddy!" Megan shrieked in panic, and came running toward him.

"Dad?" Ben whirled, his eyes wide.

"Sir?" Terry was on one knee beside Matt, trying to shield him from an unseen assailant while his gaze raked the woods behind them, then returned to the helicopters disappearing into the gray distance.

Matt pulled himself to his knees and looked at the array of concerned faces. "I'm fine. I uh...I don't know what happened. It was just..." Matt got to his feet and brushed the sand off his clothes. "I must have tripped." Better to be thought a klutz who might trip over nothing more than a bit of beach sand than a man who panics at the sight of a helicopter.

"I think we should head back to the house." Terry made it sound more like an order than a suggestion. Matt suspected Terry's heart was racing at least as fast his own, and the adrenaline rush would be roaring in his ears.

They trooped down the beach and away from the woods. The distance to the house was shorter this way and far more open. Terry hovered closer than he had before, his face impassive, his eyes vigilant. Megan glanced at Matt with a curious look on her face, but then shoved one arm through Annie's and the other through Thanh's, and launched into an off-key version of *Follow the Yellow Brick Road*. Ben brought up the rear.

When they reached the house, everyone dispersed to find dry shoes with a promise to meet in the kitchen for hot chocolate.

"It was the helicopters, right?" Terry asked, hesitating outside the door. "Been there. Done that. Embarrassing as all hell."

"I haven't done anything so foolish in years," Matt agreed sheepishly.

"Well, think of it from my point of view," Terry grinned. "Better you have a delayed home-from-the-war episode than you actually got shot. On my watch!"

"Sorry I gave you a nasty scare."

"*De nada,*" Terry shrugged. "It's part of the job. I'll be in the den if you need me. Give you time with the family without me hovering."

What I need is time with Thanh without anyone *hovering.* Matt headed to the mud-room to shuck his sodden boots and then up to his bedroom to find his moccasins. He felt colder than wet feet could account for and dug out a heavy fisherman's knit sweater. He was dilly-dallying. He dreaded going back downstairs. What was he going to tell them? How could he possibly explain his bizarre behavior on the beach? God only knew what they were thinking.

Reluctantly he left his room and headed toward the back staircase to the kitchen. Half way down, Megan's voice stopped him cold.

"I think he's got post traumatic stress disorder. You know, the thing EMTs get, and policemen or victims of violent crime and soldiers."

"Jeeze, Megan, Dad's war ended years ago."

Matt sagged onto the stairs, his legs suddenly as substantial as the vision of refugees trying to storm an embassy compound had been an hour ago.

"What makes you think so, Megan?" Greg, Matt's psychologist brother-in-law, asked in a calm, professional voice. When had Greg arrived?

"I was reading about it in psych class," Megan explained. "The stress thing, I mean. A couple of weeks ago something else happened, kinda like today."

"Tell me about it," Greg encouraged gently.

"It was my fault, I think," Megan began. "I asked Daddy how he got wounded. It was like, one minute he was there, and then he wasn't."

"What d'ya mean one minute he was there, and then he wasn't?" Ben asked, exasperation in his voice.

"Just before I asked him how it happened, he was laughing at something, I don't remember what. Then I reached out to touch the scars on his back and..." Matt heard the snap of fingers. "It was like he was a zillion miles away."

"He probably was," Greg murmured. "Probably in Vietnam, getting shot at."

"Well, it was scary. I mean really scary."

Matt wanted to get up and go on down into the kitchen and stop the discussion. He wanted to tell them there was nothing wrong with him. Nothing to worry about. But he couldn't go on pretending.

"I shouldn't have asked, I guess. If he wanted to talk about it, he would have told us years ago. And maybe this afternoon was my fault, too. If I hadn't pushed it the other day, maybe he wouldn't be thinking about it now."

"The fault is mine, not yours," Thanh interrupted. "If I had not brought him that photo and reminded him of his cousin, I think he would not suddenly be remembering things he tried so hard to forget."

"Neither of you is responsible," Greg cut in, firmly. "Any number of things could have triggered old memories. The fault, if you want to blame anything, is that there are some things that never get dealt with because they hurt too much. So, they get buried. Buried stress can sometimes show up unexpectedly, long after the event, but no one is to blame. Not you, Megan, for asking an honest question any daughter would be curious about. And not you, Thanh, for seeking information about your father's family."

"Where is Daddy, anyway?" Matt heard the anxious concern in his daughter's voice.

Suddenly there was the scrape of a chair being thrust sharply back. Then Ben's head appeared at the foot of the stairs.

"Jeeze Dad, how long have you been listening?"

"It's true, you know." Matt forced himself to stand and descend the remaining stairs. "Eavesdroppers never do hear anything good about themselves."

"I'm sorry, Dad. We didn't mean to talk behind your back."

"Don't apologize, Ben." Matt looked at each of them in turn. "Your Uncle Greg is right. Everyone has nightmares now and then. Nothing all that dreadful, except I don't get as much sleep as I'd like. And the flashbacks that you found so alarming aren't fun either. But they relate to things I did or didn't do long before you were born. If it's anyone's fault, it's mine."

Megan picked up Matt's favorite chipped mug and shoved it into the microwave. While the hot chocolate reheated, an uneasy silence reigned. Then the shrill timer went off and broke the tension.

"Hey, Thanh!" Ben asked suddenly. "You seen *Beginner's Luck*? I heard it's playing up town. Wanna go?"

Megan looked at Matt closely as she slid his steaming cup of cocoa onto a coaster, then glanced at her brother and asked, "Can I go too? I heard it's a really cool flick."

Matt felt the silent message that passed between the two. It felt like they were still talking about him. They probably thought he needed some serious couch time with their Uncle Greg. Ben shrugged. "Sure. Why not?"

"No!" Matt pulled his cocoa closer and wrapped his chilled hands around it. "Please wait. I..." He'd meant to do it differently.

He'd meant to tell Thanh first since it impacted him the most. But the time had come. "There's something I need to tell you. All three of you. You can stay if you want, Greg. You'll know soon enough anyway."

"Know what, Dad?" Ben sat down again, straddling the seat of a kitchen chair and resting his forearms across its back.

"Where is Annie?" Matt didn't need outsiders privy to a confession meant for his children.

"She went out to the airfield with Mr. Santos. He said he wanted to check on the plane." Megan slumped back into the seat she'd been in when Matt first stepped into the kitchen. Her brow furrowed as she studied Matt's face.

"Unless you'd prefer me to stay, I think I'll take myself off to see who's winning the Cowboys game." Greg pushed himself away from the counter and looked at Matt questioningly. Matt shook his head, and Greg disappeared down the hall.

Matt's heart raced uncomfortably. The courage Eve's acceptance had brought only hours before, had deserted him. He toyed with the handle of his cocoa mug. Then looked up and met their eyes in turn. Ben's pale blue, often critical eyes. Megan's, brown and sympathetic like her mothers. And Thanh's, as piercingly blue as his own.

If Matt couldn't tell his own children who loved him and would be inclined to forgive him because he was their father, how was he ever going to find the courage to tell Jeff Hall and everyone tuned into *The Scoop*?

"So?" Ben rested his chin on the backs of his hands. "What's up?"

Twenty-one

"Nothing's up. Exactly." Matt answered, sounding troubled. His brow furrowed into a worried frown as he stared steadily into his ignored cup of hot chocolate.

Ben chewed on his lip. Megan smiled encouragingly. Thanh did not know where to look. Perhaps he should not even be here. This seemed more like a family matter, and he did not belong. He watched the senator's brother-in-law disappear down the hall and wondered if he should follow the man.

But when Thanh looked back, Matt's gaze had settled on him. The older man's sharp blue gaze seemed to probe deep into Thanh, as if he were looking for answers to a question Thanh had not asked. Matt nodded toward the chair next to Ben, his desire for Thanh to stay made clear by the gesture. Thanh sat.

"A long time ago, I did something that wasn't very honorable," Matt began hesitantly.

Matt? Dishonorable? Astonished, Thanh watched a distinct tide of pink sweep up Matt's neck and into his hair. Thanh squirmed uncomfortably. Whatever this was about, Thanh did not feel like he should be here listening to a confession he had no business hearing.

"Is this about Vietnam?" Ben interrupted.

"In a way..."

Maybe that is why I am here? If it is about Vietnam, maybe he thinks I will understand or something. Thanh settled back into his chair, curious in spite of his unease.

"But you were a hero, Daddy. That's nothing to be ashamed of."

Matt shook his head. "I'm not a hero. I was just like any other Marine, doing a difficult job as best as I could. If anyone is a hero, it was my cousin Sam."

"If you're going to tell us you didn't deserve the medals you got, I'm not going to believe you." Megan tossed her head, a martial gleam in her eye, her pride in her father obvious and unswerving.

"Please. This is hard enough. If you both keep interrupting, I'll never get it said."

Megan pointedly folded her hands and leaned back in her chair. Ben returned Matt's gaze with an unreadable expression in his eyes. Thanh's discomfort increased, and suddenly he had an eerie foreboding that whatever Matt was trying to tell them would change something irrevocably.

"I looked up to Sam." Matt swallowed hard, and it looked painful. "I wanted to be just like him, and I loved him more than any man save my dad. And I betrayed him."

Thanh felt as if someone had yanked a rug out from under him. Megan looked equally stunned. Ben's mouth dropped open.

"H-how, Dad?"

Matt shoved his fingers through his hair with a quick anxious motion. "Sam Davis was not…" Matt swallowed again. "My cousin was not…Thanh's…father."

A loud buzzing erupted in Thanh's head. He felt inexplicably cold. *What is Matt trying to say? If Sam Davis is not my father, then who is?*

Matt took a deep breath and looked directly at Thanh. "I am your father, Thanh."

His confession dropped in their midst like a grenade with its pin pulled.

Megan gaped. Her gaze flicked from Matt to Thanh and back to Matt.

Thanh's breathing grew shallow and unreliable. The buzzing in his head morphed into dizziness. He must have heard wrong. *Matt Steele is* not *my father. He cannot be!*

Ben shot to his feet. His chair crashed forward, hit the table and stopped, balanced on two legs. "And you let us go through that ridiculous charade with the reporters last month? And all the time you knew the accusation was true?" Ben's face turned an alarming shade of red. "I can't believe you did this to Mom! You cheated on Mom! You bastard!"

Matt winced. "You may call me any obscenity you like, but I'd rather you didn't do so in front of your sister." His reasonable tone reflected none of the distress he must be feeling.

Thanh's heart pounded furiously. He tried to process this revelation that had just shattered everything he knew about himself.

"You think she hasn't heard the word before?" Ben challenged rudely. "She just never heard anyone call her precious daddy a bastard."

Megan appeared to be doing some rapid calculations. "But Mom and Dad weren't married when Thanh was…"

Thanh ran similar calculations through his reeling brain. He had been born, full term, on the twenty-second of January in 1976. Matt Steele had left Vietnam on the last day of April the year before. And Sam Davis had been killed on the twenty-fifth. Neither man could possibly have known Thanh's mother was pregnant.

"He's still a bastard!" Ben snapped at his sister before turning back to Matt. "So, maybe you weren't married, but you were engaged. And while Mom's at home being faithful, you're banging some Vietnamese chick." Ben stopped for a breath and shot a quick, halfway apologetic glance at Thanh. "Sorry, Thanh. I should have said he was banging his cousin's fiancée. Which is even more unforgiveable."

"She wasn't exactly Sam's fiancée."

"But she was," Thanh blurted in protest. He had the paper to prove it.

"Not when...not when we..." Matt's husky pain-filled whisper broke off mid-sentence.

Suddenly Thanh knew Matt must be talking about those five short days after Sam Davis had been killed.

"Whatever!" Ben spat the word out with loathing. "How could you be so completely irresponsible? Never mind Mom! You let that poor woman bear your bastard! Alone!"

"Your father..." Thanh hesitated. *My father!* As shocking as it was, the idea suddenly felt right. "*Our* father had already gone home before my mother even knew she was pregnant." Whatever else had happened, Thanh did not believe for an instant Matt was the kind of man who would have knowingly abandoned any child he had fathered.

"So! How long *have* you known the truth?" Ben ignored Thanh and took a couple steps closer to Matt. He loomed over his father with a look of disgust distorting his handsome features.

"I don't know exactly." Matt looked up at his son with an expression that pleaded for understanding.

"While you were busy denying it to the press?" Ben hissed in a vicious whisper. "Or was it when you introduced your bastard to Mom? Does she even know the truth?"

Thanh wanted to stop the angry attack, but he did not know how. Ben was on a rant and not listening to any reasoning.

"Your mother guessed the truth before I did." Matt's quiet answer came in stark contrast to Ben's contemptuous accusation.

Ben pounced, grasping the front of Matt's shirt and dragging him to his feet.

"Ben, stop it," Megan leapt out of her chair and grabbed at Ben's sweatshirt.

Thanh stood, too, moving to back Megan up.

"Ben, stop it," Ben mimicked cuttingly. "I can't believe you're defending this asshole. And get your claws out of me." He let go of Matt and grabbed Megan's wrists, yanking her hands away from his shirt.

"Take your hands off your sister," Matt ordered.

"You can't order me around anymore," Ben snapped.

Thanh stepped between Megan and her furious brother. Thanh had never seen Ben so angry. He looked furious enough to hurt someone. Guilt raced through Thanh like a wildfire. This was his fault. He had to stop it.

"Ben, please…" Thanh began.

Ben completely ignored Thanh's attempt to intervene as he glared at his father. "How could you do this to *my* mother?" Ben balled his fist. His body trembled as if his self-control was within a hairsbreadth of snapping.

Matt made no move to defend himself.

Thanh put a hand on Ben's shoulder. Ben jerked away, his mouth working as if he wanted to say a great deal more. Abruptly, he pivoted and strode from the kitchen. His angry footsteps echoed across the tiled hall floor until the great room carpeting swallowed them up.

"Daddy?" Megan's voice quavered.

Matt glanced at Thanh. "This isn't your fault, Thanh, so take that sorry look off your face."

"If I had not come to you, this never would have happened. You would still have your son's respect."

"Right now, I don't feel like I deserve it. Or yours, either."

"He should not have said such things. A man's father deserves respect," Thanh insisted, his throat tight with anguish. "You do not deserve such scorn, whatever the truth of the past. How can Ben dismiss all that you mean in his life over something that does not even concern him?"

"Ben will cool off." Matt sounded as though he did not quite believe his confident assurance.

"Perhaps I should talk to him." Thanh plunged his fingers into his hair and shoved it away from his face. God only knew what he could possibly say to Ben to help him see things differently, but he could at least try.

"Ben never stays angry very long." Thanh had forgotten Megan's presence until she spoke.

"I'm sorry, Megan." Matt turned to his daughter. "This can't be easy for you, either."

Megan rushed around the table and wrapped her arms about her father's waist. "I love you, Daddy. I always will, no matter what." Then she leaned away to look up into his face. "I don't know what happened all those years ago, and I don't know if I want to. But it doesn't matter. I love you, and I love Thanh." She turned and shot a warm inclusive look in Thanh's direction. Then she released Matt and hurried to Thanh. She threw her arms around Thanh's neck and hugged him fiercely. "I'm lucky to have you for my brother."

For a moment, Thanh did not know if he should return her embrace or not, but slowly he folded her into his arms. "I am lucky to have you for my sister, as well. It will take some getting used to, but it is my good fortune to find I have such a wonderful family." His gaze locked with Matt's over Megan's head, and Thanh felt his eyes begin to smart. *How come I never thought about how extraordinarily blue my father's eyes are? Or realized how much they look like mine?*

For several long moments, Thanh held his new-found sister, trying to absorb the change his father's confession had wrought. When Megan released Thanh and stepped back, he felt curiously vulnerable, yet a small bubble of happiness had settled into his being. Megan was his sister. Matt was his father. Ben might be hard to win over, but he was still Thanh's brother. Thanh had never known how it would feel to be part of a real family.

Megan's warm brown gaze touched each of them in turn. "Seems like you guys have a lot to talk about, and you'd probably like to do it without me around." Then she smiled. "So—I think I'll just go check out that football game."

~ * ~

Matt faced Thanh awkwardly across the expanse of the kitchen table. He drew air into lungs that felt horribly tight as he watched the play of emotions flickering across his son's face.

"Like Megan, I am not sure if I wish to know how it is possible that you are my father," Thanh said finally. "But now that I have gotten to know you, I am not sorry that it is you and not Sam Davis."

"I'm not sorry that you are my son, either." Matt felt unbearably embarrassed, but there were still things that needed saying. "But I *am* sorry I didn't try to find out what happened to your mother. I would have married her if…" The mule kick of pain Matt had felt last night hit him again. If he had known about Thanh, it would have changed everything. Mai Ly had not been in love with Matt either, but she was a survivor. She'd have made their marriage work. And Matt guessed he'd have come to love her eventually. But his heart had always belonged to Eve. "I would have married her if I had known."

"But you did not." Thanh shoved his hands into his pockets.

Matt took another deep breath and let it out. Guilt over the things he should have done and didn't weighed on him like a Mack truck. A memory of the embassy fence flashed through his mind again. He should have gone out looking for her, instead of just assuming she had changed her mind.

Suddenly the kitchen felt too small. Too confining. He moved toward the door, and grabbed two jackets off the hooks in the entryway. "Mind coming outside? I could use some fresh air." He held one jacket toward Thanh. Terry would be upset with Matt for going out unguarded, but at the moment, he didn't care. He had to get out of this kitchen. Away from the scene of Ben's anger.

For a moment, Thanh remained where he was, his hands still shoved deep into his pockets. Then he sighed, almost the same deep intake of breath and heavy exhale Matt had taken a moment before. "Yeah, me too." Thanh reached for the jacket Matt held in his direction.

Matt led the way. The house had a porch that wrapped around three sides of the building. Along the side, away from either door, an old wicker rocker and two Adirondack chairs were lined up against the wall. Matt avoided the rocker because it creaked badly and as nervous as he felt right now, he'd be rocking like a dory in a stormy sea, and creaking like an un-oiled door. He lowered himself into one of the Adirondacks. Thanh took the other one.

For a while, neither man said anything. A squirrel hopped erratically across the yard, stopping to dig, first in one place, then another, before finally finding a nut. He carried it to the maple tree and scurried up its trunk, disappearing into the colorful leaves.

"Are you feeling guilty more because you betrayed your friend? Or because you dishonored my mother?" Soft as the question was uttered, it stabbed hard into Matt's heart.

"Both." The wrenching admission shamed him. "I violated my promise to Eve, too. I didn't mean for it to happen, but I was not strong enough to stop it."

Thanh frowned. "You did not stop it?"

Too late, Matt realized what his comment implied. He didn't know how to undo the implication.

"Did my mother mean for it to happen?"

Matt felt trapped. He didn't want to demean Thanh's mother, but didn't want to leave Thanh thinking Matt had forced her, either. "Sam had just been killed. We were both grieving, and I think she only wanted to forget. She wanted me to make her forget. She asked me to hold her. Then things just..." Matt swallowed. "I should have made her leave, but I didn't."

Thanh raked his hand through his thick black hair again, leaving it standing on end in several places. "She told everyone I was the son of Samuel Davis. His name is on my birth certificate."

Thanh looked away from Matt, toward the tree the squirrel had disappeared into. His next words were thick with discomfort. "Were Mr. Davis and my mother lovers?" Then he turned his head and looked directly into Matt's eyes.

"They were very much in love. And yes, they were lovers."

"Then perhaps she believed I *was* his son, and it was not a deliberate lie."

"She loved Sam. She would have wanted to believe her baby was his. And we..." Matt wanted to look away, but he couldn't. "We were only together that once. The chance was so slim she would have had little reason to think it might have been me."

Matt didn't know that was the case. Sam could have been using condoms. Should have been using condoms. Mai Ly would have known if he had. But there was no reason to leave that hurtful piece of doubt in Thanh's mind. Everything he'd ever believed about himself had just been torn to shreds. Matt wasn't going to make it any worse.

"I know this is way too little and a lot too late, but I want you to know I felt a connection between us right from the start." Matt tapped his heart. His emotions had been so conflicted regarding Thanh, it was hard to sort them out. But there had been a bond. From that first moment when his gaze had met Thanh's across the table in his campaign bus.

"I enjoyed having you around. I couldn't wait to introduce you to my family and my friends. I felt like you belonged. I wanted you to belong. Then one day, while I was shaving, I found myself staring at myself. Studying my face. Especially my eyes. And I knew where you'd gotten yours. You can't even begin to guess how I felt in that moment. Like my heart might have stopped. Of course, it hadn't, but that's what it felt like.

"It seemed so unreal at first, but I knew it was possible. When I couldn't stop thinking about the chance that it might be true, I purchased a DNA kit, and I sent it away. Part of me was afraid to find out we were related, but a bigger part of me was terrified I'd find out we were not." Matt wanted to pull the young man into his arms and hold him close. He wished he'd held him as an infant, just as he'd once held Ben and Megan. Wished he'd been there for Thanh's first words and his first steps. Wished he'd been there to give Thanh his name. "But mostly..." Matt's throat squeezed painfully. "...mostly, I just love you."

Thanh's gaze held Matt's as emotions Matt couldn't interpret clouded the vulnerable blue depths.

"And I am more afraid than you can ever know that you will not be able to forgive me." Tears smarted in Matt's eyes, and he blinked them back.

"What is there to forgive?" Thanh asked, his voice gentle, his blue eyes as awash with tears as Matt's. He pushed himself out of his chair and walked to the railing, then turned back. "Should I forgive you for giving me the gift of life? Or for welcoming me into your home and making me feel like family even before you knew our true relationship. You know, you could have kept this to yourself forever, and no one would ever have known. But instead, you chose the honorable thing. The hard thing. I have nothing to forgive you for."

"You are very generous."

A glimmer of a smile tugged at Thanh's wide mouth. "Perhaps I get it from my father."

My father! The words slammed into Matt's heart with unexpected force. "Thanh, I..." Matt stopped when Thanh reached into his pocket and withdrew a stack of photos Matt's mother had given him the night before.

"I studied them for a very long time last night," Thanh said, sounding uncertain. He flicked through a few of the snapshots Ellen Steele had found of Sam, then squared the stack and handed them to Matt. "I tried to make them feel real, but I could not. And I did not understand why. But now..."

"I'm sorry," Matt said again. He couldn't think of anything else to say. How could he make up for shattering everything his son had always believed?

Thanh said nothing for a long moment. He stared at his empty hands. When he looked up again, he'd given up his battle to keep his tears in check. "I am not sorry at all. Well, maybe a little. For the trouble I caused with Ben. But you are everything I ever dreamed my father might be, and I am proud that..."

Matt shot from his chair and dragged Thanh into his embrace. Thanh's strong, young arms locked hard about Matt's middle and they clung, wordlessly trying to make up for thirty-six lost years.

~ * ~

Alone in his study, Matt found himself standing in the middle of the room, eyes shut, addressing God in silent thanksgiving.

Thank you for Eve. His gratitude was bone deep. *Thank you for all my kids. All three of them. Thank you for Megan and Thanh and for their understanding. And please, don't let Ben hate Thanh.*

Suddenly, the tears he'd been fighting all day pressed painfully at his tightly shut eyelids. He dug the heels of his hands into his eyes, trying to stop the tears from coming. "I've made such a mess of things with Ben," he cried aloud to the empty room. Then his voice dropped to a whisper. "How can I undo it?"

"Undo what, Daddy?"

Matt whirled, heart pumping.

Megan stood just inside the door, a tray with two steaming mugs in her hands.

"I didn't hear you come in." He fought to gain control of his racing heart and watering eyes.

"I thought a cup of hot chocolate would be good right about now. It always makes me feel better when things seem overwhelming and you make cocoa to share with me."

She didn't wait for his agreement before coming across the carpet and setting the tray on the table beside his chair. She pushed him gently toward his chair and waited while he sat, then pressed a mug into his unresisting hands. She took the other for herself, then settled on the stool before him.

"You're not wishing you could undo Thanh, are you?"

"Thanh's the only good part of this whole mess." Matt lifted the mug to his lips with shaky hands, sipped carefully, and then lowered it again. "I'm sorry, kitten. I guess I should have found a better way to tell you. I'm sorry you had to be a part of such an ugly scene."

"Ben's right about a couple things. I've heard it all before, and I didn't like hearing him call you names. But it's not your fault."

"This whole mess is my fault!"

"You remember the talk we had after my fiasco of a date with Randy Romin'...hands?" Megan asked, ignoring his agonized exclamation.

Matt struggled to recall the night, then remembered with a rush of embarrassment. "Mostly," he said, reluctantly.

"I never knew you could be like that. Talking about things like that, I mean. I always thought you probably never ever did anything you were ashamed of, and I was afraid you wouldn't understand how I could have let myself get into such a predicament."

"I've done my share of things I'm not especially proud of."

"But..." She looked him in the eye. "...*I* didn't know about them. I always wanted to live up to you, and I was afraid to tell you when I screwed up. I wanted you to be proud of me."

"I am proud of you, kitten." He was appalled that she could ever doubt it. "I've always been proud of you."

She touched him, her hand resting lightly on his wrist. "It's kind of hard imagining your parents ever being young and stupid. I guess you always think your parents were just born wise and never learned anything the hard way, but that night was different. Instead of tearing out of the house, ready to punch Randy out, you tried to make me see how what happened didn't mean I was wicked."

"I felt like punching him out," Matt admitted.

"But you didn't. You talked to me like you were my friend instead of my father. You made me realize you were my age once, and I felt like you really understood how I was feeling. I mean, like you *really* understood.

"When you told us about Thanh all I could think of was how crazy Randy made me feel...before he went too far that night in the car, that is. And I thought about you and Thanh's mother, and how things were a lot different then. It must have been a scary time. Then Sam got killed, and...I think maybe I do understand."

Matt felt a hot, prickling tide flood up his neck and into his hair and face. Twice in as many hours, his embarrassment had been so acute he'd blushed. He opened his mouth to say something, but shut it again.

"I'm not saying what happened was right," Megan continued, ignoring his blush. "But, I think maybe you weren't the only one to blame."

"It shouldn't have happened," Matt burst out, unable to accept her pardon so easily.

"You told me another thing." She slid forward onto her knees, pressing herself between his thighs. Her eyes, so like Eve's, held his unflinchingly. "You reminded me no one is perfect, and we all make mistakes. You told me not to be ashamed of myself, and you said success only means picking yourself up one more time than you fall."

What a humbling experience! Matt stared at his daughter, unable to think of a single thing to say to her.

"Anyway," she said, stretching up to kiss him on the cheek. "I want you to know I'm not ashamed of you, either. I'm proud of you for having the courage to admit you made a mistake. And I think it's neat that Thanh is my brother."

Twenty-two

Tony Santos pulled Ben's borrowed Subaru into the Steele's gravel drive and parked it next to the campaign bus. Full dark had fallen, and light spilled invitingly from the windows. It made a welcoming sight, but the coziness only made Annie feel like an intruder. Her father turned the engine off and turned to her.

"You've been awfully quiet this afternoon. I hope nothing's wrong between you and Thanh."

Annie shook her head. Everything was wrong, but it wasn't about Thanh. It was about her. And her mother. And TJ. "Everything's fine, Dad. Thanh's a great guy and..."

"And what?" Tony reached over to cover her hand with his big warm one.

"I'm in love with him," she blurted. Even more shocking than the declaration she'd never even allowed herself to think, tears boiled up in her eyes, and she had to fight to keep them from escaping. "I didn't want to fall in love. After Alejandro, I..."

Annie's father dismissed Alejandro with a scornful snort. "He was a louse. Thanh is nothing like him."

"I know." Annie looked out the window toward the house. Thanh was in there somewhere, probably wondering why she'd gone off with her father with so little explanation. Annie wanted to

219

go find Thanh, and wished she could just enjoy their growing relationship without this cloud hanging over her head. But she was afraid of TJ and his ability to coerce her to reveal everything she'd learned today about the Steele family. Even more, she was afraid of how quickly Thanh's view of her would change if he found out.

"I'm not an expert about love," her father said with a self-deprecating sigh. "If I were, I'd not have been married and divorced twice, nor hurt your mother as badly as I did. But I know a man in love when I see one, and Thanh is very much in love with you." He squeezed her hand. "I don't think he'd ever hurt you the way Alejandro did."

"I know he likes me, but he's never said he loves me." *And he might never say it if he finds out what I'm doing here.*

Tony barked out an incredulous laugh. "Are you kidding? It's written all over him. Use your eyes, girl."

Annie knew her father was right. Even without words, she could see Thanh's love in his eyes and feel it in his touch. He cared for her more than she deserved, and he would be so hurt if she betrayed him. She rolled her shoulders uncomfortably.

"Look, Annie…" Her father pressed a finger under her chin and lifted her face. "I'm not sure what's really bothering you. But I hope you know you can tell me anything. I might be a lousy husband, but I think I've been a pretty good father, and if you find yourself in a jam, I'll help however I can."

Annie tried to nod, but her father's hand was firm beneath her chin.

"Promise me, Annie. Promise you'll come to me if you need help. About anything."

"I promise." Annie felt small and defenseless. Even her father couldn't help her out of the fix she was in.

"Good!" He pulled her into a quick hug, then gave her a little shove. "Now go find that young man, and tell him how much you love him."

~ * ~

Annie walked quietly across the great room toward the den in search of Thanh. She heard the sounds of the television and quiet conversation. She peeked around the corner.

Megan and Megan's Uncle Greg were there. And one of Mr. Steele's secret service guys, but not Thanh. She slipped away from the door as quietly as she'd come, and hurried to the kitchen. Although several lights were burning, the generous room was empty of occupants. A couple of the pegs by the back door were bare, so she crossed the kitchen and stepped out onto the porch. But that, too, was empty. She retraced her steps back through the kitchen and into the dining room, probably the only room in the house with no lights on at all. She sank down onto the window seat built into the bow window on the far side of the dining room table, and considered her predicament.

The nook was dark and comfortable. It felt like a safe hiding hole from the dilemma she faced. She drew her feet up onto the cushion and wrapped her arms around her knees, and with her chin resting on one knee, tried yet again to figure a way out of the trap.

"How long have you known about Thanh?" The angry voice came from the hall just outside the dining room. It sounded like Ben's voice. Annie's heart jumped into her throat.

"Hush, Ben." That was Megan's mother, her voice calmer, but stern.

"I just want to know how long this farce has been going on?" Ben's voice increased in temper and volume. "How could you let Dad treat you so cheaply?"

"Your father has never treated me cheaply." The voices grew louder. Ben and his mother must have stepped into the dining room, although Annie couldn't see them.

She didn't want to be listening, but there seemed no way to extricate herself without them knowing she'd been there. She pulled her knees tighter against her chest, shrinking into the corner of the window seat and hopefully, beyond their range of vision.

"Oh, yeah! And I suppose passing his bastard off as the son of his long dead cousin and expecting you to accept Thanh into the family with open arms isn't pretty damned low?"

"Your father didn't know Thanh was his son. Not at first. It wasn't deliberate."

"How the hell could he *not* know? For Christ's sake, Mom. He knew he was screwing the woman! And his cousin's body wasn't even cold yet." The scathing words dripped with anger, but Annie could hear hurt and a sense of betrayal in them.

Mrs. Steele made a shushing sound and then said something too softly for Annie to make out.

"I don't hate Thanh," Ben answered in a less heated tone. "I actually liked the bastard. I still like him. It's not his fault, anyway. I can't even begin to imagine what he's feeling right now. Believing his father was Sam Davis all these years and then…" The pause stretched out, while Annie listened against her will. "I was more upset for you," Ben finally added in a more chastened tone.

Again, Annie couldn't make out Mrs. Steele's reply.

When the quiet became more absolute, Annie guessed they must have left the dining room, and she wondered how long she should wait before making a break for the room she was sharing with Megan. Then the meaning of their discussion washed over her like a towering, icy wave of angry, churning ocean. She pressed her face against her knees, trying to block it all out.

But the words would not erase themselves. Thanh was Senator Steele's illegitimate son, born to a Vietnamese woman who'd been engaged to the senator's cousin. Annie tried to reconcile the warm, big-hearted senator, who obviously loved his family, with a man who would have intercourse with a woman he didn't care about while he was engaged to someone else. And worse, abandon the woman after he got her pregnant. Or perhaps he had cared about the woman, but did that make it any better? He'd still left her and his child behind. He'd still betrayed both his own cousin and his future wife.

Then something Ben's mother had said came back to her. When he'd first met Thanh, the senator hadn't known Thanh was his son. There were obviously huge chunks of this story missing from Annie's understanding of what had happened, either years ago, or more recently. Who was she to judge?

Then the realization that this was exactly the sordid sort of story TJ hoped she might dig up hit her. The stakes had just gone from boyhood pranks that TJ could twist into tales of juvenile delinquency, to the kind of lurid scandal that sells tabloids and ruins reputations. She could picture TJ smirking in delight. She shivered as a claw of icy fear ripped at her insides. TJ could never know. Never!

~ * ~

Thanh stood at the side of the long driveway watching Ben pack Annie's and her father's bags into the back of the Subaru. His Secret Service shadow stood close by, keeping an eye on Ben and their surroundings. They would be dropping Annie and Mr. Santos off at the airport on their way back to Philadelphia, while everyone else returned to DC on the campaign bus.

Annie had not come to his bed last night although Thanh had lain awake a long time hoping. He was worried about her. She seemed distressed about something but whenever he asked, she just said it was nothing. Just a headache. But Thanh suspected it was something more than just a headache. Only he did not have a clue what. He did not even know if it involved him or their relationship.

She had not been privy to any part of the scene in the kitchen yesterday afternoon, so he did not think it was the changed circumstances between Thanh and his father, which had not been discussed at any point during the evening.

With the exception of Ben, they had all gathered around the kitchen table to play a spirited game of Trivial Pursuit, which Thanh, surprisingly, had won. Annie had lost abysmally, her mind clearly distracted, or so it seemed to Thanh. Now that he considered it, Annie had not been her usual bubbly self all weekend. The noise of the small airplane on the way up had not lent itself to easy discussion, but in the car between the airport and Everett, Maine, it had been Megan who had done all the talking.

The only clue Thanh had was that Annie had mentioned feeling out of place when she had come to him in the den the first night. He had dismissed her feelings then as being due to having just been introduced to the entire Steele family, which had been rather overwhelming. He had felt overwhelmed himself. But before they had a chance to talk about it, she had slipped beneath the covers and conversation had ceased. She had been gone when he woke.

During their walk through the woods to the beach, Annie had dallied behind everyone else, talking very little. Megan had been so full of stories about Sam Davis and their father growing up, Annie would not have had a chance to say much even if she had wanted to. But then she had taken off with her father to check the plane with no explanation at all. Something seemed amiss.

Annie came out of the house and down the front stairs, her steps hurried and her head down. She looked up and met Thanh's gaze.

She changed course and came toward him, her hand outstretched, but he ignored it and pulled her into his arms instead. "I wish I knew what is troubling you," he whispered into her ear.

Annie shook her head against his shoulder and tightened her arms about his waist.

Thanh kissed her temple, then her cheekbone. "I also wish you knew that you could trust me."

She huffed out a little bit of a laugh and turned her head to look at him. "Of course, I know I can trust you." But the laugh was strained, and her eyes looked haunted.

Thanh bent his head and kissed her briefly on the mouth. "There is no time right now, and this is perhaps not the place," he whispered against her lips, "but I want you to know you can tell me anything. Nothing could change how I feel about you." He drew his head away and looked down into her eyes. He loved this woman with every fiber of his being, and it distressed him that there was something standing between them that he did not understand.

At the beginning of their relationship, he had thought it was the hurt inflicted on her by a man named Alejandro. But Annie had seemed to get past that, and the last few weeks had been the happiest of his life. He had thought they had been happy for her as well.

"I love you." He hadn't meant to say it aloud. Not yet. But the swell of emotion couldn't be kept bottled up any longer. In amazement, Thanh watched Annie's eyes fill with tears. It was not the reaction he had expected. Apparently this was not the time or place for that declaration either, but she needed to know that whatever caused her pain, caused him pain as well, and that he wanted to share it.

"I love you, too." Annie's response was so faint, he almost did not hear it, but he read it on her lips and saw it in her eyes. His heart soared. Whatever it was that haunted her, they would get through it. Together.

He hauled her back into his embrace, hugging her hard against him. "In that case, there is nothing we cannot fix together. Smile for me and give me one more kiss before you go, and I will see you tomorrow in DC."

If anyone had doubted their feelings for each other before, Thanh thought they could hardly do so any more. The kiss went on for a long time. Annie clung to him, opening her mouth beneath his and kissing him as she might have done when they were alone in bed at night. Before she could completely unman him, he put her from him and gave her bottom a pat.

"Better get moving. I think your father is getting ready to ask if my intentions are honorable."

Annie laughed at that. A much happier, more normal laugh than he had heard all weekend. She blew him one last kiss and climbed into the back of Ben's car.

"Don't forget your books." Megan came hurrying down the path and knocked on Annie's window. Annie rolled the window down and Megan handed the books through the opening. "Don't forget we have a lunch date next week."

Thanh did not hear Annie's reply because Ben had appeared at his elbow.

"Uh, Thanh. I meant to talk to you earlier, but...well...one thing and another..." Ben looked down at his sneakers, then across the yard to where his father stood, and finally back at Thanh. "I'm sorry for some of the things I said yesterday. I was out of line."

"You were upset. I understood." Thanh began, but Ben went on in a rush of words.

"I never expected...well, what Dad told us was kind of the last thing I ever expected to hear from him. He's not that kind of guy.

At least, I never thought he was. And it was kind of shocking to find out my father wasn't exactly who I always believed him to be. I was angry for my mother, too, but that wasn't even my place to butt into." Ben swallowed hard and met Thanh's gaze squarely "Anyway, I got to thinking, if it was shocking for me, I could only begin to imagine how shocking it was for you. I mean to grow up believing one thing and find out it was all a lie."

"Your father is still the man you have always known. Nothing about what happened over thirty years ago changes the father he has been to you all your life. Or the husband he has been to your mother."

"Well, that's what I wanted to say, but you put it better than me."

"You know, it is not me you should be telling this to. It is your—our father."

"I talked to him this morning. After church. Maybe you didn't notice because you were walking with Annie, but Dad and I kind of lingered in the cemetery longer than anyone else. Anyway I couldn't get that reading from James that we heard this morning out of my head."

"The one about forgiving?" Seven times seven, Thanh thought it went.

"No, that was the other one. I was thinking about the one that said to confess your sins to one another and pray for one another, and you would be healed. And then when we were walking among the stones, I saw Dad looking at me, and he looked so hurt. And I realized he'd done the confessing, but I hadn't done any praying and until I did, there wouldn't be any healing for either of us."

Ben flexed his shoulders as if his jacket was too tight. "I'm not sure I've ever believed all that much in the healing power of prayer, but I couldn't stand the look in Dad's eyes. Especially knowing I'd put it there. We don't agree most of the time, but he's always been a good father, and I know he loves me. He'd never knowingly do anything to hurt me, or Megan or Mom. Or you either, come to think of it. So I prayed." Ben made a wry face and glanced away from Thanh toward the gray rolling ocean beyond the dunes. Then he looked back at Thanh and went on with a look in his eyes that seemed to say he couldn't quite believe what he was saying.

"And it was like God talked to me. I mean I didn't hear any voice or anything like that. That would have really freaked me out. But I felt—different." Ben tapped his chest. "I wasn't so angry any more. All that craziness from yesterday, it was just gone. So, I figured, if Dad was big enough to tell us the truth, then I ought to be big enough to tell him I was sorry for the way I behaved, and make an effort to understand what it must have been like for him."

Thanh felt as though Ben had lifted an enormous load off his heart. If his advent into their lives had estranged these two men he had come to love so much, Thanh was not sure how he would have lived with that. He felt the ominous gathering of tears and blinked them back.

"What did he say?"

"Not a lot. We just hugged, and I think he was trying not to cry. I'm glad he didn't. I don't know what I'd have done then. I don't think I've ever seen Dad cry."

Thanh had. And those tears had meant more to Thanh than all the words that had been said. "It has been a rather emotional weekend for all of us." Certainly the most emotional weekend of Thanh's life. From tears to joy and back. More than once. He had gained a father he had never expected to have, a brother and a sister he already loved, and Annie had told him she loved him. *My cup runneth over, indeed!*

"Yeah," Ben agreed, his shoulders relaxing. "You can say that again. So, are we good?"

Thanh had heard the expression, but it seemed so inadequate. "Yes. We are good," he agreed, reaching up to put a hand on his brother's shoulder.

Ben slapped Thanh's back in return, his gaze flicking from Thanh's face to the sea and back. Then he flung his arms about Thanh and gave him a proper hug. "Welcome to the family, Thanh. Dad's planning to come completely clean, you know? I hope you're ready because your life will never be the same again."

Ben gave Thanh one last manly slap on the back and released him, then bounded around to the driver's side of his car and folded his lanky height into the seat.

Thanh watched the car back slowly down the drive and into the road. Ben tooted once, and the car started forward. In another moment, they were gone from sight, but Thanh lingered beside the drive, trying to process Ben's about-face. Megan had assured him that her brother never stayed angry for long, but the outrage had seemed too deep to be so quickly assuaged. Thanh wondered what Ben had said to their father in the cemetery that morning. He hoped it was as generous as the admission he had just made to Thanh.

The bus engine rumbled to life with a cough of blue smoke. Mrs. Steele came down the front stairs with Skip at her heels, his plume of a tail waving happily. Megan followed, her backpack bouncing against her back as she passed her mother and leapt into the open door of the bus. Thanh wondered where his father was.

"Sir?"

Thanh turned to find Bharat Sahir beckoning to him. He was taller than Thanh by three or four inches, and heavier built with dark eyes and black hair. He was one of his father's secret service detail, but not one Thanh knew very well.

"Yes?" Thanh did not think the man had ever addressed him before.

"The senator said I'm to hang with you until you get your own guy sometime tomorrow."

"My own guy?" Thanh was confused.

"Your own detail," Bharat explained.

"I get a detail? But why?"

"The senator has informed me that you are his son, and that means you get protection. Same as Ben and Megan. It's just protocol. You'll hardly notice we're there."

Apparently, Ben's word of warning was coming true already. Life really would not ever be the same. What next?

Twenty-three

Tony Santos tied down his little plane, while Annie transferred their luggage to her car. As his daughter pulled out of the lot at the College Park Community Airport, Tony suggested stopping for supper at a diner he liked that was on the way to her apartment.

Annie didn't feel very hungry, but stopping at the diner would be better than having to fix something for them both back at her apartment, so she agreed. Her father guided her through a maze of little streets, and suddenly they were on Georgia Avenue, and she recognized where they were.

Ten minutes later they were seated in a corner booth and handed menus. Tony didn't even open his.

"I thought you were hungry," Annie commented looking up from her own search for something she felt like eating.

"I always get whatever the special is. Don't need a menu for that." Her father grinned at her.

"Okay. Then that's what I'll have, too." She folded her menu and set it aside.

"What'll it be? The usual?" A buxom, artificially auburn-haired waitress with a badge on her breast that read *Pam,* asked. She leaned her hip against the corner of the table and winked at Annie's father.

"Times two," he answered winking back.

Pam gathered up the menus and sauntered away, hips swaying.

"Do you know her?"

"Who? Pam? She's a regular, and I eat here a lot, why?"

"I was wondering if you flirt with every woman you meet?" Annie didn't know if she should shake her head in mock disapproval or laugh.

"Can't help it. It's my nature," Tony agreed. "Besides, I get better service that way. You should try it sometime."

"What?" Annie raised her eyebrows dramatically. "Flirt with Pam?"

"Well, no. Flirting with another woman probably wouldn't be to your advantage, but lighten up. Smile more. Enjoy life."

Annie didn't know how to respond to that so she didn't say anything. She'd always known her father was something of a flirt. He'd even flirted with Mrs. Steele over the weekend, and several of the ladies at the party on Friday night. Now that she thought about it, all of the ladies he'd bestowed his charm on had seemed to enjoy it. Maybe he had a point. But she hadn't inherited his confidence. Or his charm.

Considering her father in this new light, she saw a glimmer of the man her mother had fallen in love with all those years ago. And that thought brought her to the sudden consideration of what Matt Steele might have been like back then. And how he might have gotten caught up in a relationship he hadn't meant to have. And fathered a child he'd never known about.

Annie was no longer just not hungry, she felt nauseous. Then the food arrived. Her father thanked Pam, asked for water and flicked his napkin open, then placed it in his lap. Apparently he really had been hungry because for several minutes, he tucked into his meal without speaking and with only occasional glances at Annie. But then he looked up, his eyes alight with pleasure.

"So, what did you think of the Steeles? I've got to tell you, I was pretty impressed," he added before Annie had a chance to say anything. "Matt Steele is so down to earth. So like someone who might live next door. I still can't believe he could be our next president, and I've actually met him." Tony shook his head as if making sure he was really awake and not dreaming.

"They were all very nice." Annie forced a smile to her lips.

"Think about it, Annie, I've actually sat in Matt Steele's dining room talking economics over dinner like I was an equal. And to think I almost didn't agree to flying you guys up there. I have to tell you, I was worried about all the extra protocol, those guys checking out my plane, and me and everything. But, wow!" Then he frowned and peered at Annie more closely.

"You haven't even tried it." He waved his fork in the direction of her still un-touched meatloaf and mashed potatoes with gravy.

"Yes, I have," Annie protested. She bravely brought a forkful of the mashed potatoes to her mouth, and even managed to swallow it without too much difficulty. Her father's enthusiastic assessment of the Steele family made her role in their undoing seem even more sinister. "So, how long do you plan to stay in DC before heading back to Arizona?" she said in an effort to change the subject.

"That kind of depends on you," he responded, setting his silverware carefully on the edge of his plate.

Annie glanced at him and saw an intense look of concern furrowing his brow. "W-why on me?"

"It rather depends on how long it takes me to find out what's bothering my daughter and figure out how to fix it."

"Nothing's bothering me. I told you already. I'm just not—not feeling too good."

He squinted at her, and then shook his head. "I think I know you better than that. If it's not your relationship with Thanh, then it's something else. And I'm not going home until I know everything is right in the life of my little girl."

"I'm not your little girl any more, Dad." If only she were. If only this were about a dress she was dying to have that her mother had said no to. Or a failing grade in school. If only she'd never volunteered at the Cabot campaign headquarters.

"Life is full of ifs, Annie. If I'd done that. If I hadn't done this. But brooding over the might-have-beens doesn't help you solve problems."

It was as if he'd been reading her mind. He pushed his plate away, and when Pam, hovering close by, would have swooped in to remove it, he waved her off. He stacked Annie's nearly untouched plate on top of his own and reached across the table to take both her hands in his.

"You might as well spit it out. I've got broad shoulders, and I'm not going away until you tell me what's got you so tied up in knots.

The tears Annie had been fighting all weekend surged back. She blinked, shook her head and blinked again. Her father's hands were big and strong, and her own seemed fragile folded into their comforting warmth.

"It's a long story."

"I've got a long time.

~ * ~

Tony Santos didn't interrupt, even to ask for clarification when Annie knew she was talking in circles. When she finally stopped babbling, all he said was "I see." But she could sense the wheels turning in his head. "I could ask what on earth possessed you to be taken in by that arrogant upstart, but that's just another *what-if* so I won't. Are you planning to go back?"

Annie shook her head.

"Good. I'm absolutely sure I don't like you being anywhere near that TJ slimeball."

"But, Dad, he knows where I live. He seems to know everything about me. He knew about Thanh before I was really even dating him. He knew the first time...the first time Thanh spent the night, and he knew I was going to Maine this weekend. How can he know so much about me unless he has someone following me? It won't matter if I don't go there, because he'll just come after me."

"You're not telling him anything."

"But how am I going to avoid him?"

"You aren't. You're going to tell him to go to hell." Her dad squeezed her hands. He leaned forward to peer up into her downturned face. "Look at me, honey. You are going to tell him you aren't going to be his tool. We'll find another way to protect your mother."

Annie wished she could believe him, but if TJ knew everything about her, she couldn't see a way to shield her mother. Even if her mother tried to hide, TJ would be sure to find her. It would be breaking the law for anyone to help her, and there was no way her mother could disappear on her own.

"I could marry her. If she'd have me."

Annie jerked her head up to look at her father in disbelief. He looked dead serious. "She hates you. At least she says she does."

"She didn't hate me once." Her father's voice faded to a wistful tone, and his eyes lost their focus. "And I loved her very much. More than I ever loved either of my wives."

Annie gaped at him, trying to fit this idea into her thinking. It would be a way out of this fix, but she suspected her mother would never agree. Even to secure her right to stay in the country. But what if she did? She could stay in her little apartment in Virginia, and Annie's father would be in Arizona. It wasn't as if they had to live together. Nothing about her mother's life would have to change.

"She wouldn't have to live with me." Again her father seemed to be reading Annie's mind. "Well, maybe just for a few weeks, until this election is over, and TJ has nothing left to gain by harassing her."

Annie shook her head. "It wouldn't work."

"Of course it would."

"Why would you do it? Even if Mom would agree? I mean, the way she's treated you all these years? Why would you want to, even for a few weeks?"

Her father didn't answer right off. He looked as if he were choosing his words, or marshalling his arguments.

"Well, mostly for you, honey. You must know I'd do just about anything for you. But for your mother, too. I did love her once, and I guess part of me still does. I don't want to see her hurt, either, and I expect that dealing with the INS would hurt a great deal, especially if she lost her battle with them. They aren't in a very forgiving mood right now."

Annie wanted to believe this might be her way out, but she was afraid to hope too much. Her mother could be extremely difficult sometimes.

"What if she says no?"

"I expect she will, at least at first. But she loves you, too. If she realizes there's no other way, maybe she'll change her mind. But we won't know unless we ask, will we?"

~ * ~

There were lights on in Annie's apartment when she and her father pulled up out front. That could only mean one thing. Her mother was already here. Awaiting her return and eager to hear all about the Steeles and Thanh.

"It looks like we will find out sooner rather than later," Annie remarked as she pulled the keys from the ignition.

"Guess so." Her father sighed heavily. Then he got out of the car.

As she watched him collect her bag from the back of the car, Annie wondered if her father was dreading the coming scene or eager for it. He'd been in a strangely mixed mood on the drive home from the diner. One moment chatting normally and the next staring absently out the window, having broken off in the middle of whatever he'd been saying.

As she fitted her key into the door, her father chuckled ruefully. "Wish me luck, Annie. They say the third time's the charm." He stepped through the door ahead of her.

They found her mother in the living room, the Sunday paper scattered in sections on the floor around her. Mrs. Luong looked up with a smile of welcome on her face. Then she saw Annie's father, and the smile froze. She got slowly to her feet.

"I did not know you would have your father with you, or I would not have come." She turned toward the kitchen. "I will get my things and leave."

"Please, Mom." Annie stopped her. "We have to talk. I'm in some trouble, and Dad has offered to help. But I need to explain it to you."

Annie's mother slowly sank back into her chair. A frown of concern creased her brow as she studied first Annie, then Annie's father. "Trouble? What kind of trouble?"

Once again, Annie struggled to explain the last nightmarish weeks of her life. Leaving out the details of her affair with Thanh, which she knew her mother would pounce on with relish and become completely sidetracked by. But when she got to the part of offering her father's solution, Tony Santos got up and came to touch Annie on the shoulder.

"What?" She looked up at him.

He crooked a finger, signaling his desire for her to get up. She rose and stood uncertainly, wondering at the odd look on his face. He leaned close and whispered in her ear. "A man's kids aren't supposed to be around when he does his proposing." Then he winked at her and gave her a little push toward the kitchen.

"But it's not like…"

"You have no idea what it might be like to be asking the woman you've loved for over three decades to marry you."

Annie's heart seemed to do a somersault. Her father had mentioned loving her mother in the past. He'd even suggested there were still traces of that old love left in his heart. But as she looked into his eyes now, she saw a bottomless well of emotion. Deeper than anything she'd ever seen in him. About anything, including herself. And suddenly she felt like an interloper. Without another word, she turned and left the room.

Twenty-four

Matt Steele strode through the subterranean labyrinth of shops and vendors between the Capitol and the Russell Senate office building with Joe Venuto keeping pace, and the new agent, Zack Corsair, who had replaced Bharat, two steps ahead. Matt had only a day and a half in DC before he'd be on the road again and it felt like he had at least six days worth of work to get done. This morning's Appropriations Committee meeting had been critical, and it had gone on much longer than he'd anticipated, and he still needed to get in touch with the assistant producer from *The Scoop*.

"Senatah Steele. Good day to yah." A grinning black man shot up from his stool as Matt passed. "Them shoes do looks like they need a shinin'."

Matt paused and glanced down at his shoes. Jamar was right, they did need shining. Matt hesitated, reluctant to take the time, then shrugged.

"Trouble is, I'll be paying you good money for a shine that won't last the day in this rain," Matt complained good-naturedly as he hiked himself up onto Jamar's chair.

"No such thing, Senatah. You just trust Jamar."

The dark, elderly man went to work on Matt's shoes with the air of a tradesman who takes pride in doing even a simple job better than anyone else.

"Heard you on TV the other night," Jamar interrupted his work to peer up at Matt.

"Which night was that, Jamar?"

"I forget. Friday, maybe Satiday. I think you were in Boston." Jamar went back to layering a coat of polish on Matt's shoes. "You know what I'm thinkin'? I'm thinkin' every last body is expectin' the impossible. Ever take notice how everyone wants their piece o' the pie, but nobody ever wants to do the bakin'?" With hands that moved in quick, light strokes, he brushed the polish to a high gloss.

"Well put, Jamar."

"I got to thinkin' 'bout them lobbyists, and if you ask me, I'd say, throw the buzzards out. Buzzards, I tell you. They just hunkerin' in to see they get the biggest piece of the carcass." Jamar dropped the brush, grabbed a long piece of soft cloth and proceeded to buff Matt's shoes to a gloss even his boot camp DI would have approved of. "There you go, Senatah."

Matt climbed down from the chair and handed Jamar a folded bill.

Jamar pocketed the money. "Hear what I'm sayin'? Throw the buzzards out, and we'll all be better off."

"I'll work on it," Matt promised as he moved away.

Leave it to a simple, poorly educated man to boil the problem down to a singly obvious conclusion. If all the lobbyists actually could be thrown out of Washington, implementing any reasonable plan to fix the economy would be far easier.

"Jamar's got a point," Joe commented wryly. He punched the button for the elevator.

"If it were only that simple," Matt replied as the door opened and Joe ushered him inside. Zack Corsair followed Matt and Joe onto the elevator and punched the button before anyone else could enter.

"Where did they corral you from?" Matt asked the new agent.

"Paintball range," came the brief reply.

"Paintball? Don't they give you enough opportunities to play war in training?"

"That was different. Paintball's a lot more fun. Ever tried it?"

"No, I haven't." Matt's blood ran cold at the thought of playing at war. He'd had more than enough of war. Real war. Including real, red blood, his own and others' splashed all over his utilities.

"You ought to. It's just like the real thing. Everyone gets themselves up in camo gear and you actually get to..."

"It isn't anything like the real thing." Matt cut in sharply. "The real thing is pure hell, and there's nothing fun about it."

The elevator door opened, and Joe stepped out. Matt paused, trying to get his sudden surge of anger under control, then followed.

Zack gaped at Matt with a suddenly sober expression of chagrin, as if he'd just realized he might have been speaking to his new boss a little too informally.

Matt forced himself to moderate his tone. "Sorry, I didn't mean to jump down your throat. It's just that I've been there. Done that. For real."

"I'm sorry, Senator. I didn't think..."

"Maybe..." Matt forced a half smile onto his face. "Maybe if I hadn't seen some of the things I've seen, I'd have thought paintball was a great game, too. Especially when I was your age."

Matt studied his new guardian agent and told himself to just let it go and shut up. But some inner compulsion prompted him to go on. "The thing is, I have seen action, and I learned the hard way that war is not a game. It's violent, and it's shockingly brutal. Being shot at is nothing short of terrifying. And once you've killed another human being, you are never the same. You stop dreaming about being a hero before you're five steps into the fighting, and you pray no one ever finds out you're really scared shitless.

"Consider that the next time you're out there taking your buddies down with your paint loaded ammo." Realizing he was close to making an idiot of himself, Matt finally shut his mouth and turned on his heel.

He'd covered half the distance to his office door before Zack recovered from Matt's outburst and hurried after him. Matt stormed into his office without his usual easygoing greeting and stalked wordlessly toward his private sanctuary. His staff, unnerved by this volatile and unprecedented mood, took one look and hastily went back to their work. Only Murdoch had the temerity to speak to him.

"You asked for this stuff," he said without elaborating and thrust a bulky file into Matt's hand. "If you want me, I'll be in Elliot's office."

Matt jammed the file under his arm, dropped his notes and tape recorder on his secretary's desk and let himself into his personal office, shutting the door with a shaking hand.

He leaned against the heavy oak panels for a moment, appalled to find himself trembling. He'd thought he had gotten past all this anger over his emotion-filled weekend. Gotten the anger out of his system along with the confession. He waited for his heart rate to return to normal and his hands to steady.

Gramma used to say, count to ten, he reminded himself. He was vaguely surprised when it actually helped. He let his shoulders relax and felt the tight bands around his chest loosen. Finally, he crossed to his desk and sat down, forcing himself to put the disturbing conversation with Zack out of his mind.

Murdoch's file, labeled, Hall, Jeff, *The Scoop*, held a number of things. As usual, Murdoch had been satisfyingly thorough.

A short bio on Erika Emory had been included. A Princeton graduate in 2002, Emory had distinguished herself at that school as the only conservative member on the school news staff. Oh two!

That would make her what? Hard to believe that sassy slip of a woman could possibly be thirty.

Jeff Hall was another matter. He was forty-six, experienced, confident and a disciplined interviewer—make that interrogator!—Jeff Hall had a reputation for insightful interviews with men and women from all walks of life and from all layers of the political spectrum. Hall was fair and even-handed, but he had a knack for extracting information no one else even suspected, often information the interviewee had no intention of sharing.

Matt swallowed the panic that threatened to choke him and took out his date book. Then he found Erika Emory's business card, picked up his phone and placed a call.

A pert voice answered on the second ring.

"Miss Emory? This is Senator Steele."

"Senator!" She didn't disguise the surprise in her voice. "You changed your mind?"

"You were very persuasive." Actually, it was his need for free national airtime to set the record straight in his own words, but she didn't need to know that. "But you didn't say exactly when the open slot was."

"Wednesday," was her immediate eager reply. "We tape in the morning. Is that going to be doable? I'm sure your schedule is pretty full?"

Matt checked his book. "I'm due in Chicago at two p.m." His flight out of DC could be changed. "I'm assuming you need me in New York?"

"Jeff doesn't do road trips, so yeah, it'll have to be New York. Nine a.m.? I'll fax over the information you'll need." Matt heard her scribbling frantically. What could she possibly be writing? "I'm looking forward to seeing you again, Senator."

The phone clicked. Slowly, Matt replaced the receiver. His heart rate must be close to two hundred, and a cold sweat had suddenly soaked through his shirt. He hoped he was doing the right thing.

Jack would have a cow when he found out. Hell, Rick would be out for blood. On second thought...

Matt dialed Jack's cell.

~ * ~

Asher Elliot sprawled across the king-sized bed in Rolly Miller's DC suite watching Blair Cabot drone on about his expertise in international affairs based on having turned a small New England foundry into a worldwide conglomerate. Ash snorted with disgust. The man was nothing more than a ruthless opportunist who didn't care who got hurt on his way to the top.

Ash had wanted his affair with Rolly to be publicly acknowledged for years, but he'd understood the reasons it couldn't be and respected Rolly's right to choose. The plummeting poll figures over the past two weeks proved Rolly's arguments, and the choice hadn't been his. Ash knew it could be laid at the door of Blair Cabot and that little weasel he called his campaign manager. Ash hated them both for what they'd done to Rolly.

Some time ago, Ash had overheard a young female employee, who obviously didn't like Cabot any better than Ash did, telling his cook how her grandfather had once worked for Cabot Industries, as it had been known back then. He'd worked there his entire career, first for Blair's father and then for Blair. But then, with no warning and little reason, he'd been let go along with most of the staff in shipping. The old man had been sixty-two at the time and had never been able to find another job. Which he had always blamed on Blair Cabot.

Ash rolled over and climbed off the bed as that conversation reeled through his mind again. Why *had* the old man been let go?

Could have been something he'd done or not done, of course. People got fired all the time for poor performance. But that didn't seem entirely likely, given that he hadn't been the only one. Might be worth looking into. The one thing Ash did have was money. And influence. If there was anything smokey about the way the old man had been let go, it might be enough to start a few smoldering little fires.

Suddenly, Ash wanted revenge. If Cabot had done anything even remotely improper, Ash wanted to make it public knowledge. Dent the little bastard's image a bit. Twitter was a wonderful medium for starting rumors and bringing down the mighty. Just look at what happened to that representative from New York! Of course, that guy had asked for it, but still…

Ash dug into his pocket for his cell, flipped it open and dialed his home number. His cook answered the phone.

"Mr. Elliot!" She sounded surprised to hear his voice. "I thought you were in Washington."

"I am. Look, Mrs. Kelly, I need to talk to that girl, Margo or maybe it's Melissa, the one that helps you out in the kitchen. Is she there?"

"Well…yes, but…"

"Could you put her on, please?"

"Sure thing, Mr. Elliot." He heard the phone clatter down onto the granite counter and footsteps moving away.

A moment later a timid voice asked, "Mr. Elliot?"

"What's your name?" Ash realized it sounded rather rude the way he'd blurted it out, but he was too eager to make an effort to soften it.

"Melissa Kinney." The voice was even more timid.

Ash wasn't a harsh employer, and he didn't like having his employees afraid of him so he took a deep breath and softened his tone. "Look, Melissa, I'm sorry to interrupt whatever you were busy with, but I need to know your grandfather's name. The one who once worked for Cabot Enterprises?"

"Grampa Dave? But why?" She sounded completely confused.

"I just need to talk with him about what it was like working for Cabot. Ask him a few questions. Nothing bad."

"He lives way up in New Hampshire," Melissa said, as if this distance were an impediment to talking with her grandfather. "And he doesn't like Mr. Cabot very much."

"But he has a phone, doesn't he?"

"Well, yes..."

"Could you give me his number?"

"Sure. Just a minute." More shuffling sounds, then, "Six-O-three is the area code." Then she gave him the rest of the number, her voice still registering confusion. "Grampa isn't in trouble is he?"

"Your grandfather is not in any trouble. I assure you. And thank you, Melissa." Ash hung up and fingered the card on which he'd written the number. How best to go about this? Fly up there and talk to the man in person, or call first?

One thing he wasn't going to do was tell Rolly what he was up to. Rolly wouldn't approve. It wasn't his style to seek revenge. But it was definitely Ash's style!

Better to just go up there, Ash decided. He crossed to the desk and sat down in front of Rolly's laptop to dig up an address to go with the phone number.

~ * ~

When Annie Santos heard the knock on her door, she thought it was Thanh and hurried to answer it.

"Well, Miss Santos? How did your weekend go?" TJ Smith pushed his way into the front hall in that moment of shocked immobility before Annie realized it was not Thanh coming to supper.

Annie gaped in panicked dismay for another too-long moment, and TJ continued on into the living room where he sank onto the sofa as if he'd been invited to make himself comfortable.

"Mr. Smith. I—What can I do for you?" Annie followed more slowly and refused to take a seat, hoping to make it clear he was not welcome.

"Tell me about your weekend," TJ asked in a cheerfully friendly voice as he leaned back and crossed his ankles.

Annie continued to stand. "No."

"No?" TJ's eyebrows lifted in surprise, his smile still in place.

"I'm not your mole." Annie remembered the words her father had told her to use. "And I will not be threatened into doing something I consider wrong." Her heart raced with increasing panic, but she stood her ground and stared down at her nemesis.

TJ got to his feet and stepped close enough to loom over her. He was short and paunchy, but the sudden hard gleam in his eyes made him seem suddenly larger and more formidable. Her breath caught in her throat, and she backed up involuntarily.

"And what about your mother?" His voice had become oily and repulsive, all of the earlier bonhomie gone along with the smile.

"My mother will be f-fine." Annie tried to make her declaration firm, but her fright showed, and she knew it.

"You don't seem so sure about that." TJ moved toward the front door. "But, I'm an understanding guy. I'll give you an extra day to rethink your position. And in the meantime, perhaps I'll pay a little visit to your mother."

"You leave my mother alone." Annie hurried after him and slammed her hand against the door when he would have opened it. "You leave my mother alone, you slimeball." Another of her father's words, but not one he'd advised her to use aloud.

"I've been called worse by people in a better position than you are, Miss Santos. Your vehemence rather suggests there is something you are trying to hide. I wonder what it could be?" TJ lifted on eyebrow as if expecting her to capitulate.

Annie said nothing.

TJ shrugged as if her recalcitrance was only a minor set-back. He turned the doorknob and pulled the door open in spite of Annie's hand pressing it shut. "Until tomorrow, Miss Santos. And a bit of advice? I wouldn't go to either your lover or the senator for help. Harboring an undocumented alien would get the former sent back to his miserable little country and would cost the latter the election." He stepped onto the porch and trotted down the stairs to his car, which sat idling at the curb while his driver read a paperback book.

Annie sank onto the bench inside her door in defeat. What was she going to do? Her father had made it sound so easy to stand up to the bully, but it had been one of the hardest things she'd ever done. And it hadn't gained her anything. If only her mother had seen reason and accepted her father's proposal.

Annie buried her face in her hands. Suddenly the picture of her father's disappointed face appeared in her mind's eye. And her mother, hands on her hips glaring defiantly at them both. Why couldn't her mother be reasonable?

"Annie?" Thanh stepped into the foyer with Bharat close behind. "What are you doing sitting here with the door wide open? Are you all right?" He dropped his briefcase, then squatted in front of her and tipped her face up with two gentle fingers.

Annie looked at Thanh, then glanced at Bharat, who was moving past them into the living room, then back at Thanh. The last threat TJ had made echoed ominously in her head. *The former would be deported.* If she told Thanh what was going on, she might not only lose his love, but if he did anything to help her mother, he would lose any hope of gaining his citizenship. He'd be sent home to Vietnam, and he'd lose the family he'd just found. She couldn't do that to him. Her choices had been reduced to two: save Thanh, or save her mother.

"I'm fine." Annie got to her feet and moved away from Thanh's gentle touch. "I was just… Someone from the campaign came by, and they just left. That's why the door was open." It sounded lame even to her, but she was a lousy liar, and she couldn't think of anything plausible.

Thanh caught up with her as she started down the hall toward the kitchen. "Annie. Stop." He turned her with a hand on her shoulder. "I know when I am being lied to."

"I'm not lying. Someone did come by. And they just left."

"But you are not all right." Thanh's brilliant blue eyes bored into hers as if he wanted to read her soul.

"I'm a little worried about my mother." Best to stick as close to the truth as possible.

"Your mother is ill?" Thanh frowned in concern. "Should you be taking care of her instead of cooking me dinner? Is there something I can do?"

"N-no. I mean, she's—she's not ill. She's—It's nothing you can help with."

Thanh's frown eased, but a hurt look appeared in his eyes. He dropped his hand back to his side and studied her for several painful moments. "I am disappointed, Annie. I love you, and I thought you loved me in return, but perhaps I assumed too much. I thought that loving someone meant sharing everything with them, the good and the not so good. You obviously do not feel as I do, or you would trust me."

"I do trust you." Annie's heart felt like it was breaking. "I just…"

Thanh shook his head sadly. "I do not think you do." He reached out to wipe a tear off Annie's cheek.

Annie fell into Thanh's arms, hugging him hard around the waist. He felt so solid and so dependable, and she wanted to blurt the whole sorry story out and have a good cry while he assured her everything would be okay. But she couldn't.

She couldn't risk having him try to help her and get himself into trouble.

"Annie, please," Thanh tipped her face up. "Tell me what is wrong."

Annie slipped her arms free and cupped his head with both hands, pulling his mouth down to hers. She kissed him hard, opening her mouth and trying to blot out everything else.

Thanh's arms tightened, and his lips moved warmly over hers, matching her passion. She crushed herself against him, moving her hips against his, cradling his head with her fingers laced into his hair.

But then Thanh lifted his head with a groan and took her upper arms in his hands. He separated himself from her and held her several inches away. "We cannot solve whatever your problem is with sex." He was panting, and his body had responded to her wanton attack, but his eyes told her he meant to turn her advances down.

"I love you, and I love making love with you, but this is not the way to fix whatever is wrong."

Annie felt bereft. She could not ask Thanh to help her, and she could not even bury her fear in lovemaking.

"Tell me," he commanded gently.

"I can't."

"Cannot or will not?" Thanh dropped his hands and stepped away from her. Thanh's blue eyes were as piercing and probing as before, and now filled with disappointment.

"Can't," Annie insisted.

Thanh flinched as if she'd hit him. "Bharat?" Thanh raised his voice to call out to the man who'd come in with him. "We will not be staying for dinner after all." Thanh retrieved his briefcase from the floor where he'd dropped it on entering and glanced back at Annie. "I love you very much, Annie. I would do anything for you. I thought you understood that. I really want to help you out of whatever trouble you are in, but I cannot if you will not trust me. You know where to find me if you change your mind."

He turned, and Bharat, who had just materialized from the living room, opened the door and stepped out onto the porch. Thanh followed him, and the door clicked softly. Slowly Annie sank onto the floor. Now she had no choices left.

Twenty-five

"What the hell's the matter with you, Matt?" Rick Winfield paced, as usual, like a caged lion. The rest of Matt's inner circle lounged comfortably around the table in Matt's bus where they had gathered to squeeze in a quick meeting before Matt's next engagement.

"I'm sorry, Rick. I'm not sure if I understand the question," Matt hedged, hoping Rick would give him a clue what had gotten under his skin this time. No way could he have heard about the date with Jeff Hall. Not yet anyway.

"What's not to understand? I asked if you had anything to add. You've hardly said anything."

"You've had plenty enough to say for both of us." Snickering greeted this remark.

Rick began to gather up the papers scattered over the desk in front of him. The rest of Matt's staff got to their feet and began to make their way to the bus door, heading off to their own next destinations.

"Look, Matt. We have to discuss the polls." Rick wasn't done yet.

"What about the polls?" Matt asked, then disappeared into his traveling bedroom to change into his old Marine Corps uniform.

When Rick would have followed, he shut the door in his manager's face.

The organizer of today's Veterans' Rally had gotten the bright idea to have the speakers appear in uniform. Each represented a different branch of the armed services, and she'd thought it would be a nice touch. *Women luuuve uniforms*, she'd drawled, when Matt had been ready to turn her down. Rick had pounced on the idea and the decision had been taken out of Matt's hands.

"The polls are bad. And getting worse since Rolly was outed. Cabot reaped the benefit from that little bombshell. I guess we know who leaked that tidbit to the press." Rick raised his voice on the other side of the door.

Matt felt like telling Rick, *I told you so*, but he refrained. Besides, Matt was getting ready to tattle on himself, and if anything, the truth about Thanh was going to make the numbers even worse. Rick was going to have a conniption.

"God dammit! Are you listening?"

"I'm sorry." Matt sucked in his gut and fastened his trousers. Not too terribly tight, thank God.

"You need to get off this retrenching bandwagon you and Hal are on lately."

"Can't do it."

"I don't understand you." Rick backed away abruptly as Matt strode back into the main room, thrusting his arms into his uniform jacket.

"It's really pretty simple." Matt sighed. "Both parties have been on a path that is just plain unsustainable for way too long. We spend all our energy blaming each other and drawing lines in the sand and none of it on finding ways to reach across the aisle and making the difficult changes that must be made. Hal and I have decided it's time for that to stop, and we are appealing to that vast middle of the road majority who've seen this coming for a lot longer than the supposed experts. That's Cabot's draw, and if we stick to your program, the polls aren't going to improve."

Matt turned toward the door. Rick was too steeped in traditional Democratic dogma. He'd never get it. The fact that they hadn't been on the same page for months was rapidly coming to a boil. Just so long as Rick hung in for a couple more weeks. That was the best Matt could hope for.

Rick glowered as if there was a great deal more he wanted to say, but there wasn't any time left. "I'll see you on the plane in the morning, then." He pulled on his suit coat.

"Actually, you'll see me in Chicago," Matt corrected him. "I'm flying to New York tonight, then to Chicago."

"New York? What the hell are you going to New York for? And how come I haven't heard about this before now?"

"It's personal business," Matt said, hoping to squash further questions.

Murdoch stuck his head in the door. "Eve's here."

"Sorry, Rick. I've got to go. See you in Chicago."

Rick wanted to argue. Matt could see it in his eyes. He felt, rightly in this case, that anywhere Matt went right now was his business. But he wasn't going to find out about Jeff Hall and *The Scoop* until it was over.

"Aren't you supposed to be meeting with somebody…" Matt looked pointedly at his watch. "Like about ten minutes ago?"

Rick stared hard at Matt, his pale gray eyes icy with indignation. "You are really stretching our friendship, Matt."

"I'm sorry you feel that way." Matt took one last glance in the small mirror hung beside the door just so he could make sure he looked his best every time he stepped outside. He tugged the jacket down under the belt, then straightened the array of ribbons.

"Why can't you…"

Matt stepped down onto the pavement, leaving Rick fuming in his wake.

Joe Venuto moved in on Matt's right, and Zack hovered on his left, doing their best to place as much of a buffer between Matt and the waiting press as they could.

"Senator, can you comment on your running mate's speech last night in Atlanta?"

Matt kept moving, ignoring the microphones being thrust at him. Jack appeared ahead of Matt and threw up one arm to ward off a microphone.

"Senator Steele!" A woman's voice pierced the general clamor. "Is this to be a new direction for your campaign?"

"Senator," another journalist persisted. "Could you at least tell us if you are backing Weymouth's statements?"

"I am fully supportive of Hal Weymouth's views." Matt paused to answer the question. He would have said more, but they had reached the car where Murdoch stood holding the door. Matt stooped and slid into the back seat. Jack turned to the frenzied group still waving their mikes.

He made the kind of statement that sounds clever and yet says nothing, then he too, ducked into the car.

Murdoch slammed the door and sprinted around the car, nimbly avoiding an opportunist trying to gain access through the driver's door. Joe jumped into the front with Murdoch. As the car pulled away from the curb, Matt wilted with the realization that by tomorrow at this time, the frenzy would be even worse.

~ * ~

When Hal Weymouth's plane rolled to a halt on the tarmac, Matt waited for him with Eve on his arm. Safely isolated from the crush of press cameras and mikes by a couple hundred yards of asphalt,

Matt, Eve, Weymouth and his wife Kate, waved and smiled at the crowd lining the fence, before climbing back into the waiting limo.

As the limo sped back along the parkway, Matt asked Kate how the ladies' breakfast had gone that morning. And he made a sincere effort to listen to her reply without letting his mind wander to Rick's increasing disaffection. The growing hostility troubled Matt.

Rick was only beginning to realize his worst nightmare. He'd tied his reputation to a horse he could no longer control and in whom he no longer believed. Tomorrow, Rick would be blindsided by an event he would consider a total betrayal. The blow would be swift and painful and completely unexpected.

As the limo and its flanking motorcycles drew to a halt before the John Paul Jones Memorial, Matt dragged his attention back to Kate and Hal. "I'm sorry for having to whisk you straight to the Veterans' Rally without any opportunity to freshen up. But at least you've got the right kind of shoes for a hike."

"Don't worry about me," Kate answered cheerfully. "I love a parade, as they say. And at least Hal's gear arrived so he could get himself decked out before we left." She smiled, an infectious grin that invited Matt to grin in return. He put Rick out of his mind.

The Mall was packed with veterans in and out of uniform. Airmen, sailors, Marines and soldiers from all of the wars of the past sixty-plus years lined the paths and spilled onto the grass. A sea of people covered the ground up to and surrounding the Washington Monument, flowed around the World War II memorial and all the way down both sides of the reflecting pool.

Matt saw the uniforms of Seals, Rangers, and dozens of other specialized units. Officers and enlisted men, some with chests full of medals, some with none. Round white sailor caps bobbed above a sea of equally white uniforms, flanked by Army drab and Marine and Air Force blue. Matt could recall only a couple of times he'd seen as many military people in one place. It was an impressive sight.

A Marine band played a stirring march that soared out above the hubbub of a million conversations. As the entourage of speakers stepped onto the temporary platform, the voices faded to a murmur and the band finished with a resounding crescendo.

The mayor of Washington, a veteran of the first Gulf War, proudly stepped to the mike dressed in the plain drab fatigues of a Marine grunt. He had to wait several minutes to allow the wave of applause to die before he could begin his introductions.

Hal stood as the mayor began, and Kate stood with him. Hal was a veteran of a half dozen skirmishes since the US involvement in Vietnam and had spent most of his career serving aboard aircraft carriers. Matt thought about the woman who'd planned this affair and decided she might have been right. Hal, at least, was at his most impressive in the sharply-creased white of a Navy Commander. He appeared even taller than usual, his face shaded but handsome beneath his billed and braided cap.

When Hal finished speaking, several more military dignitaries gave short rousingly patriotic speeches that were greeted by roars of approval from their various branches.

With applause echoing in his ears, Matt stared out over the sea of heads toward the slight rise of land that blocked his view of the Wall.

He hadn't been back to the Wall since the day he'd first seen Thanh. What had seemed like an ideal setting for garnering the support of the veterans three months ago, now loomed frighteningly difficult.

Neither Rolly Miller nor Blair Cabot had ever served in any branch of the military. Like Clinton, Rolly had actively avoided the draft, and Blair Cabot was too young. Matt's campaign strategist saw today as an easy victory. Only last month, Matt had agreed.

But as the moment when Matt's turn to speak drew closer, he began to sweat. His dress uniform clung damply, stifling and oddly unfamiliar. He felt he didn't belong in it. He wished there were not so many honors displayed so ostentatiously across his chest. He didn't feel worthy of them.

"Matt?" Eve's fingers tightened on his arm.

He looked down, forcing himself to breathe evenly.

"Is something wrong?"

He nodded. "I was just thinking I'd have been more comfortable in fatigues."

Eve grimaced. "But you wouldn't have looked as impressive."

"I don't feel impressive. I'm no better than any of the thousands of other men and women here this afternoon."

"Most of them are hoping you will soon be their Commander-in-Chief," she reminded him. She let her hand slide down his arm and laced her fingers through his. "Don't let them down."

Matt heard his cue and got up to move to the podium. He hesitated, staring off to his right, toward the unseen black marble wall. Forgive me, Sam, he begged silently, as he gazed at a tiny American flag being waved above the heads of the crowd.

Forgive yourself.

Sam's voice sounded clear and very much alive inside Matt's head. For several long moments, he hesitated, frozen into shocked immobility between his seat and the podium. The crowd continued to roar its desire to hear him speak, but he could barely hear them.

Forgive yourself. The words echoed in his heart.

Suddenly, Eve stood beside him. She slipped one hand into the crook of his arm and with the other touched, first her chest, then his. Her special smile, the one that began with a flicker in her eyes then spread to the rest of her features, glimmered, then grew.

Ignoring the roaring crowd, conscious only of the roaring in his head, Matt bent his head to hers and kissed her. Then they walked together to the podium. The applause swelled, then slowly subsided and ended with a few last sporadic claps. Eve squeezed his hand, and Matt cleared his throat. He stared out over the sea of faces, took a deep breath and began to speak.

He stumbled at first, realizing he couldn't use the polished speech he'd rehearsed. But then the words he needed to say began to flow. He put his heart into them and offered them up.

"…And in closing, I would like to share this with you.

"As any officer knows, it is often, perhaps more often than not, lonely at the top. As an officer in the United States Marines, I often felt that loneliness. The men I commanded in Vietnam had each other. The men I served under often seemed removed and uncaring. But one night, after a particularly vicious night attack on our base, I happened to overhear one of my privates describing the action in our sector to another soldier.

"It was not the highly colorful and wildly exaggerated feats he ascribed to me that caught my attention, however. It was the fact that he called me 'good people.' Just a regular guy, not like some officers he knew.

"I wished I had overheard that comment at the beginning of my tour, for I would have felt better about my leadership. I suddenly realized I belonged to them as much as they belonged to me. We were in it together.

"And that is how I would wish to begin my tour as your Commander-in-Chief. Standing shoulder to shoulder. As equals. Individually, even the greatest among us is powerless, but together, we are the best the world has ever known and I am proud to be one of you."

Matt stepped down from the podium with only one thing in his mind. Relief.

In those few panicked moments on the way to the podium, he'd felt like a fraud. He wasn't the man they thought he was. He wasn't even the man he'd thought he was. He hadn't felt worthy of their respect. The speech he'd meant to give said all the wrong things, and he'd had no idea what to say.

But then Eve had reached out to him, and the words had come. From his heart, they had said themselves. And they had been the right ones.

While he was speaking, he'd remembered another important lesson. One he'd almost forgotten in the years since his days as an officer. The secret of leadership isn't always in standing above everyone else, but rather in standing with them.

~ * ~

Ash Elliot took his seat in first class and buckled his seat belt. His trip to New Hampshire had not been wasted. David Kinney had been happy to talk about his former employer. He didn't like Blair Cabot much, that had been clear. But far from being embittered by the treatment he'd received at Blair Cabot's hands, Kinney had apparently moved into early retirement with a fair amount of satisfaction and turned to gardening to fill his time. He also hadn't forgotten the odd collection of coincidences that had preceded his being given his pink slip.

Kinney had invited Ash in, put a fresh pot of coffee on to brew and settled in to relate everything he knew.

And he'd known quite a bit.

Ash opened his briefcase to haul out the leather folder he'd jotted down notes on once he realized there was a lot more to the story than he would ever remember on his own. He ignored the bustle of economy class passengers brushing by with their wheeled suitcases and whining kids and read through his scrawled, but detailed notes.

Kinney had been the manager in the shipping department at the time Cabot Industries was moving into the international market. The foundry in Epping, New Hampshire had been casting engine blocks for shipment to Israel for several years, but three shipments had gone missing. Kinney had been told not to worry about it, just reship, and the company would eat whatever loss insurance didn't cover. And he'd done as he was told.

Except after the third such shipment, he'd begun to dig around on his own time, trying to figure out where the missing engine blocks could have ended up. Engine blocks weren't exactly a hot commodity that invited theft, and that invited questions. The last truckload had run into some kind of trouble between Epping and Boston, and the driver turned up dead three days later in a marsh outside Ipswich, Massachusetts. And yet, the bill of lading for the shipping company, a newly purchased subsidiary of Cabot Industries, had confirmed receipt of the shipment at the pier in Boston on time, but delivery in Israel had never taken place. No one seemed to know who had actually been driving the truck when it unloaded its cargo on the pier in Boston. And no one had any record of the crates being offloaded in Israel or anywhere else.

The insurance claim had been filed and paid, but before Kinney could dig any deeper, he'd been given his marching orders. Along with most of the shipping staff under his management.

In two apparently unrelated incidents just months after the last of the lost shipments, Blair Cabot's second in command had committed suicide, and the head of accounting for Cabot Industries had been killed in a mugging in South Boston. The accountant's death was considered random, bad place, bad timing, but the Executive Director had appeared to have a good life, a wife he adored, two teenage sons doing well in school, and no financial problems. No reason for the suicide was ever determined, and if it had actually been a homicide, no suspects had ever been questioned. At least, as far as David Kinney knew.

Ash wondered how he could parlay any of this into rumors that held enough water to dampen Cabot's campaign. He read through his notes again, jotting down comments in the margins. Then he sat back, lips pursed in thought.

An announcement crackled through the speakers that the flight was being held, waiting for several passengers on a connecting flight that had been delayed in Chicago due to bad weather. Ash whipped out his cell phone and hunted through his contacts for the retired detective from Boston PD he'd met at a gay rally in DC four years back. Perhaps it would be productive to dig into the investigations surrounding these three seemingly separate deaths. The mugging had been in South Boston, the suicide in Andover, Massachusetts, and the truck driver had been found on the north shore. If three different police departments had done the investigating and nothing had triggered a wider involvement, perhaps something important had been missed?

The chance acquaintance answered his phone, and Ash introduced himself. They spent a few minutes catching up and talking trivialities, then Ash got to the point. Talking fast and persuasively. Nodding from time to time as if his listener could see him.

A half a dozen new passengers arrived breathless and harried looking, and the flight attendant walked down the aisle asking everyone to turn off all electronic devices preparatory to take off. Ash glanced at the woman and made a gesture that he would comply in a moment. He listened to the man on the other end for another half minute. A smile tugged at the corners of his mouth.

"So? Think there's anything to it?"

Twenty-six

"Are you responsible for this?" Matt Steele pointed at the screen of his laptop and glared at his campaign manager. Rick had stopped by Matt's house unexpectedly, only moments after Matt had seen the tweet his brother-in-law had called to give him a heads-up on.

Rick approached Matt's chair and bent over to peer at the computer screen.

SAVVYDETECTIVE: Old records for Cabot Enterprises reveal shady shipping deals and mysterious deaths - http://tbg.98.dec/24Mjts37.

"What is this?" Rick straightened. A frown marred his brow.

"That's what I was asking you," Matt replied, trying to keep his cool. He and Rick had fought over revealing Rolly's dirty laundry, and Rick hadn't been happy to be overruled, so Matt figured maybe Rick just didn't ask permission before starting rumors about Blair Cabot.

"I don't know anything about it," Rick reiterated vehemently. "Did you check out the link?"

"I did. It's to an article in *The Boston Globe* from nineteen ninety-eight." Matt clicked on another screen, then stood up and handed his campaign manager the laptop. "Might as well read the whole thing."

Rick took the laptop and began to scan through the article. Then his eyes widened and returned to the top of the page, and he began reading more carefully. A moment later, he sank into Matt's vacated chair with a low whistle.

"This is incredible. How come we never heard about any of this?" Rick glanced up at Matt, then back at the computer. "Three deaths and a missing shipment, and it never occurred to anyone they might be connected?" Rick began reading aloud, "'*Cabot Industries seems plagued with misfortune, but the owner and CEO, Blair Cabot, assures us that his company will get through this and come out stronger. He is setting up trust funds for the children of the slain men, including those of his COO who took his own life.*' Sure sounds smoky to me."

"So, you really didn't start this?" Matt sat down on the sofa opposite Rick.

"I wish I had!" Rick sounded as if he were relishing the possibilities. "If any of this can be traced to some underhanded stuff going on in Cabot's company, it could slow him down. Hell, even if it's nothing but circumstance and rumor, it could throw a monkey wrench into the campaign. I bet TJ is crapping his pants right now!"

Rick looked back at the computer and read the fourteen-year-old news article again. Matt studied his manager and decided Rick really hadn't had a hand in this latest deal. He might be singing off a different page than Matt was, but Rick had never given Matt reason to think Rick would go behind his back.

For a fleeting moment, Matt considered leveling with Rick about the date to appear on *The Scoop* tomorrow morning. Then he dismissed it. Rick would be furious. He might as well be furious when it was too late to talk Matt out of it. Always easier to ask for forgiveness than permission.

Matt heard the doorbell chime, but didn't get up. Zack or someone else would answer the door, and if it was for him, they'd come get him.

"So what brought you over here? I didn't think I'd see you before tomorrow afternoon in Chicago."

Rick looked up, his face blank. As if he had no idea why he had come. Then his expression cleared. He reached into his jacket pocket and drew out a stack of index cards. "I forgot to give you these." He handed them to Matt. "Bios on the folk we'll be meeting tomorrow."

"Sir?"

Matt glanced up to see Zack standing in the doorway.

"There's a young woman here to see you. An Annie Santos? She seems upset."

Matt got to his feet. "Show her in." As Zack moved back toward the front hall, Matt glanced down at Rick and removed the computer from his lap. "I won't keep you." Whatever Annie was upset about, it didn't involve Rick. Matt wondered why it even involved him, rather than Thanh. Suddenly his heart stuttered, and then beat harder. What if something had happened to Thanh?

He wanted to rush out into the hall and reassure himself, but he refrained. Rick tugged his pant legs down, then headed for the door with nothing more than a brief wave. Matt suspected he would spend the night Googling everything he could find on the subject of Blair Enterprises and the events of nineteen ninety-eight. A moment later, Annie entered and Rick was forgotten.

"Senator Steele, thank you for seeing me."

Matt frowned. "I thought I told you to call me Matt?"

"M-Matt, sir. I need your help." Annie grabbed his hand and clung as if she were in need of physical support as well.

"Thanh?" Matt barely got the name past his lips. "Is Thanh all right?"

Annie hesitated, then flushed. "As—as far as I know. He—I haven't seen him since last night."

Matt experienced a sudden flood of relief. Whatever Annie had come for, it didn't involve serious injury or trouble for Thanh. He felt magnanimous. "Tell me why you've come, then. I'll do whatever I can."

Matt drew the young woman over to the small sofa and pressed her down onto it. He took the seat opposite and waited. Now that she had his attention, she wrung her hands as if undecided, but then squared her shoulders and lifted her chin.

"This is embarrassing." Annie flushed under her tanned skin and squirmed as if she were uncomfortable. "I got myself in a kind of a bind. I was working for Mr. Cabot's campaign. You see, I thought he was the answer to our economic problems. But—" she emitted a short humorless bark of laughter. "God! I can't believe how deluded I was. Anyway, to make a long story short, and please, I hope you won't detest me. It's partly why I wouldn't tell Thanh anything. I couldn't bear it if he hated me."

She was babbling, but beneath the nervousness, Matt sensed a desperate urgency and a lot of fear. "Annie, slow down. No one is going to hate you. Least of all, Thanh. He loves you very much, and I doubt there's anything you could do or say that would change that."

Annie nodded and met Matt's gaze. "But he might not want anything to do with me. If he knew everything."

"Maybe you're selling him short. He's probably very hurt if he thinks you don't feel you can trust him."

"I do trust him. I'm just afraid he's going to hate me when he finds out."

She was talking in circles. They were never going to get to the bottom of the problem at this rate. Matt glanced at the clock. "Maybe you should just tell me what it is that has you so scared, and then we can see what to do about it."

"My mother has disappeared. And it's my fault. I wouldn't tell them anything, and they've taken her. I'm sure of it."

"Who's taken her?"

"TJ Smith. Blair Cabot's campaign manager."

Matt felt an icy river of premonition sluice through him. "Why on earth would TJ want to abduct your mother?"

"Because I wouldn't rat you out."

"Rat me out?" Premonition turned to confusion and dread.

"It's a long story."

"Well, perhaps you need to start at the beginning so I can understand."

Annie nodded. "But I need to hurry. My mother might…" Annie broke off and tears brimmed in her eyes.

Matt took the young woman's hands in his in an effort to calm her. "Take it easy, Annie. The sooner you tell me the whole story, the sooner we can figure out how to fix this problem."

Matt tried to keep himself calm and not leap to the conclusion that this was about him and the scandal for which he was responsible.

"Okay." She drew in a long breath and let out a shaky sigh. "I was working for Mr. Cabot, and Mr. Smith found out that I was seeing Thanh. So, then he coerced me into letting my relationship with Thanh get serious enough so I would get invited into your home. He wanted me to spy on you.

"I didn't want to, and I told him no. But then he threatened to have my mother deported if I didn't do as he asked. My mother's health isn't that good. She'd never make it on her own. I couldn't let them send her back to Vietnam. You have to see that. I just couldn't. But then I fell in love with Thanh, and I couldn't—I couldn't go through with spying either." She sucked in another shaky breath and looked at Matt with pleading in her eyes. "I just prayed that I wouldn't find out anything worth telling. Only, then Thanh brought me to Maine."

"I see." The leap in Matt's head hadn't been that far off the mark. This *was* about him. Annie had gotten an earful over the weekend. She must have overheard some part of the revelations about Thanh. "So you know I am Thanh's father?"

She nodded, tears still running down her face. "I heard Ben talking with your wife. I didn't mean to listen, but he was yelling, and I couldn't not hear him. Afterward, I realized there was a lot he left out. But even so, I knew enough to really hurt you and your family. I didn't know what to do. I didn't think there was anything I could do except refuse to tell TJ anything. And I didn't. Honest, I didn't tell him anything. But now my mother is gone, and I think he has her. He's been trying to call me on my cell, but I refused to answer because I don't know what to tell him. He came to my apartment yesterday. He said he was going to visit my mother while I thought about it. I begged him not to, but she's gone, and I can't think of anywhere else she could be."

Dismay pierced Matt's heart. How many more people were going to be hurt by that one transgression committed so long ago? But he didn't have time to dwell on self-recrimination. Annie's mother had to be found, and found quickly.

"What's your mother's name?"

"Cam Luong. She calls herself Mrs. Cam Luong, but she's not married. She never has been. When she came to this country expecting dad to marry her, she found out he already had a wife. But he acknowledged me and got my citizenship established, and he supported us both. He supports her still, but she never got legal status. She could have gotten it back then, but she didn't. And TJ said he'd get her sent back to Vietnam."

"Well, he won't. And we'll find her. I promise." Matt gave Annie's shoulder a squeeze.

Matt started to rise, but Annie caught his hand and stopped him.

"TJ warned me not to go to Thanh. He said if Thanh helped to hide her it could get him deported. That's the other reason why I couldn't tell Thanh what was wrong. He—TJ…"

"TJ what?" Matt kneaded Annie's shoulder encouragingly. "What else did he threaten?"

"He said I shouldn't tell you either, but I didn't know who else to go to. My father would do anything to help. He even offered to marry my mother, only she wouldn't agree. But I can't find him either."

"Why did TJ tell you not to come to me?"

"B-because if you helped to hide her, it would be illegal, and he'd see that you never got elected."

"Trust me, Annie. Neither TJ nor Blair Cabot can hurt me because of your mother. I'm glad you came to me. Now, if you'll just give me a minute, I need to make a few phone calls."

Matt crossed to his desk and dialed Murdock. As succinctly as he could, he told Murdock what the problem was and told him to turn over every rock he could and find out what Smith and Cabot were up to. He also asked him to call the INS and feel around to see if Mrs. Luong had already been turned in to them. "And call me as soon as you know anything."

Matt returned to Annie. "Megan and I have a proven remedy for problems." He held out his hand, and Annie took it.

She followed him through the great room to the hall and then to the kitchen, where he invited her to take a seat while he busied himself filling an electric kettle with water and turning it on to heat.

Annie had no idea what he was about, but his calm take-charge attitude gave her a sense of peace for the first time in days. His confident assurance filled her with renewed hope.

In a few minutes, he returned to the table with two steaming cups of hot chocolate.

"Cocoa?" Annie asked, perplexed.

"Megan swears hot chocolate will fix anything." Matt took the seat opposite hers and took a sip from his mug. "Try it."

Annie brought her own mug to her lips and sipped. He'd been thoughtful enough to add just enough milk so it didn't burn the tongue. She took a bigger sip and felt the comforting warmth slide down her throat.

When she looked back at him, he was studying her with a concerned expression in his eyes.

"I'm sorry you've had to deal with this. Sorrier than I can put into words."

Annie wondered why he was apologizing.

"And by tomorrow this time, neither you nor your mother will have anything to fear. It is, as you said, a long story. For both of us. Mine began thirty-five years ago. And tomorrow the world will know most of it. I'm being interviewed by Jeff Hall on *The Scoop* tomorrow morning. And I'm afraid Thanh will be living in a fishbowl, at least until the next big scandal erupts. Unfortunately, the press probably won't stop there. They'll likely be chasing you around asking for your opinion as well"

"It's none of my business!" Annie was horrified that her opinion might be solicited. Whatever had happened between Thanh's mother and Senator Steele was none of her business. And who was she to judge, anyway? The story of her own birth was just as questionable. "I—I'm not judging you, sir."

Matt took another long swallow of his hot chocolate, then set it aside. "The rest of the country will, though. And probably not favorably, for the most part. I *am* Thanh's father. And I *did* leave him behind in Vietnam. In my defense, I didn't know I'd gotten his mother pregnant, and I had no way of knowing because Thanh was conceived in a moment of grief and poor judgment only days before I left Saigon for good."

"There were thousands of babies left behind when the Americans left." Annie jumped to Matt's defense. She knew quite a few of them personally. "I'm one of the lucky few who ever knew who my father was. And most of our mothers did what they did because they wanted to, not because they were forced into it. So that hardly makes you a…"

"What I did was still wrong. And I am so sorry you got caught up in this mess."

Matt Steele's humility touched Annie deeply, and she began to understand why Thanh thought so highly of him. And loved him. If she hadn't been so consumed with her own guilty secrets, she might have realized before now, how things had changed over the weekend. Thanh must have only just found out that Matt was his father, but unlike Ben, Thanh hadn't been angry. Connecting with his father had completed something in Thanh. She'd seen the new but unexpressed happiness in his face and sensed it in his demeanor. She'd just been too overwhelmed with her own problems to wonder about it.

Annie brought her mug to her lips and took another swallow. She had never met a man in such a revered position who seemed so capable and yet so humble at the same time. The realization warmed her as much as the hot chocolate.

~ * ~

Thanh left work on Tuesday in a wholly different state of mind than he had on Monday. Yesterday everything had been right with his world, and he had been filled with anticipation and joy.

Yesterday, when he left work, he had been filled with the wonder of having a family for the first time in his life. He had a father who acknowledged him with tears in his eyes and love in his heart. He had a brother who welcomed Thanh in spite of the shock and hurt he blamed on their father. He had a stepmother who accepted him into the family regardless of the circumstances of his birth. And a sister who made him feel like he had belonged all his life. Thanh had a family that did not consider him as nothing more than the dust of life as any fatherless boy in Vietnam was viewed.

He had a woman who loved him, as well. A woman he could envision spending the rest of his life with. And starting his own family. Giving his new father grandsons and granddaughters to love and spoil.

Thanh had known something was bothering Annie, but she had told him she loved him, and he had believed they could fix whatever haunted her. He had met Mr. Santos and Mrs. Luong, and they both liked and approved of him. It would have been good to have in-laws he liked, who liked him in return. Yesterday he had been on top of the world.

But today things were very different. He still had his new family. That had not been taken from him. But Annie and he had argued. Their first argument had left him uncertain and more than a little worried. He had begged her to trust him, and she would not. Perhaps he should not have left as he had. Perhaps he should have made love to her as she so desperately wanted him to. Perhaps he was expecting too much of her.

Falling in love was easy. At least it had been easy for him. But trust was harder to learn. They had not known each other all that long when he considered it. Perhaps he should have given her the space to keep her secrets instead of rushing off in a fit of ill-humor and ill-disguised disappointment?

The thought of returning to his apartment to spend another evening alone seemed impossible. Facing the same four walls he had stared at for hours while sleep would not come the night before was not a pleasant prospect. His heart ached with longing. Perhaps he should return to Annie's apartment and apologize? But apologize for what? What would he tell her? Would she even listen?

While the perhapses and what-ifs still jangled in his head, he found himself pulling into his father's driveway. Another first in his life—he was not alone. He had someone to share his hurt and confusion with. *If only my father is home and not off on the campaign trail.*

Thanh parked in front of the closed garage doors and sat in his car wondering if he should burden his father with this when he clearly had enough worries of his own. Bharat had already climbed from the car and stood with one hand on the roof glancing up the street, then down. Perhaps Thanh should tell him to climb back in. But he did not. An urge far stronger made him get out and head toward the front door and help.

A new agent Thanh had not met before opened the door at Thanh's knock.

"I need to see Senator Steele." Thanh had wanted to say he needed to see his father, but he could not reveal that relationship to someone he did not know.

"I'm Zack Corsair, the senator's new agent. And I believe you must be Thanh Davis. Do you have any identification? I hate to ask, but it's required."

Thanh dug his wallet out and handed over his driver's license. The agent nodded, handed the license back and beckoned him in. He made a motion to have Thanh wait, and turned toward the kitchen.

Zack stuck his head around the partially open kitchen door. "Sorry to bother you again sir, but Thanh Davis is here to…"

Before Zack's announcement was completely out of his mouth Thanh shouldered his way past the agent.

"Dad! I need to talk to you!" Thanh jerked to a stop in the middle of the floor, his troubled eyes shifting from his father to Annie. "Annie! You are here?"

Matt Steele got to his feet. "I think you two have a few things to sort out, so I'll leave you to do it." He reached across the table to touch Annie's cheek with a gentle finger. "You can trust my son. I did, and I'll never be sorry. Tell him everything." Matt straightened and moved toward Thanh.

"I'll be in my study if you still need to talk. And tell Annie I'll let her know as soon as I hear anything." Matt put a hand on Thanh's shoulder and squeezed it reassuringly. Then he left.

~ * ~

Asher Elliot set the phone into the cradle carefully. He was grinning like a jack-o-lantern and feeling even happier. Revenge was sweet indeed. He woke his computer up and logged onto Twitter, then opened another new account and spent considerable time creating an entire life history for his new man. One that would lend credence to the rumor he wanted to start. He sat back and considered what to write. Finally he bent over the keys and started typing again.

COLUMBO: Re: Cabot Intl-COO death not suicide. Was it the Colonel in the study w a gun?

Twenty-seven

"God give me the courage to go through with this." Matt's whispered words hung, unchallenged in the crisp air-conditioned chill of the Green Room.

Edgy and impatient, he paced. Where, he wondered, had his confidence gone? Only the compelling conviction that had driven him to accept this interview in the first place remained.

Everything about this impersonal, low-ceilinged room felt like it was closing in on him—the huge cluttered cork-board, the uncomfortable vinyl furniture, the glare of the fluorescent light, the bare floor that echoed his footsteps with hollow loneliness.

Abruptly he sat, folding onto the smaller of the couches with a sigh. He started to rub his sweat-soaked palms on his knees, then stopped himself before he could destroy the creased perfection of his gray slacks.

Christ, he hadn't felt so nervous in his entire career. Nervous? Now that was understating the situation. Terrified more nearly hit the mark. The past two days had been so incredibly chaotic he'd not had time to worry about the interview with Jeff Hall.

Now, in spite of his conviction that he was doing the right thing, apprehension clawed at his insides.

An insistent thudding noise made his head hurt, and Matt wondered why Zack wasn't checking to see what was causing it. Then he realized the sound he heard was the pumping of his own heart echoing in his head.

"Fifteen minutes!" A harried voice outside the door cut into his spiraling dread.

I've gotta get a grip. If I get elected, I could very well end up having to deal with far more calamitous and frightening things than this.

He got to his feet and then stepped into the adjoining bathroom to wash his hands. He dried them with a paper towel from a stack piled haphazardly on top of the dispenser and gazed at his reflection in the mirror above the sink. The resemblance to both his sons struck him with a visceral intensity that caught him off guard. Ben had Matt's blonde hair and fair skin, the same square chin and his dimple. Thanh had Matt's eyes. It seemed so obvious now that Matt wondered how come everyone hadn't guessed Thanh's parentage already. But the realization calmed him and renewed his conviction that he needed to be here.

The one thing he'd promised his constituents, right from the first political race he'd been in, had been honesty. He would not promise his constituents one thing to get elected, then pursue a different course once in office. Nor would he pay lip service to things people wanted to hear if he didn't believe they were right. He had an obligation to be just as honest about his personal life. About the man he professed to be.

He ran thoughtless fingers through his carefully arranged hair. A lock fell across his brow, and he tried to push it back, but it refused to stay. He thought about Eve. She'd be sitting in the front row, silent but faithful in her support. He dragged a slow uneven breath into his lungs to collect himself. Then he returned to the Green Room.

Zack stood with the door half open, addressing someone outside in the hall. Matt's heart began to race. Fifteen minutes couldn't have passed yet. He closed his eyes and offered up another plea for composure. When he opened them again, Ben stood just inside the door, and Zack must have stepped out into the hall.

"Ben!" Matt's anxiety was suddenly overshadowed by surprise. "How did you know I was here?"

"Mom told me. I drove over because I knew I had to see you before you went on the air," Ben began. He fidgeted with the flaps on his blazer pockets.

"Well, I appreciate the support, but you didn't need…"

"Dad," Ben interrupted. "I was wrong that night when I was yelling at you in Maine. I…" Ben struggled to go on. His troubled gaze held Matt's with difficulty. "I wanted to tell you…" Ben broke off again and swallowed, his Adam's apple bobbing in his young throat.

"It's okay, Ben." Matt put a hand on his son's shoulder. "You already apologized. And besides, it isn't you who did anything wrong."

"Oh, but I did! I rushed to judgment. We hardly ever agree on stuff lately, but you've always been the perfect dad." Ben's words began tumbling faster, like water finding a breach in a dam. "You never missed my games. You were there for all my big events and for most of my small ones. You helped with my homework, you coached my little league team, went camping with me when I was in boy scouts. You never lost patience with my vacillation over choosing a college and drove me to every single campus, however inconvenient it turned out to be. You did it all, and instead of being grateful, I resented it. I felt like I'd never be able to live up to you. Then suddenly you weren't perfect anymore, but I couldn't accept that either." Ben tugged at his unaccustomed tie. "I owed you a chance to explain. You always gave me the benefit of the doubt, but I wasn't big enough to give you the same consideration. I was a jerk."

"You were upset," Matt offered, horrified at this picture of an unapproachable man Ben was painting.

"Well, so were you, but you kept your cool. I wouldn't have blamed you if you'd decked me, but you didn't. You let me say unforgivable things, and you didn't even try to defend yourself."

"Ben, there's no need…"

"Megan tried to reason with me," Ben forged on, unheeding "She's going to make a great lawyer, by the way. And Thanh's a better man than I am."

"Don't be so hard on yourself, Ben. I don't blame you for feeling betrayed and shocked. My behavior all those years ago deserved both."

Ben winced. "But I had no right." He jerked at his tie again.

"You know, Ben, I hated my mother for months when I first found out what the word bastard meant." Matt realized he'd never told another living soul about that brief but miserable part of his youth.

"It's not the same thing," Ben insisted. "I'm not a little kid. I know what it's like to be twenty and horny as hell. I know how easy it is to forget everything else when something or someone gets you totally turned on. Only thing I don't know is what it was like to be you, in that place, at that time. I can't even begin to imagine what you might have been living through, and I'll probably never know what combat does to a man. I had no right to judge you. You're twice the man I'll ever be."

Matt squeezed Ben's shoulder, completely speechless at his son's sweeping apology and acceptance. As he gazed into his son's eyes, Matt saw a new maturity in them, and realized they were equals. His son was accepting him, not just as his father and mentor, the parent who sired and raised him, but as a friend. Not perfect, not always in charge, sometimes vulnerable, often wrong, but worthy of love and understanding. And worth admiring. Matt's heart swelled with the unexpected gift.

"I'm sorry, Dad," Ben whispered. Then he shrugged away from the hand that still kneaded his shoulder with painful intensity, and wrapped his arms about Matt in a bear hug that had been a long time coming.

They stood, locked in a fierce embrace without words. Matt felt redemption and peace settle over him. "I love you, Ben. Thank you for coming today. You can't know how much it means to me, and I don't know if I can put it into words. Not nearly as well as you just did, anyway."

Ben loosened his grip and stepped back. A faint smile touched his lips, and the anguish was gone from his eyes. "I love you, too, Dad."

"Time!" The warning accompanied a sharp rap on the door.

"I'll walk with you," Ben offered.

"I'd appreciate that." Matt put one arm about Ben's shoulders as they started down the hall with Zack leading the way. "I admire the courage it took to tell the perfect dad he wasn't perfect after all, but that you still love him anyway."

"Not half so much as I respect the courage it took for you to tell the truth about Thanh. No one would ever have known if you had kept it to yourself."

"I'd have known."

"That's the part I respect most," Ben said as they stopped walking. "You're putting everything on the line for a principle. I don't know if I could do that."

Matt smiled at Ben. "When you believe in something enough, you dare anything. And when your day comes, I know you'll find the courage, too."

"Go slay the dragon, Dad. I believe in you."

~ * ~

Matt stepped into the circle of light and shook hands with Jeff Hall, then settled into his chair. Eve had chosen his clothes, a soft cable-knit sweater that reflected the blue of his eyes with dove gray trousers and loafers.

"It makes you look like the boy next door," she'd said, kissing him before they left their room.

"I'm hardly a boy," he'd reminded her.

"But you want to look approachable, right?"

Apparently it had worked for Ben. Perhaps it would make a difference to the rest of the world.

As Jeff Hall reeled off an impressive sounding bio, Matt took a deep breath. *So, here I am. My family is whole. My heart's at peace. But I've no script, and the best interviewer in the country is sitting next to me, ready to take me apart. I'm ready to admit my mistakes, and get them behind me. But then I'm praying Hall will give me a chance to lay out our economic plan and challenge the American people to follow us.*

~ * ~

"I quit!" Rick Winfield announced as Matt cleared security at O'Hare International Airport and entered the main concourse. Several heads swiveled in their direction. Those that hadn't already been focused on Matt as he came into view, anyway. Zack and Joe stuck close at his side, and Jack forged the way ahead like the cowcatcher on a high-speed locomotive.

Getting onto the plane in New York had been pretty much standard, but at that time, only a few people knew what had been revealed in his interview with Jeff Hall. The time it took for his plane to arrive in Chicago had changed all that, and the clamor was deafening. Matt tuned it out. But he couldn't tune Rick out.

"I'm outta here!"

"Please don't say that. I need you."

"You don't need me. You don't even listen to me. Or ask my advice. If you had, I'd have told you to keep your mouth shut about your bastard." A vein throbbed in Rick's temple, and his face was bright red. Rick had a volatile temper, and Matt had seen him furiously angry on several occasions, but never like this. Never with so little awareness of the fact that he was throwing a very public temper tantrum. Never with so little regard for the consequences.

"Rick, can we discuss this at the hotel?"

"No! I'm through discussing anything with you. I'm flying back to DC in half an hour, and my formal resignation will be on your desk tomorrow."

Rick almost threw the briefcase he carried at Jack. "Here's everything you need to carry on without me." Then he stalked off.

Cameras clicked and whirred as the hovering crowd of reporters captured every nuance of the episode to be aired on every television station, discussed by every talking head and rehashed by every political pundit from country yokels to the big names in New York. Matt had known his unvarnished confession would reap a whirlwind. He'd known a succinct outline of the economic plan he and Hal supported and were prepared to fight for would stir up a hornet's nest, especially in his own party. And he'd known Rick would be outraged, but he hadn't been prepared for Rick's defection. That hurt.

Matt allowed himself to be hustled through the airport, ignoring everything and everyone as he tried to absorb this setback. He felt a hand on his back. Joe Venuto's, steering him past a row of barricades lined with a cheering mob of people. Zack's shoulder bumped against Matt's as Zack fended off several reporters who would have accosted Matt before he reached the automatic doors. Then they were out of the airport, moving toward the waiting car.

It was cool in Chicago. The sharp air filled Matt's lungs. He took another deep breath and took note of his surroundings again. More reporters, but farther away, not a threat. Not yet. Terry stood by the car, holding the rear door open. Matt nodded a *thank you*, then slid into the seat. Jack followed him, and Zack jumped in front.

"You've been promoted," Matt informed Jack as the car pulled away from the curb. "You always wanted to be in charge. Right?"

"Hey!" Jack's voice registered both dismay and sympathy. "I'm just the media jockey. I don't know anything about running a campaign. You've got the wrong guy."

Matt met Jack's pleading brown gaze and understood the panic filling his breast. "It's pretty much on autopilot. You've been close enough to all the planning. You'll do fine."

"What about Ken McColl? He's the strategist. He'd be a better choice than me."

"And his wife is due any day now. It's been a difficult pregnancy, and she needs him close by. I'm sure he'll be readily available by phone to answer any questions that come up that you can't handle."

"But…"

"Jack. Do I have to beg? Or offer up my firstborn grandchild?"

"Look, Matt, after that interview with Jeff Hall, you're going to need me twenty-four-seven running interference with the press. You need me to keep this story from spiraling out of control and to counter the spin everyone else will be putting on your economic plan. You don't need me running the campaign."

"Then who do you suggest?"

"Murdock."

Murdock! Matt pictured the wiry black with the mischievous eyes and athletic grace, and realized Jack was right. Reuben Murdock was technically in charge of advance operations, but he coordinated both Matt's and Eve's schedules, dovetailed those with Hal and his wife, accompanied Eve when she was on the road alone, manned the fort when Matt was out of town and still had the energy and smarts to fix anything Matt needed fixing. He'd been Rick's right hand man, although never in so many words. And always with a smile and an *On-it-Boss* attitude.

"You're right."

"Of course, I'm right." Jack breathed an obvious sigh of relief. "I'll get him on the next plane out here." He slipped his cell out of its belt holster and hit a speed dial number.

~ * ~

SAVVYDETECTIVE: disagreemt over arms smglng deal! //RT @ COLUMBO: Re: Cabot Intl-COO death not suicide. Was it the Colonel in the study w a gun?

~ * ~

POLBRAT: Col Cabot -Whats w arms smglng? Isnt that treason?

~ * ~

TJ barged into Blair Cabot's private office without knocking "Who's Colonel Cabot?"

"Colonel Cabot?" Blair glanced up, a blank look of incomprehension on his face.

"This Colonel Cabot!" TJ slapped a sheaf of computer printouts onto Blair's desk.

Blair shuffled through them, then looked up again. His brow still furrowed in confusion. "I don't know any Colonel Cabot."

"Well, he appears to be connected to Cabot International. And it's being suggested that he killed your once-upon-a-time Chief Operating Officer. That the death wasn't a suicide as determined at the time, *and* that it was a cover-up for some kind of shady arms shipments."

Blair went suddenly ashen, and TJ felt the shock of that involuntary admission clear down to his toes. He'd been so sure that this whole Twitter thing was a hoax.

"There are no colonels connected with Cabot International. And Bill Candace did commit suicide." Blair stood, clearly pulling himself together and trying to get a handle on things.

"Then who the hell are they referring to?" TJ did his best to keep his voice even, but inside he was appalled. More than appalled. He'd believed in this man. He'd put his neck on the line for him, done things he wasn't too proud of. Like blackmailing one young woman and threatening an old one. Outing Rolly hadn't bothered him. He had no patience for the entire gay movement. It was an aberrant lifestyle that sickened him. But leaning on Annie Santos had been another thing. He'd done it for Blair Cabot.

He'd done it because he honestly believed Blair Cabot was the best man for the job. He'd done it because it was time to break the grip of the two party system. He'd done it because Matt Steele had been close to overtaking Cabot, and TJ was determined not to let it happen. But this?

TJ's gut churned with outrage.

If this had any truth to it at all, it would destroy everything.

"Who is the colonel?" TJ spit the question out between gritted teeth.

"I'm telling you…"

TJ's cell chimed, announcing a new tweet alert. TJ glanced down at it and felt the blood drain from his own face so fast he felt suddenly faint.

STREETWISE: OMG! And he's rning for Pres? //RT @ POLBRAT: Col Cabot -Whats w arms smglng? Isnt that treason?

TJ couldn't believe this was happening. Silently he held his cell out for Blair to read. When a ready denial didn't spring to Blair's lips, TJ sank into a chair, his legs no longer strong enough to hold him up. He closed his eyes and wished the black cloud hovering on his periphery would swallow him up.

"I can explain." Blair's voice seemed to come from a long way off.

"Explain what?" TJ opened his eyes and glared at Blair. "Explain why you never thought this would come to light? Explain how it's not really what it seems? Does it even matter?"

Twenty-eight

Thanh sat in his father's comfortable recliner in the den of the Steele home in McLean, Virginia monitoring the television, the computer and the phones. Annie, exhausted from a night of worry with no word about or from her mother, had fallen asleep on the couch opposite him.

Thanh got up, set his laptop aside and crossed to the couch. He touched Annie's face gently with the back of his fingers. He worried about the dark circles under her eyes and the pale look of her skin. Usually a warm honey tone, her flesh appeared far too pale, and he could see blue veins in her temples. He removed a throw blanket from the back of the couch and covered her with it, tucking it around her with care.

He thought about the emotional scene they had lived through just last night. He had been horrified by the level of anxiety and fear she had tried to shoulder on her own and wished he had pressed her harder to confide in him. Finding that she had kept it to herself because she loved him too much to chance losing him had filled him with conflicting emotions. Dismay that she had not believed he would still love her if he knew her weakness had been liberally mixed with the exhilaration of knowing his love for her was returned with such intensity.

Once her story had been told, however, and his reassurances accepted, they had gotten busy making phone calls and tracking down leads suggested by Thanh's father and the man named Murdock that Matt had called on for help. With something to do and someone to share the worry, Annie had begun to recover some of her usual resilience.

Thanh bent and kissed her lightly on the forehead. She stirred but did not waken. He returned to his chair and settled back in, hauling the laptop onto his knees to restart the interview he had already watched once before. It was a lengthy interview that had been posted to a Facebook account two hours ago by a user named ManFriday. Fortunately, Thanh had thought to download it to his laptop, because half an hour after he had discovered it, the posting had been taken down.

Thanh glanced back at the television, but nothing new was happening there. Then he picked up his cell phone, checking it yet again to make sure he had not missed the call he was anxiously awaiting. If it had not been for that call and worry over Annie's mother, Thanh would have been on the phone with Ben, or Megan or any one of his friends discussing the mind-boggling and totally scandalous events unfolding in the news.

Thanh and Annie had spent the night at the Steele home because it had been so late when they finished tracking down all the leads on the list provided by Rueben Murdock. Murdock had stopped in to check on their progress around noon, but then Jack had called ordering Murdock to get out to Chicago on the double. If it had been up to Thanh, they would have involved the police by now, but Annie had been frantic to avoid that option. Now, considering the appalling allegations coming out about Blair Cabot, Thanh wondered if perhaps he should call nine-one-one in spite of Annie's pleas.

Except Thanh was praying that Murdock's last hunch might turn out to be right. After Murdock had called on his way to a meet-and-greet in Chicago with Thanh's father, Thanh had made another flurry of calls. Now he was hoping against hope that a suite booked in the name of Mr. Anthony Santos at the Riviera Hotel and Casino in Las Vegas meant Annie's father was checked in there. And that he knew where her mother was as well.

A reporter in a green windbreaker appeared on the TV. Behind him a scene from somewhere in Manhattan, judging by the NYPD insignia on the door of the police cruiser the reporter was standing next to. Beyond the reporter, the balding, paunchy form of TJ Smith wearing a wrinkled trench coat and a day's growth of beard could be seen being escorted toward a navy blue Yukon with dozens of flashes going off as reporters chased after him. Thanh turned the sound up to hear what was being said.

"...Cabot has not been seen at any of his scheduled campaign stops. His campaign manager, TJ Smith, was tracked down at the New York headquarters of the Cabot campaign twenty minutes ago and asked to go in for questioning. He is not, we are told, a person of interest at this time, but it is hoped he will be able to shed some light on his candidate's whereabouts. Smith insists he has no idea where Blair Cabot is and has not seen him since early this morning when Mr. Smith says he confronted Mr. Cabot about the flurry of posts to Twitter, Facebook and other social networking sites. Mr. Smith refused to answer any further questions from the press, but perhaps he will be more forthcoming with the FBI.

"That's all from here, Roger." The reporter with the microphone signed off, and Roger Stephens, the talking head from the local station, returned. Thanh hit mute again. He had heard it all already.

All that anyone knew for sure, that is. And a lot more that was pure conjecture with nothing to back it up. Pretty much nothing else had been on the air since the story broke.

The original tweet had suggested that three deaths more than a decade ago might not have been as unconnected as had originally been assumed. Thanh wondered who the colonel was. He had Googled Cabot Industries but had been unable to find any colonel anyone connected to the company. Blair Cabot himself had never been in the military so the insinuations that he was the colonel were probably misleading. Thanh had then Googled Colonel Mustard when he had seen that name appear in another tweet, but the only Colonel Mustard he had come up with was from a board game called *Clue*, which Thanh found totally confusing. Perhaps it was a cultural thing he did not understand.

A tweeter who went by the name of *Columbo* had sited four more murders possibly connected to the original three. All within a month of each other and all less than two months before Blair Cabot had announced his decision to run for president.

Thanh had gone to the various sites listed. With growing horror, he had read that the captain of the shipping company involved in the missing Cabot International shipments had died in a boating accident a little over two years ago. Then Thanh read the obituary of the captain's first mate, who had had a heart attack only two days before the captain had sailed out of Boston for a day trip on his personal yacht. A third article told of an undercover cop who had been working on a case involving illegal shipments of arms to known terrorist organizations. The cop had been struck by a hit-and-run driver and left for dead. Paralyzed and unable to speak, he now lived in a veteran's home in Chelsea, Massachusetts. The last article was about a customs agent from the Boston office of the US Customs Service, who had apparently had an accident while riding his mountain bike in New Hampshire. His body had not been found for almost a week so it was not known how long he might have suffered before dying of his injuries.

If all four men had been shot, perhaps their deaths might have been connected two years ago, but the apparent randomness had clouded the picture. Thanh could not believe it was just coincidence. All of the men had been intimately involved with the mystery surrounding the missing shipments from Cabot International. There had to be a connection, and it could not be good.

Thanh started the interview again. Officer Dalton was once a strapping man, over six feet and over two hundred pounds, judging by the photo of him in uniform taken three years previously. He was still over six feet, but in a wheelchair who could tell, and much of the once-muscular physique had wasted away. But he was a good-looking man, with intelligent gray eyes and a determined expression. He still could not speak, but apparently he had been rehabilitated to the point where he could communicate via a small computer device. And the computer-generated voice had a very damning story to tell.

Thanh had heard only the start of the story when his cell phone rang. He snatched it up and pressed it to his ear without taking the time to notice the caller ID.

"Hello."

"Thanh?" It was Tony Santos. *Thank God!*

"Where are you? Is Annie's mother with you?"

"She is, and we are truly sorry to have worried you all. Cam didn't think Annie would even notice she was gone so she didn't think it necessary to leave a message. Also, having met that TJ scoundrel, Cam didn't want to put Annie in the position of knowing anything until the knot was tied, just in case. Is Annie there?"

Thanh had already shoved the laptop onto the little table beside the recliner and gotten to his feet. He hurried to the couch and sat down, shoving his hip against Annie's sleeping form to make room for himself.

"Annie! Wake up. It is your dad." Annie stirred and stretched. Her eyes opened, but she looked dazed as if she had been dreaming. "It is your father, Annie."

Annie jerked to a sitting position and grabbed the phone from Thanh's hand, her eyes wide with apprehension. "Dad?"

As Annie listened to her father, Thanh watched her relax, her shoulders losing some of the tension they had carried for the last twenty-four hours. Then a small smile lifted the corners of her mouth, and she began nodding her head.

"Oh, Dad. I'm so glad. Can I talk to Mom? Congratulations, Mom....What?...No....Of course. I think it's wonderful....I love you. Tell Dad I love him, too. And thank you so much for calling. I was so worried about you....Yes, Mom. I'm really happy for you. You should know that. Love you." She touched the *End* button and handed Thanh his phone. She was beaming from ear to ear. "They got married after all."

"So I guessed." Thanh leaned over to capture her lips with his. Murdock was a genius. The Riviera of all places! With its casinos. And its wedding chapel.

Annie returned Thanh's kiss, slipping her arms around his neck and pulling him down as she sank back onto the sofa cushions. Thanh willingly followed. He could tell her about the rest of the news later.

~ * ~

Later turned out to be less than fifteen minutes. Thanh dragged himself back to sanity and pulled away from Annie, out of breath and thoroughly aroused with the phone jangling for a third time on the far side of the room. The house phone, which only moments before had gone to the answering machine when Thanh and Annie had ignored its second round of insistent ringing.

Thanh scrambled to his feet and hurried to pick up the phone before whoever was so determined to interrupt what had been a very enjoyable interlude got shuttled to voice mail a third time.

"Steele residence. This is Thanh." His voice sounded almost normal. At least he hoped it did.

"Turn on the television," Ben shouted in excitement.

"It is already on." Thanh glanced over at the big flat screen and nearly dropped the phone.

"Do you believe this?" Ben crowed in wicked delight.

"What is it?" Annie joined Thanh, tugging her clothing into some semblance of order.

"I do not think Blair Cabot or his evil henchman will be bothering you any more, Annie. They have far bigger problems to deal with." Thanh watched in utter amazement as the once impressive figure of Blair Cabot, his hands cuffed behind his back, was folded none-too-gently into the back seat of a dark sedan by a big man wearing a vest stenciled with the logo of the US Marshals' service.

"Why in cuffs?" Thanh asked of no one in particular.

Ben laughed again. "Hey, who's there? Is that Megan?"

"Megan is out. It is just Annie and me here."

"Did you find her mom?" Ben was instantly solicitous.

"Yes. In Las Vegas. I will never know how Murdock figured it out. Mrs. Luong changed her mind about marrying Annie's dad, and they are enjoying the hospitality of the honeymoon suite at the Riviera. A story with a happy ending."

"Well, put me on speaker then. Annie needs to share this."

Thanh held the phone away from his ear and found the button for speaker.

"Hey, Annie," Ben's voice came out slightly distorted but gleefully exuberant. "Good news about your mother. I'm glad they found her and all is well. And you are really, *really* never going to believe what happened to your guy."

"I am having trouble believing it, and I have been reading all the postings." Thanh continued to gape at the television.

"Cabot was arrested about twenty minutes ago," Ben reported cheerfully. "They dragged him off a South African Airways flight to Johannesburg. And when they searched him, they found he had another ticket, under an assumed name with a false passport. He was headed for Sudan."

"Did he resist arrest?" Thanh was still reeling from the idea of a man who might have been elected president in a matter of days being led away in handcuffs.

"Don't think so, but someone said the arresting marshal's brother was a civilian peacekeeper killed by a terrorist using a gun made in the US and sold illegally. The guy was probably more than happy to be shackling a man who could have been the one who organized the transporting of that gun. Probably why Cabot's head just happened to bounce off the roof of the car when he was being tucked inside, too. The bastard!"

Annie sank onto the ottoman, her face a study in utter shock. "I believed in him," she muttered. "How could I have been so mistaken?"

"Cheer up." Ben laughed. "You're in the right camp now. Just don't forget to vote for my dad next Tuesday. He's still got to beat Rolly Miller, and you can bet your last dollar Miller will be reclaiming most the votes he lost to Cabot a couple weeks ago. And then some, depending on how people react to my father's interview yesterday."

"You mean the story about Thanh?" Annie looked up at Thanh with worry lines creasing her brow.

"Well, that too, but I was thinking more about the economic upheaval dad has in mind. Well, I've got to get a move on. You'd think they might suspend classes in light of all the ruckus over Cabot, but they didn't. I gotta go."

Thanh pressed the speaker button and pulled the phone back to his ear. "Thanks for calling Ben. Sorry I did not answer the first time, but Annie and I were..." Thanh broke off, realizing he might have told his brother exactly what he had been up to if Annie had not been sitting right next to him. "Anyway. Thanks."

"Oh! I almost forgot. Everything *is* okay between you and Annie now. Right?"

Thanh hesitated. They had not told anyone yet. Not even his father who was back on the campaign trail. Nor had Annie mentioned it to her own parents during their brief conversation just a short while ago. But Ben was his brother.

"I was wondering if you would be my best man?"

Ben whooped. "Absotively! Congratulations, old man. Wow! That brings up something else. God, I'm going to be *so* late! I saw Dad at the studio before the Jeff Hall interview, and we had a good talk. A really good talk. But that's another story. Afterward, while we were waiting for his flight to Chicago, he told me you were passed out on the couch when he left, so he didn't get a chance to tell you himself. There's something he wants you to have. He hoped you might need it before he got back to DC again. So, if you go into his office and look on the shelf over his desk, there's an old leather trunk. Inside it you'll find a little blue box. There's a note with it."

"A note? To me?" Thanh could not think of a single reason why his father would have left him a note, never mind a gift.

"That's what he said. Look, I'm late, gotta run. I'll be talking to you, Bro. And congratulations again. I'm really happy for you." He chuckled and hung up.

Thanh looked down at Annie, torn between helping her get over her shock and finding out what was in the trunk in his father's office. He opted for Annie and sank down beside her, drawing her into his arms and inviting her to talk things out.

~ * ~

Thanh sat at his father's desk with the battered leather trunk open on the blotter. He held the small velvet box in one hand and his father's note in the other.

To my son, Thanh,

I am certain your other father, the man whose name you bear, and who you thought of as father for most of your life would want you to have this. It was meant for your mother and perhaps now it will belong to Annie. I have no idea why Sam had it engraved as he did; that is a secret known only to Sam and your mother. But in light of what happened all those years ago between your mother and me, and more recently between you and me, and between you and Annie, it seems more than appropriate. I wish you luck,

Love, Dad

Thanh read the letter twice, then set it carefully on the desk and opened the box. Inside, nestled in pale blue satin, was an engagement ring. An unusual ring. Not a simple diamond, but a beautiful blue sapphire with two sparkling diamonds flanking it.

With shaking fingers, Thanh slipped the ring from the box and tipped it under the light on the desk to read the inscription inside. "Love forgives everything."

Twenty-nine

Election day dawned cool and grey on the east coast. Matt Steele began the day very early at his home in McLean, then after a brief visit to his DC headquarters to thank all his supporters for all their hard work and devotion, he flew to Portland with his wife, Eve, and their son, Ben. During the drive between the airport and his residence in Levitt, Matt stopped at half a dozen polling sites to shake hands and answer the never-ending barrage of questions. He thought it odd that few people seemed to question the sweeping economic changes he had insisted were unavoidable if the country was going to survive the current financial crisis. Most of the clamor was about Thanh.

Even more surprising, the curiosity about Thanh and his place in Matt's life didn't carry condemnation with it. Over and over, Matt heard admiration for his honesty. Sometimes reluctant. More often it was outright approval that finally a politician had stood up, admitted his mistakes and was ready to accept responsibility. People just wanted to know more about the newly acknowledged son. How long had he been in the country? Where did he live? What was he like? Did he have a wife? Kids? A job? Matt wondered if it would have made a better impression had Thanh accompanied him today. But Thanh had a class to teach, and he wasn't a registered voter, so he'd stayed in Virginia. He'd be watching the returns with his fiancée and staying in touch by phone.

When the car finally crunched up the driveway of the home Matt and Eve had purchased before Ben was born, Matt was relieved. At least for another hour, he could put his feet up and try to relax. If that was even possible on a day like today. He and Eve and Ben would head down to the local high school to cast their votes as Matt always had, at six o'clock. He would have preferred to return to his home and watch the returns in his own living room, but Murdock had overruled him, and Matt would be headed back to DC as soon as he'd voted so he would be on hand to accept victory or concede defeat in person and thank his people one more time.

The cool air that started the day off had given way to unseasonable heat for November, but the sky had darkened and rain was predicted. On the porch overlooking the ocean, Matt unbuttoned his collar and leaned back in the Adirondack chair, closing his eyes. The past months ran through his mind like an old-fashioned movie, jumping erratically from one frame to the next.

He felt again the surge of emotion as his nomination was announced at the national convention. He remembered the exhaustion of endless trips as snippets of airports and hotels flashed past. He relived countless speeches and felt his hand being shaken by thousands of others. It had been an experience like nothing else.

He recalled his brother-in-law's words when he'd called earlier.

"Congratulations on taking me completely by surprise, old man. I thought I knew everything about you. I was impressed. Jean said to tell you she's never voted Democrat, but she's going to make an exception."

Matt's mother had called earlier as well. Her comment had been typical of her. "I knew you had something up your sleeve." Nothing much got by his mother.

It had taken a moment before he recalled who Father Eagan was when his cell revealed an unknown caller just before lunch.

"Now I know why Bill Nickerson thought so highly of you," the priest from the veterans' home had said. "Good luck, my son and God go with you."

But the most surprising call of all had come just a few minutes ago.

"Senator?" the quavering voice had demanded with determination."

"This is Matt Steele. How may I help you?"

"You already have," the unfamiliar voice answered less querulously. "I just wanted you to know I voted for you, and I'm holding you to your promises. I haven't believed a word I've heard for years, but you sound like a man I can trust. And thank you for answering my letter."

Matt muttered a confused thank-you, and the line clicked. It took several minutes before he realized he'd just been speaking with Edna Jordan, the author of the letter that had changed the course of his campaign. He smiled in satisfaction.

"I won't let you down," Matt murmured, too softly for his secret service detail to overhear.

~ * ~

By the time Matt and his family arrived at the high school, rain had begun to spit from the skies with steady persistence. He unfolded his golf umbrella and held it over himself and Eve. Ben ignored the rain with sublime indifference. Before long, his blond hair lay plastered to his head, and the shoulders of his jacket were dark with rain. Anxious officials offered Matt the opportunity to move into the building, but he refused.

During the afternoon, Ben had repeatedly described the long lines shown on television as voter turnout reached record highs.

Matt prayed the heavy turnout was a positive sign. Or as one enthusiastic supporter had shouted when Matt stepped from the car, "Way to go, Steele. Time and more to put our money where our mouths are!"

Slowly, the line inched forward and they were almost under the canopy that jutted out over the main door. A woman who clearly did not support him began a chant that was taken up by others wearing buttons with the legend *Give me a Miller*.

Supporters took up the challenge and started shouting, "Reclaim the American Dream!"

"I think our side's winning," Ben commented, grinning. "At least they've got stronger lungs."

Matt heard a sharp crack and reacted without thinking. He hit the pavement taking Eve with him, hardly aware of the searing pain in his shoulder.

"Shit!" Joe Venuto swore as his weight landed on top of Matt.

"What the hell? Ooof!" Matt heard Ben's grunt of surprise as his own agent took him to the ground without ceremony.

"Matt!" Eve sounded panicked and breathless.

"I'm hit," Matt said disbelievingly. "Dammit, I've been hit."

"Don't move, sir!" Joe eased his weight off Matt, but kept his body close as a shield. Zack's broad shoulders loomed at Matt's other side. His eyes darted, first one way and then the other, his gun drawn and gripped in two hands.

People began to realize what was happening. Pandemonium broke out. The screaming confusion masked the final round that ricocheted off the pavement. It tore through Matt's upper arm and plowed into his jaw. It completely missed the protective shield of his bodyguard and was probably just a lucky hit from a hastily aimed second attempt.

The momentum jerked Matt onto his back. Eve scrambled to her knees. Matt tried to lift his head but the pain in his face nearly caused him to black out.

Eve pressed her hand against his jaw. The world spun madly. Rain fell in his face. It steadied his whirling senses.

"I'm sorry," he mumbled through his shattered mouth.

"Shhh," Eve sobbed. Her agent tried to move her away, but Eve hung on.

"Hurts to 'reathe," Matt gasped. Pain everywhere.

"You're going to be okay. You have to be okay," Eve pleaded, still trying to stanch his bleeding jaw and fend off her bodyguard.

"I di'n't 'uy it'n Nam," he rasped, "an' I'm not goin' to now." He struggled for another breath.

Scuffling sounded beyond Zack's shoulder. Out of the corner of his eye, Matt saw another man face down with a blue-clad knee thrust into his back. The officer snapped a cuff on one wrist. Matt tried to turn his head for a glimpse of his assailant.

The movement was a mistake. The agony it unleashed took his breath away. What breath he had. Every effort became more difficult than the last. He closed his eyes.

"Matt!" Eve shouted his name.

Matt forced his eyes open in response to the desperation in her voice. "Eve," he began, but even just her name was almost more than he could manage. He choked on his own blood.

Sirens wailed in the distance and grew closer. Matt forced himself to keep his eyes open. He swallowed the pooling liquid that threatened to drown him. The coppery taste so familiar. So frightening. Darkness menaced until all he could see was Eve. The sirens blared louder, then suddenly died with the screech of brakes. Doors slammed. Running feet.

"Eve!" He wondered if she could even hear him. *Eve. Eve.* His head spun woozily. *Eve.* She was his song, his talisman. As long as he didn't lose her, he could make it.

"I'm here." She leaned closer and kissed the mess that was his mouth. "I'm right here." The blond agent hovered close at Eve's back.

Matt closed his eyes. They were so heavy.

"Matt!" Eve pleaded. "Matt, look at me."

He dragged his eyes open again. A half a dozen faces spun crazily above him.

"Doc!" Matt sighed in relief. *The medic will fix me up*, he thought, confusing the moment with another long ago.

"I'm just an EMT, sir, but we're going to get you to a doctor just as soon as we can."

Matt wanted to give in to the encroaching oblivion. Eve clutched at his hands. He tried to squeeze back. He needed to tell her something. But what? His mind drifted. He thought he heard choppers. And more gunfire. He was no longer sure where he was.

A sharp stab bit into his arm and sobered him abruptly. An intense young woman held an IV bag above his head. Matt blinked to clear his confusion. He wasn't in the Nam. He was in his own country and someone wanted him dead.

He heard voices talking to him, but they kept fading. They asked questions, but he couldn't answer.

"He's going into shock. Push that IV."

The world spun. Darkness hovered dangerously close.

"Eve." Her name came out barely audible, even to himself.

"Don't try to talk. Just be still and let the man do his job." Eve tightened her grip on his left hand. Her face seemed so far away. Everything seemed to be floating. He seemed to be floating. Drifting.

Suddenly, Matt knew he was dying.

Oddly, he wasn't afraid. Only sad that he would have to leave Eve alone. *Hal can carry on*, he thought vaguely. *I did my part.*

"Sir! Sir, can you hear me?"

Matt shifted his focus toward the voice. He moved his lips but nothing came out.

Hands busy around him. Enclosed his neck in a brace. Shoved something beneath him. His body jerked sideways, and excruciating pain cleared the fog in his brain. Then blessed warmth spread over him.

Dying wasn't so bad without the icy chill. Surprising that so small a thing as warmth could be so important.

He closed his eyes and let the warmth seep into him, stealing consciousness and pain.

Then he jerked his eyes open again. "Eve?" There was something he'd forgotten to tell her. He couldn't remember. "Eve?"

Eve's face appeared, hovering close. He *had* spoken aloud.

"Eve," he gasped as she began to move away. Or maybe he was moving away.

His vision narrowed again, blotting out everything but her. He tried to form the words but his lips refused to cooperate.

With immense effort, he dragged his hand toward his chest. It trembled. With determination he touched his thumb to his heart. Then, with a groan ripped from deep inside him, he held the thumb out toward Eve. Then he surrendered and the blackness swallowed him.

Epilogue

An excited crowd gathered for the launching of the new destroyer at the Bath Iron Works shipyard in Maine. There was always a crowd for a launching, even in winter when bitter winds charged up the Kennebec River dotting it with frothing icy whitecaps. But today the weather was sunny and warm. Spring, which comes to Maine with reluctant tardiness, abounded everywhere, and people who were tired of being shut in, came to Bath to stand on the bridge and watch the navy's newest ship float free of the dry dock in which she'd been created.

Tugs milled about the blue water waiting to guide the new ship on the first leg of her journey to the sea. Motorists craned their necks for a glimpse through the solid line of spectators, and sleek gray gulls soared overhead impassively searching for their next meal.

The awaited moment approached. Within the confines of the shipyard, activity quickened. Lined up along the edge of the new destroyer's deck, sailors stood to attention. Dignitaries took up their positions on the platform below her looming bow. Then the color guard marched in and the ceremony began.

Eve looked up at the tiny figures above her, outlined against the brilliant blue of the sky. The sailors, dressed in smartly creased jumpers, their white hats tipped low over their brows, stood at sharp attention, looking proud and eager to serve their new mistress.

"Remember when Dad used to bring us to see the ships launched when we were kids?" Megan reminisced. Then she turned to Thanh and Annie. "It was a lot different then. We used to walk up to the middle of the bridge. That was the best view 'cause you could watch the ship slide down the rails and splash into the water. All the tugboats tooted to tell each other what they were doing. It just isn't the same since they built the dry dock."

"I thought it was just more exciting because we were kids," Ben answered, as the color guard moved forward to present the flag. "All Megan ever talked about was wanting to ride on one of the tugs."

"I'd still like a chance to go out on a tugboat."

"So, join the Merchant Marine."

Megan gave her brother a playful elbow. She pointed up at the sailors. "Look at how many of them there are. You think they're all crew? Maybe I can get a tour later."

Ben rolled his eyes toward Thanh. "There's not much to see inside her yet. But maybe you're more interested in the sailors."

"Hush," Eve turned in her chair and gave them a stern look over one shoulder.

Eve turned back to the front and gave her attention to the first speaker. At least she tried to. Her mind was a long way away. It wasn't until the President of the United States took the podium that she stopped thinking about that rainy schoolyard all those months ago and paid attention to his words.

Dressed in sober gray, his shoulders broad, he towered over the men around him. His eyes, shadowed by the brim of the hat he'd been given with the new ship's name on its peak, looked calmly out over the cheering crowd.

He spoke of the generations of men and women who'd served their country from the first brave stand at Concord to those still in uniform today. He talked of the fine tradition of the shipbuilders of Bath, and the hundreds of warships they had sent to sea. Then he told the story of the man this ship was being named for, a gifted young athlete with the talent to be anything he aspired to be and who had chosen to become a Navy Seal. A sailor who had ultimately chosen to sacrifice his life to save those of his men and complete the mission he'd been sent to do. As the speaker told the story of this brave young man, his own passion and patriotism infected the listening crowd, bringing tears to the eyes of many. Then he exhorted his listeners to honor the memory of this fallen warrior by keeping the American Dream alive.

Eve smiled, remembering Matt, his eyes bluer than his sweater, earnestly pleading for that dream with his heart and soul in every word, instilling a far more critical audience with the same kind of passion and patriotism. She'd been so proud of him. And she was proud of the two and half years of incredible change his courageous stand had brought about.

Her eyes watered, and she blinked the tears back. Suddenly, it was her turn. Confidently she walked to the edge of the platform where she took the bottle and cleared her throat. Briefly, she glanced back at her family. Ben looked unusually solemn. Megan wiped a tear from her cheek and Thanh's blue eyes met hers and winked.

Raising her arm, she brought the bottle down against the arching bow. Cheering erupted, and the band began to play. The crew of the new destroyer saluted as one. Tugs tooted from the river beyond, and the great doors of the dry dock began to open. In moments, the new destroyer gracefully entered the water she was born to ride with pride.

Only then did Eve dare to turn her head to meet the piercing blue gaze beneath the commemorative hat. Reaching up to remove the cap, the man ran his hand through his unruly blond bangs. Then he touched his thumb to his chest, wagged it in her direction and smiled.

"I love you, too, Mr. President," she whispered.

Meet

Skye Taylor

Skye. Taylor considers life an adventure and willingly admits that she often dances to a very different piper. She claims that motherhood is the biggest and most rewarding adventure of her life and she is proudest of the five wonderful people her children have grown up to be. But now that they are on their own and have presented her with twelve terrific grandchildren to spoil, she has spread her wings and flown as far as the South Pacific where she spent two years in the Peace Corps. She's jumped out of perfectly good airplanes and earned a basic sky diving license, and she gets dressed up in the garb of an 18th century Spanish citizen to volunteer at the historic tavern in the oldest city in North America. Having been born and lived most of her life in New England, she is now a transplanted Yankee soaking up the sun, warmth and history of St Augustine, Florida where she lives with her furry buddy, MacDuff. She spends most of her free time writing novels, volunteering in the living history Spanish Quarter and walking on the beach. Besides her children and grandchildren, she loves traveling, chocolate, the ocean, anything that flies, reading, NCIS and history - not necessarily in that order.

Made in the USA
Middletown, DE
23 September 2019